By R.J. Price

Seat of Magic
Trouble
Sit Pretty
Dark Spirits
Highest Lord

A Seat of Magic Novel

Landscape Magic

R.J. Price

Copyright 2017 R.J. Price

Front Cover Design by Masoumeh Tavakoli

This is a work of fiction. Any resemblance to actual events or people, living or dead, is purely coincidental.

All Rights Reserved. This book may not be reproduced in part or whole without written permission except in the case of small quotes for reviews, articles, or essays.

Chapter One

They sat in the war room in awkward silence.

The table they sat at was old. Some antique thing that was little more than a few rough planks nailed together and then into four feet. Time and use had worn the table's surface to an almost smooth finish. The chairs they sat on were mismatched, from different eras.

Er and Url sat together, with Gamen across the table from them. Van sat near the opposite end, obviously feeling out of place from the warriors sitting at the table. Jer sat at the other end, almost at the head of the table.

Jer didn't know how he knew that, just like he didn't know why they were all sitting in awkward silence. He did know that the silence affected the warriors at the table, and Van, being a queen, simply remained silent because the others were also silent.

Van adjusted in his seat, which creaked under his weight as he moved. Jer turned to Van as the other warriors looked down the table at him. The Western Baron went red, then paled considerably and attempted to ease his weight back into the chair without causing more noise.

The war room hadn't been used since before Jer was born. Possibly even before his father had been born. The last war that the palace had marched to had happened when Telm was a girl. It had been so long ago that the room had been overtaken by the servant women. They had grudgingly given it back to the warriors, but only after Jer had found Telm and had her command the servants to leave.

Because apparently being steward to the court and brother to the mate to the throne meant nothing to them.

The doors to the war room opened, and Av walked in, glaring at the doors as he went.

"Those things are supposed to creak," Av growled under his breath.

Amused, Jer waited until Av made eye contact with him before he spoke up. "The women thought it frightening that it creaked when they came and went, so they oiled the hinges."

Av pulled to a sudden stop, surprise playing over his features. Either he hadn't realized he had spoken, or the women taking over the war room was news to him.

Behind Av, Aren walked in.

Even though Er and Url's backs were to the door, the two stiffened at Aren's entrance.

The queen walked past Av and to the table, pulling the warrior out of his startled silence. Av's eyes watched Aren move to the head of the table and take the seat that should have gone to him. There was hunger in those eyes as they flitted from Aren, then to the others sitting at the table, looking for any sign of rebellion.

"Van, you surprise me," Av said as he walked to Aren, stepping behind the queen and setting a hand on her shoulder. "Why wouldn't you bring Ella with you? She does, after all, represent that which we need to discuss: War."

"I am the Baron, thus I will speak for my people," Van said quietly, though he didn't sound sure of himself in the least.

This was a warrior thing. It was what they were bred to do. Queens only mucked things up, made things worse because they were always stopping to whine about innocents and commoners and how slaughtering one's enemies was foolish.

"You brought Aren," Van said in a higher pitch than he normally used, accusing Av of a double standard.

"And she knows that here, in this place, it is my word that is law, not hers," Av said sternly.

Aren shuddered and pushed back into the chair. Av set his free hand on her other shoulder. So much could be interpreted from that silent shudder.

Jer tried to dismiss the motion, but found himself focusing on it the more he tried to ignore.

"It's too late now," Url murmured, keeping his eyes on the table. "At least for this meeting. Van can bring her for the next one, or the one after."

"Very well, what are we discussing at this meeting?" Av asked. "Does anyone know how to plan a war?"

"Uh…" Jer cleared his throat and adjusted in his seat. "I have Laeder looking it up for us. Unless he marches onto palace land, we have to gather an army then march down on him. To do otherwise is stupid, foolhardy, foolish, and only an imbecile of the highest order wouldn't at least try to make some military strategy before marching into war against commoners who have obviously been planning this thing for years and might do something like the anvil. Or, so I've been told."

"What is an anvil in war?" Av asked.

"Like a smithy's hammer strikes an anvil, so would the army march on the enemy," Van said from the other end of the table. "Perhaps as the only one of us who is not a warrior, it was in my best interest to study matters of war and history. Jer is correct, commoners who march against ranks have plans and great numbers. Conscripts usually."

"What's a conscript?" Aren asked.

"A man forced to war by his lord," Van said. "I have a small army of conscripts. All commoners, prisoners who would have been put to death otherwise. They serve in small functions against the western lands."

"I thought palace lands were all there was to this land?" Aren said, sounding confused.

"There are lands outside of palace lands," Gamen said sternly.

The Eastern Baron looked around the table as if asking the others if Aren were truly that stupid.

"No, I know there are lands across the sea," Aren responded. "But there are other lands attached to what was once palace lands, that is what you're telling me?"

"Yes, that is what I'm telling you," Van said.

The two queens met eyes and Aren frowned. It was very much a look that Jer expected to see on the face of a woman her age. Confusion at learning something that changed her view of the world. It was incomprehensible to her that there were other lands attached to her land.

The lands.

Jer reminded himself that what had once been palace lands were split still.

"Then we need an accounting of men," Aren said slowly. "Palace lands have few ranks. A majority of those ranks reside here, at the palace and the village an hour's walk away."

"There's also the commune," Av said to the table. "But those are queens and healers who were outed by Em. Many of them are powerful, but we would not want them going to war. They are too damaged to see the difference between the enemy and their own men."

"I have many ranks," Van said quickly. "Good, strong blood. Ella has made her wishes known. She will ride with the army."

Er made a scoffing sound. "You have many ranks of different sorts. The North is where your army will come from, Av. Good strong blood, warriors mainly. Let Van provide the healers. We will provide the fighters."

"Except…" Url said, glancing over at Jer.

War took time. Bringing an army together took months or even years. Av didn't have the patience to sit about while men gathered. Jer was surprised his brother had even managed to come to a meeting to start planning a war.

"Except?" Aren asked.

"We are warriors, Lady Aren," Er said quickly. "The relationship between queen and warrior is different in the North. Certainly, there are the youth who will demand to go to war and those warriors who call to blood more strongly than others. But if you want real loyalty, if you want men to follow you, you need to draw them in."

"You—" Gamen gaped at Er from across the table. "You want her to do a calling?"

"That is how it is done in the North," Er said.

"Yes, but your queens call your warriors to protect them. They march up to the men they grew up with, grab them by the ear and tell them that if a single hair is hurt on the heads of the commoner children, they will be held personally responsible. A queen from an outside land cannot call warriors."

"Olea did," Van said.

The table was quiet a moment.

"Olea is a queen above any other," Gamen responded quietly, keeping his eyes on the table. He looked up only to glare at Er. "What you propose is taking an untried, unblooded woman north and praying that she can handle her magic enough to stand toe-to-toe with your queens. You pray that she will be able to draw warriors in. The girl can barely control the lights. She has no grasp of what it truly is to be a queen, and you want the fate of the lands to rest on her being able to call warriors? Are you mad?"

"The throne created me, just like it did Olea," Aren said to Gamen. "I am her replacement, and if the throne found me lacking in any fashion, it would have simply used me to draw her here, then killed me and forced itself upon her. I do believe that your words be ignored."

"Olea is not you, you are not Olea," Gamen said. "That is a woman who walks into a room and commands attention, even when she was young, on her first visit to the North. You simpered in the corner and waited for a warrior to come and claim you. You, Lady Aren, are a damsel-in-distress. Lady Olea was given that label and cast it off, daring any man to try to place it upon her again."

Aren's mouth opened to protest. Then it closed again. Jer saw something pass over her features, but couldn't tell what it was that she was thinking. The room felt darker, gloomier. Like a hole that would swallow them all, if they didn't get out, and get out now.

Jer found himself standing before he realized what he was doing. He had to fight the instinct to run, to keep himself in place as the others looked at him for an explanation.

"Yes, Er, you're mad for proposing the idea as if it were as simple as going north," Jer said, then turned to Gamen. "But you're a damned fool for saying such a thing to a queen. You grew up around several queens. Av making such a mistake, all right, I could see that. But you, Gamen? No woman deserves to be spoken to in such a manner unless she tells you outright that you're an imbecile of the highest order, and even then, you do not use an emotional barb."

Gamen looked furious, but they were all on edge. They had gathered to plan war, and they all knew that war was still a long time off.

The baron of the East gritted his teeth but forced himself to relax. "I apologize for my outburst, Lady Aren."

"Now, that being said…" Jer turned to Aren and saw that she was on the brink of tears.

He didn't understand why Gamen's words had affected her in such a manner, but he knew he couldn't focus on that. If he did, he'd end up attacking Gamen, and then Av would realize what was going on and probably hurt Jer in his attempt to reach the Eastern baron. Instead, he focused his attention on Av, who was watching Jer with that look on his face.

The one that made the guards check their weapons. The one that said that Av was very aware of his mate's mood and whatever was said in the next few moments would determine whether Gamen remained amongst the living, or was borne to the spirits.

"It will be months before the warriors gather, and the two of you are newly mated," Jer said finally. "I would strongly encourage you to visit the North, which has just rejoined palace lands. Speak with the youth there, see if they want to go to war and if you can rally them, by all means. But also just take some time with one another. If I recall correctly, the North has a tradition as such, yes?"

Er flinched when Av turned his attention from Jer to Er. The Northern Baron swallowed hard and ever so slowly turned to Av.

"Honeymoon, it's called," Er said to Av, keeping his eyes somewhere about Av's shoulders. "I would be delighted to host the pair of you for it. It lasts a month, normally and, as Jer says, if you do rally the youth, then so be it. It would gladden many hearts to see the one who sits the throne walk amongst them rather than simply have her send commands."

"I want to see my palace," Aren said distantly.

"It's mine, and you can't have it back," Url growled half-heartedly.

The growl drew Aren out of her mood. Anger replaced the sullen silence of before as she glared at the warrior who dared claim what she thought rightfully hers.

"I would just like to point out that we did not take the entire palace, just some of it," Er said very quickly.

Van looked at Jer and opened his mouth to speak. Jer gave his head the barest shake. Van would direct them back to talk of war, and they needed to avoid that for the moment.

Talk of war would fuel Gamen's annoyance and might drive Aren back to that point of tears. None of them needed to deal with that aftermath.

"Why don't we draw this meeting there?" Jer asked, turning to his brother. "We can all come to the next meeting with actual numbers. You know,"—he turned to the barons—"those little symbols that tell others how many people will be in the army to fight the war?"

Except he was talking to three other warriors and an already irritated queen. Van glared at Jer as the other warriors growled at him.

"Jer's right," Av said. "We need to know how many ranks you will all be sending for this war. We may need to conscript commoners."

"We wouldn't conscript, we'd make a call," Jer said. "Lords like sending their younger sons to battle and such, on and so forth."

"Whatever it is he just said," Av said. "You need to bring us numbers, and think. If you can't do that, then you're no use in war. And if you aren't going to be useful, you will serve at the back of the army with the prostitutes."

"Prostitutes?" Aren squeaked out.

"Yes, darling, prostitutes, or loose women in general," Av said quietly.

"Breeders are very likely," Jer said. "Those wanting strong blood for their children. Women following an army always happens and if we provide women willing to go to bed with the ranks marching on the enemy, there is a lesser chance of the warriors being—"

"Overcome by instinct," Van finished.

"Do we have to feed *them* too?" Aren demanded of Jer.

"Um…" Jer frowned at Av, who looked up at the ceiling. "Not really. They earn their keep. The army won't exactly have the coin to pay the women. We will pay them from the treasury but only if they return, and on the way, they have to earn their food."

"That's so wrong."

"The men are earning their food by killing people," Jer said.

"But they get fed all the way out," Aren responded.

"If we hire prostitutes, we can talk to them about it then," Av said. "Like anyone hired for a task, we will draw up a contract that is suitable to their desires as well as our own."

"What about protection for them, should they change their minds?" Aren asked. "If they quit."

She was asking a table of men.

"Or the women who might travel with them? If healers go, they will protect themselves, but what about the commoners who tag along as cooks and washers? Who will keep commoners safe when the army marches through? Who will hold the warriors to their honour? How many villages am I going to have to allow to be razed? I'd rather none at all. It is not the fault of the commoners that their baron has decided to go to war with palace lands."

"The men will care for themselves," Av said finally. "There would be no cooks, or if there are, they will be men."

"Who will protect the squires, then?" Aren asked. "The young boys, the adolescents who are of legal age, technically, but far from home and no longer under their fathers' protection?"

"No one is going to be seducing boys," Gamen protested.

"Your boys will be going to war, Gamen. What if Jer becomes lonely and takes one of them to his bed?" Aren asked.

"Jer doesn't do a one-night stand," Av and Url said at the same time.

"Then any other warrior in the army. You just said you need to put prostitutes in the army to keep the men from razing villages and I would forbid them from doing just that. You cannot send along an army of prostitutes to keep an army of men busy. There would not be enough women to go around."

"By the spirits," Van said in a disgusted tone. "I think she's actually right."

"I want to know who will protect the innocents when those who are meant to protect them fail at doing so."

"I will," Av said. "As well as the men sitting here at this table. As well as Lerd, who will no doubt join us, and Ella. And who knows how many other warriors who will follow us with loyalty beyond that of a promise to bleed a man of his life."

"That is why a queen does the calling," Er said gently. "In order to draw those who would do her bidding above all else. That is one reason why I want you to come north. Those sitting at this table, yes, would do their best. But those who call to a queen are a great deal more likely to stay loyal, and you have few loyal to you. Let me show you off to a land of warriors. They could all call to you and then there'd be no concerns about the innocents.

"Come north with us. See the land that has rejoined yours."

Aren was quiet a long moment, then she said, "I will think about it."

Chapter Two

Aren lounged in an armchair. Her back was against one side, bare legs dangling over the other. Av watched her, several feet away. His arms were crossed before him, irritation in every line of his body.

He wanted to touch her, but she hadn't given him permission.

It wasn't that they had agreed to do this, that she would give him permission to touch her. It simply seemed to have happened once they entered the room. Perhaps Av had picked up on her mood in the room when Gamen had called her a damsel-in-distress.

She didn't want to be a damsel-in-distress. She hadn't just waited around for Av to save her. She had had every intention of leaving the palace on her way to independence. He was the one who had stopped her and gotten in the way.

Aren sighed and looked away from Av.

"You're naked," he said pointedly.

"I felt the dress was constraining," she responded, running a finger up her leg, then down it.

She liked how that felt. She wondered what it would feel like if it were Av's finger on her, instead of her own.

Aren looked back at Av, whose eyes were on the finger as it trailed up her leg, towards her belly. She saw the intake of breath, the flush to his skin.

"Why are they sending us north?" Aren asked, lifting her hand and dropping it onto the back of the seat.

"Get me out of the way, likely," Av said, shifting closer to Aren. "The last time Jer took me hunting I almost stabbed him, I was so eager to bleed something. War is, well, it takes time to organize, as he pointed out. It would be best to have something to do, and up north they would be better prepared to deal with one with my mood."

"So this honeymoon thing that Er mentioned is a story?" Aren asked.

"Oh no, it's very real. Nearly any lord up there will open his home to a newly mated couple. They get a private room, fed and clothed, and get to spend the next month or so worrying about nothing more than one another."

"For year matings as well?" Aren asked.

"No." Av shook his head. "But I think it would be appropriate for us."

"But there's Anue and Danya and—"

"I don't want you to talk about other women when you're naked," Av said through gritted teeth.

"Oh?" Aren asked.

She trailed her finger down her leg and watched Av's breath quicken. There was something about driving that reaction out of Av that delighted her in ways she could not put words to. Just before her finger touched her hip, she lifted it and set it on the back of the chair once more.

"Prostitutes?" she asked.

"Those are women."

"Prostitutes can also be men," she said pointedly.

"I don't know about armies specifically, that's a Jer thing."

"You will be leading the army," she said. "You need to learn how an army works."

"B-but I don't want to!" Av protested. "I just want to stab people."

She groaned and dropped her legs off the side of the chair. "You sound like such a child."

"I sound like a child?" Av demanded.

"You grew up on palace lands, of course, you haven't actually grown up. You're stuck in the adolescent mentality and not planning for the future. Why weren't you finished in another land?"

"That's for lords and ladies," Av said with a growl. "I am neither of those things."

"Well, your parents should have sent you somewhere so that you could shed this stupid belief that stabbing people in the face is the way to go. How is it that Jer grew up and you never did?"

"He's been through a lot," Av protested.

"And since becoming a man the only thing you've done apart from him, the only difficult thing you've ever done, was put your mother on a pyre."

"I take offence to that!"

"We're going north," Aren said with a shake of her head.

She stood and walked to the bathing room for the robe that hung on the inside of the door. As she pulled it on, she turned back to Av. The man was frowning at her.

"I will never understand women," he said.

"I'm annoyed with you."

"I get that. I don't understand why."

"You'd rather just stab people," Aren said, then huffed out a breath. "I thought I had mated a leader, but apparently all I did was found myself a follower. Great, exactly what I need when I sit the throne."

"I don't follow anyone!" Av bellowed.

"Well, you can't lead without a thought between your ears."

Av just stared at her. Aren moved around him, tying her robe furiously as she laid eyes on Wena standing by the door, eyes downcast.

"I didn't realize you were there," Aren said, feeling heat flushing her face.

She had just been naked; how long had Wena been there?

"If you'd prefer, I can knock upon entrance," Wena said to the floor.

"That might make me think someone wants to visit," Aren grumbled.

"I will think of something else," Wena said.

"Good, because I don't want to subject you to that again unless you are helping me with a bath."

"How long was Wena there?" Av demanded from behind Aren.

"She is my servant, not yours," Aren snapped back at him.

"Warriors start fighting when war is mentioned," Wena said quietly to Aren.

"Then why did she start the fight with *me*?" Av asked.

"Do I look like a wise old woman?" Wena snapped back. "Do I really? I look like I'm older than I am, is that what you are saying, Lord Av?"

"Stop!" Aren said, stepping between the two of them. "Wena, go see Telm about us heading north for a month, see what we need to know about everything."

"As you wish, Lady Aren."

Aren waited for Wena to leave, then turned to Av, who shook his head at her and looked confused.

"First you argue with me, then she does," he said with a motion to the door. "Is the entire staff going to beat me about the head every time we have a little tiff?"

"Probably, yes."

Av swore.

"Since I was taken by the throne, I have had to do a great many things which I did not want to do. Such as staying at court, almost being mated to Laeder, being claimed by a warrior as if I had not a thought in my mind—"

"I told you that you could say no at any time."

"And be subjected to another attempted mating to a lord I have no interest in?" Aren asked. "I am interested in you, Lord Av, but make no mistake, I had no choice but mate you. Now that we are mated I have expectations of you. I expect you to lead all the time. Not some of the time, all of it. Which means leading the army we are sending south to die for us. You cannot lead an army if you have no idea how it works."

"I can lead, I do lead," Av protested.

"Learn how an army works, learn why we need a cog and what it's doing in that place, and then learn how much it costs and how cheap we can get it before its construction would be more trouble than the coin we saved."

"You know I don't have a head for numbers."

"And you know that I never wanted the throne. We don't always get what we want."

"Don't get to see you naked and I have to learn numbers," Av grumbled. He stopped, still as could be for a moment before he whimpered out, "Did you fake it all?"

"What?" Aren demanded.

"The sex, did you fake that?"

"Oh, for the love of— no! I find you attractive, I am interested in you, but what did I tell you when I was first taken by the throne?"

"You had no intention of ever mating because you wanted to be free," Av said. The warrior mulled over his words. "So you do like the sex, all of that is real, but if it feels like there's no love, it's because there isn't. You had no choice but mate me, or live a very complicated life. That makes me feel very stupid."

"You didn't mate me for love," Aren said.

"No," he said slowly. "No, I suppose you're right. I mated you because you are mine. Our vows said nothing about love. I'm glad we settled that out."

"Don't be crude," Aren said. "Our vows said nothing about love because we don't love each other. That doesn't mean we won't end up loving each other and it certainly doesn't mean the honeymoon is over before it began. And certainly, we have more to build on than most couples do going into a mating. My father mated my mother to keep himself out of debt, and she mated him because he was the only one who would put up with her. And then they still had to have children."

"We at least have lust, you mean?" Av asked.

"We could have a great deal more."

"But only if I change things about myself."

"Oh, Av. We both need to change. We both need to grow up. That love of myth and legend, it doesn't exist. We aren't country folk who have the option of falling in love and then falling into bed. We will make strong children one day, and that's the best we can promise one another. Anything else is just extra."

"I see," he said quietly.

"What are you thinking about?" she asked. "I can't tell, your face has gone all still, and you seem to be brooding something over."

"I'm very, very confused," Av muttered.

"You should have just agreed to learn how an army runs," Aren countered.

"That part I get, if I had just done that we wouldn't be having this conversation, but it's one we still needed to have. I suppose I was chasing after what my parents have, but having that with you is impossible, I see that now."

Aren felt a cold wash over her. "What are you saying?"

"That my parents loved one another devoutly."

"Just because a mating doesn't start with love doesn't mean that love won't grow."

"Why are you panicking?"

"I'm not panicking," she said quickly.

"Really? Because your wrist seems attached to the wall."

Aren turned to the wall, where the manacle was trying to latch onto the plaster. It couldn't find purchase, but she could feel the magic reaching outward, trying to find something solid to latch onto. She snatched her wrist away from the wall and held it protectively against herself.

She had been panicking. She had been on the verge of some terrible feeling because Av said that they would never have what his parents had.

Why? Why had she felt like that?

"Did I upset you when I said that we wouldn't have what my parents had?" Av asked.

"Yes."

"Why?" he asked.

"Because they loved each other, and if you can't love me then no one can, and I'll die sad and alone and—" And suddenly she was crying.

Why was she crying? Why couldn't she stop crying? She would not cry over something so stupid. She would not cry.

Aren wiped away her tears and looked up. Av had come to stand less than a hand span away. The pity on his face made her start crying again, and she didn't understand why.

"I hate feeling!" she screamed.

"I know, feeling hurts," he said, pulling her towards him. "Van did mention something about relearning things and it causing confusion and frustration, but I expected things to melt, not for you to cry. All because you believe you're going to die sad and alone and unloved?"

"Yes," she said weakly against him.

"That's kind of a stupid thing to think. Even if we had never met, Anue loves you. Mie loves you, like only a young warrior who hasn't seen how dark the world can be could. I'm pretty certain Url has a very strong feeling towards you, but I wouldn't quite call that love yet. I hope. Otherwise, I'll have to stab him."

Aren almost giggled despite the tears. She rubbed at her eyes, not liking the conflicting emotions.

"I need to talk to Danya."

"That's fine by me, but you have to know that she can't come north with us. Someone might take pity on her and try to do what they think is the right thing."

"What do you mean, the right thing?"

"She's physically blind, and most people are stupid. I don't want to risk her life taking her north, and I'm pretty certain Telm won't allow it. If Olea has met her yet, oh goodness me, it would be a bloodbath just suggesting it."

"But I need Danya, she helps me," Aren said.

"You need her alive more than anything else. A month without her isn't going to kill you, and I'm pretty certain she'll tell you the same thing. You've spent longer away from Mar."

"Mar can't do what Danya can do. I've told Danya things, which I'd never tell Mar."

Aren looked up and saw something pass over Av's face. She wasn't entirely certain what it was, but she was fairly certain that she could make the leaping conclusion without being too far off the mark.

"Oh no, you do not get to try to talk to her and figure out what we talk about."

"I don't need to talk to her to know because I've spoken with her before. She has a way of calming a body and pointing them to the truth."

"Exactly, she helped me lots with feelings and stuff."

"When you came back after the winter, you giggled. I'm not going to argue against you seeing Danya when you're both in the same place," Av said quickly.

"And you will not try to get information from her."

"I swear I will not try to question Danya on what the two of you talk about. Considering the two of you haven't spoken since coming back, not really anyhow, the exercise would be pointless."

"That's because I forgot about her for a little bit."

"And for some reason, she didn't take offence to that. So a month away will not be that difficult."

"Maybe it won't be..." Aren muttered.

"By the way, why did your wrist go to the wall?" Av asked.

"Nothing, no reason, just nervous habit is all."

"Aren, if there's another reason, I need to know about it, there's no other way I can protect you."

"There is no other reason."

"If you say so," Av said carefully, as if considering his next words. "I should probably see my father about making arrangements for him to look after Anue. You should see Danya and Anue. Probably see to Mie as well. If you leave without telling him, he will never let you forget it. I did that once, and the next time I saw him he punched me right in the crotch. Highly unpleasant, and I imagine with his strength it would also be unpleasant for a woman."

Chapter Three

Jer sat across from his father, then turned to frown as his uncle sat beside him.

"Honeymoon makes it sound happy and festive," Jer said accusingly.

He didn't want, nor did he need, Aren and Av coming down on him once they discovered that the 'honeymoon' was to settle disputes outside of the view of friends and relatives. It would give them the time to become acquainted with the idea that they were now mated to one another and it had not been about love.

"They started fighting," a female voice said from the door before it closed very quickly.

"Wonder what he said?" Ervam muttered under his breath.

"Why do you assume he said it?" Er asked.

Ervam gave Jer a questioning look. They hadn't had a chance yet to talk about what had gone on inside the war room.

"As you said, they walked in united," Er said, drawing the trainer's eyes to him. "Aren was cleaved off when Gamen accused her of being a damsel-in-distress. I do believe the lady was blind to her own inaction, or at the very least thought she was standing for herself."

"You don't show her the cage," Ervam snapped.

"Which is what your boy here pointed out, thankfully without showing her any more," Er grumbled, adjusting in his seat. "Gamen's on edge, the barons have always led their armies, and now they are only invited to war through me. Which usually means they serve beside me, but I won't be going to war. And if anyone can find out why, that would be fabulous."

"Probably the leg," Ervam said quietly.

"How would she know about my leg?" Er demanded.

"What's wrong with your leg?" Jer asked.

"Nothing," the brothers said as one.

Jer hoped that when he and Av were their ages, they would be able to speak as one despite years apart. He also hoped that they could do it a great deal more convincingly rather than relying on a silent threat to keep someone from questioning further.

"What is up with that united front? Em and I fought like cats and dogs when we first mated, for ten years, constantly."

"They are putting on a good public face. I'll give them that," Ervam said.

"They've only just started fighting," Jer reminded the pair of them.

Er shrugged. "She's been told she can't act the way she wants without a mate; she now has one. He's been told many times that without a queen a warrior cannot act in the fashion in which he wishes to act. Now he has a queen and is mated to her. I'm certain that we will see a change in them."

"The court thought Aren was firm when she came back from the winter?" Ervam said with a chuckle. "Wait until they see him act at the slightest rebellion."

"Should I be warning the servants?" Jer asked.

"Goodness no, they know," Ervam said sternly. "Telm would as well. And Av will settle down eventually, but for now, he has a new toy that no one else has."

"As long as they make it through the honeymoon," Er grumbled. "Once the flurries settled and Olea realized we were mated, she nearly took my head off. The only thing that stopped her was Ervam here. Put her through a wall."

"Please tell me it was a paper wall or something," Jer said.

"Thin wood," Ervam muttered. "Er's the one who then attempted to put me through an actual wall."

"Queens like the chase and the whole mating bit. But when the dust settles, they realize their chosen mate didn't bring them flowers or trinkets, he didn't sweep her off her feet in a non-literal sense, that they've never danced or introduced one another to the other's parents, didn't do what women do with their lovers. They get angry," Er said sternly. "I don't blame them, not one bit. But the one man who wooed one of my daughters had weak blood and no place mingling his line with ours and no actual desire to do so, he was false. The instinct a queen has at hopping into bed with a man is a clear indication of how long their relationship will last."

"Technically Aren didn't hop into bed with Av," Jer said. "Av threw her into bed, and she just neglected to voice consent. We know she didn't have a problem with it because he's still alive, and Telm…um…Telm did that thing she does."

"Starts eyeing the young men as if she's going to bite them," Ervam said, filling in for Er. "After so long with her, I *think* that's her sex-face."

Er grimaced. Jer made a face as well at the thought.

"Given her history with men, it wouldn't be a wonder that she looks like that," Jer muttered.

"Have you ever heard of the warrior tossing the queen and not the other way around?" Ervam asked his brother.

"You and Mirmae?" Er asked in response. "Let's face it, you were trying to run in the other direction, and that woman had her eye on you despite every other warrior trying to get in her way. We tell our boys she did the tossing, not you, as a lesson that with the rise of the queen rank amongst our people, they will not always choose warriors and the rest of us must learn to stand back and let them."

"Warrior tossing a queen, you just gave an example of a queen tossing an entirely different rank!" Ervam bellowed.

"Oh, right," Er said with a frown.

"Why do you want to talk about Mother?" Jer asked his uncle.

"Must have been Gamen's comment," Er said.

"He compared Aren to Olea," Jer said pointedly.

Ervam sighed loudly. "He didn't." The trainer made a disapproving sound as the two warriors turned to him. "Av. He must have compared their relationship to mine and

Mirmae's. Er's always been a little more sensitive to a queen's moods."

"Olea says that's why we have such a good relationship," Er grumbled defensively.

Av walked into the room without knocking. "Good, you're all here. We've agreed to head north. She has concerns about Anue and Danya. She seemed to say that she wanted to bring Danya with us."

"What happened?" Ervam demanded.

"We argued and all of a sudden she started saying she was going to die alone."

"Everyone dies alone," Er said.

"I didn't tell her that, that's madness," Av said with a snarl. "I told her that there were people who loved her. The problem was that she started weeping over this idea, which I didn't tell her, that she said herself. When I asked her why, she repeated it and started crying again. By the spirits, what did I mate?"

"A half-broken queen," Jer said.

"Who is learning to feel again," Ervam said. "She's shut out her emotions for so long that there are bound to be explosions as she does feel."

"Olea cries if she thinks you meant anything about her not being good enough," Er said cautiously. "Doesn't matter that you didn't. Just bursts into tears."

"It got better over time, didn't it?" Ervam asked his brother.

"Certainly, it doesn't happen as often, but she decided to deal with the emotion by getting angry," Er said. "Sometimes that's a good thing. Sometimes it's a bad thing. I can definitely handle an angry woman better than a weeping one, but still. Why do they cry at the drop of a word?"

"Women!" Av said loudly.

"Women from disturbing pasts," Ervam said pointedly.

"Please," Av said. "You had a disturbing past. Jer had a disturbing past. I don't see him weeping any time someone mentions that he's sad and alone without Em."

"I'm not alone," Jer said in his defence.

To which, three sets of identical eyes focused on him. He should have known better than to leave off the sad portion of his words. Ranks picked up on that sort of thing, and while it was usually queens who would pick apart the words, warriors sometimes caught on when their loved ones were involved.

"What?" he said, deciding to play stupid.

"Please tell me that you don't cry because Em is gone," Av demanded.

"She was a large part of my life, Av. Despite everything, we had a child together. We spent most of our days together. There is a great deal of history there that cannot simply be forgotten."

"You have Laeder!"

"Whom I love dearly, but my mate has been dead only a season. Mother died more than ten years ago. I don't see you getting upset with Father."

"I did," Av said.

"He did, and then he broke a rib," Ervam said with a growl.

"That was not because you were still grieving, that was because you were stupid," Av said sternly.

"He broke your rib?" Er demanded. "A warrior broke the rib of a trainer? Ervam, have you been to see a healer yet? A proper healer?"

"I'm fine, Nae saw to me," Ervam responded.

They were all silent for a long moment.

"No, Danya cannot come north with us, at least not until she is better situated with using her magic to see," Er said quietly, changing the topic. "Anue should stay here. Stability is key for a young queen, especially one who has been removed from a home. We've done rescues before. Moving them about, even for visits, can lay the foundation for a life of believing they belong nowhere."

"There's no question about Anue staying here," Av said. "She'll be safer here. I think Aren's concern is raising her sister. I also think that she doesn't believe that she and I raising Anue is acceptable."

"Aren is going through a lot right now, and burdening her with an impressionable child is not going to help her or the child," Ervam said quietly.

"Well, the only ones we trust that much would be yourself and Telm," Av said in response.

"That's fine. I can care for Anue at least until the pair of you get back from the North, and then we can revisit the issue."

"Er just said she needs stability, you're already raising her," Av said.

"I never wanted a daughter," Ervam countered. "They're mean, manipulative, violent, and the queens tend to make things even more uncomfortable when they start using magic. And then I have to deal with the boys trying to get her into bed and the men trying to mate her when they've no damned place doing anything of the sort."

"Mm, well, you'll be looking after Anue, so get used to the idea," Av grumbled.

Av sighed and dropped into an available chair. He stared off at nothing as Jer watched him struggle with something.

"She thinks I act like a child," Av said finally.

"You do," Er responded.

"She thinks it's because I grew up on palace grounds and have never seen the outside world," Av responded, turning to the baron. "That I've never done anything difficult in my life and so never grew up."

"It's very possible," Er said quietly. "When I get together with my childhood friends, we still cause havoc, and Olea has, more than once, said that we're worse than my children. Did you also get a lecture about being a leader?"

"She called me a follower and then questioned what sort of children I might produce," Av said through gritted teeth.

"Why?" Ervam asked. "Your blood is excellent, producing strong warriors generation after generation. The few queens who have been born were also good, strong queens. I was considered the runt of the family, and I produced two strong warriors."

"One that's stupid and the other was cowed by a woman and then the court," Er grumbled.

"I'm not stupid," Av snapped.

"You were cowed by a woman and then the court!" Er shouted back.

"Did you just call *me* stupid?" Jer demanded, not believing what he was hearing, not understanding how he had somehow been dragged back into the conversation.

"And Aren hasn't cowed me," Av protested.

"Em cowed you, then the court did once she died," Er responded sternly.

Av was quiet a moment, then he nodded. "I suppose I deserve that."

"I'm still not stupid," Jer shouted.

"You are, you're a moron," Er said dismissively before he focused on Av. "What did you say to her to start this?"

"She said I had to know how an army worked and I said I just wanted to stab people," Av said.

Er flinched and sucked a breath in through clenched teeth. "She's right, you do need to learn that. No doubt you said no because of the numbers involved."

"And the reports and reading," Av said, looking frustrated. "I can read, I can do numbers, but not that well."

"That's why queens and warriors are supposed to work in tandem," Er said. "I'm not all that great with numbers, but Olea is. However, if I didn't know that I needed wheat to feed the army, she'd tell me the same thing. We can work on that while you visit. It will settle her mind if she sees you learning from someone who has seen battle, even if it was more skirmishes than an actual war."

"I don't need to know how many bundles of wheat I need, do I?" Av asked.

"It would be helpful to at least have a rough idea," Er said. "If your second comes to you and says you need to raid a village because you only have so much food left, you need to know whether you truly need to raid that village. And if it's an enemy village, you need to know when to unleash the bleeders and when to trade."

"What's a bleeder?" Av asked, frowning at Er, then looking around the baron to Jer, who could only shake his head in response.

"Palace warriors may call them something else, but they are the warriors who haven't quenched their bloodlust. There are always bleeders in a group, and you need to be able to pick them out and know when to let them loose in a village, even if it means a few commoners will die. Don't let them off and they'll go home and murder their own families, ravage their village, and start civil uprising before they can be put down. It's a balance."

"Jer didn't know what a bleeder was either," Av said, motioning to Jer.

"I am steward, not mate to the throne," Jer growled through gritted teeth. "I know about how much wheat we need and how long it should last, as well as how to transport it so that you can make it to the other side and be able to stab people."

"Bad food means sick men, means a weak army," Er said to Av sternly.

"Who doesn't know that bad food means sick men?" Av asked.

"The concern isn't knowing that, it's knowing how to prevent that. Just as you know getting stabbed is a bad thing for your health, but you need to know how to stop it from happening."

Av mulled over Er's words. The room was quiet as Av focused on the floor, a frown creasing his brow. Finally, Av looked back up at Er.

"This seems unnecessarily complicated."

"When you're fighting against a commoner army which will, without a doubt, be larger than your own, you need to think before you strike. They count on you striking blindly and plan accordingly."

"So we make it look like we're striking blindly but instead sweep in behind them. Destroy the hammer and then attack the anvil."

"Only works if a queen goes into battle," Er said. "And there are not enough queens to risk such a manoeuvre. Van may supply us with a few, but none of them would be strong enough."

"The hammer is made up of men on horses," Jer filled in for Av because his brother was looking confused again. "A queen, if she knows what to do, can cause widespread panic amongst horses and cause them to buck their riders, then stampede."

Av blinked at Jer, wide-eyed. "A queen can do what now?"

"You need to learn about military history," Er said sternly. "If you do, you will learn a great many uses for a queen. Especially in battle."

"*If* the queen knows how to use her magic to do such a thing," Ervam said loudly. "You all forget that this all is begun with the word 'if' which is much like saying, 'if the sky turns purple then it will rain ale.' Even if we had a queen we were willing to risk in battle, there isn't one capable of doing such things. Not on palace lands and certainly not in the North, where the expertise of their magic is focused on keeping you warm and the lights going, on melting sidewalks and roads of snow and ice to allow the city to function.

"The way of the queen is, and will continue to be, one focused on improving the comfort of the commoners and ranks alike. One hasn't gone to battle in centuries, if not thousands of years, and we will not press one into battle now. We'd be better off taking a damned lapdog into war, at least those buggers have sharp teeth to nip at the heels of our enemies."

Chapter Four

"You're beginning to become aware of what was done to you in the past, and that can cause a lot of tears," Danya said as she and Aren walked through the gardens. "I used to cry a great deal, but I usually managed to hold them back until I was alone. Then again, I did spend a great deal of time alone. Rewel liked to go off and talk to the Others, even though they couldn't talk back to him."

"Does that mean I'm just going to start crying every time we get into a debate?" Aren asked, stopping at a rose bush.

The small buds had hardly begun to grow, but she knew the bush was a rose bush. So many in the front gardens were rose bushes, especially white ones. The bushes had been a favourite of Em's, and she couldn't bring herself to command they all be dug up and replaced.

She had simply told the gardeners that if a rose bush died, it was to be replaced with something they found appropriate for the area, something with colour if at all possible.

"That's a very good possibility, but you have to remember to keep talking," Danya murmured, fingering the leaves of the rose bush. "In my experience, when men see a woman cry, they believe they have won. They don't understand that there is an entirely different thing going on, or that the tears might even mean that she wishes to crush their skull in her hands."

"Now you sound like a queen," Aren said with a chuckle.

"I like to think that's simply the response of any woman when a man believes he has won because she begins to cry." Danya hesitated, head cocking to the side slightly. "Telm is looking for you. She will be headed this way shortly."

"Hopefully our time away will give you both time to recover a little more. Or for you to get your feet under you."

"It's also a good idea for you to visit the North," Danya said pointedly, moving away from the bush.

Aren followed Danya, not certain why they were moving on when Telm was looking for her. Danya led her deeper into the garden, away from the palace.

"Yes, I'm told I should meet the people of the North and show them the type of queen that I am," Aren grumbled, more to herself than to Danya. "But the North believes their queens a rank apart from those on palace lands. They run the water on purpose, not just linked in like I am here."

"Queens across palace lands do the same thing for their homes here, but the magic is used in a small home and normally only for water, at least from what the healers have told me of the other queens they have met."

"Only the oldest homes still have pipes though, few recall how to make them, and those few are booked up for decades, nearly their entire lives," Aren grumbled again.

Danya stopped and turned to Aren, lifting an eyebrow in question.

"I went to ask about building a home before I came to see you. I was told I'd have better luck purchasing an estate than I would at getting the pipes necessary to build a home to my comfort level."

"So build one without pipes."

"That's what I said!"

"But he balked at the idea?"

"He asked if Telm was aware that I was asking such stupid questions."

"Asking what questions?" Telm asked, coming around the corner as if her name caused the woman to appear.

"Asked about building a house without pipes," Aren said with all the annoyance she could muster.

"Pipes are expensive, and those who can lay them mainly replace pipes, not lay new ones. You would still have to choose an area where there were already pipes in the land for them to replace because how they work on the other end is something that is lost to us."

Aren made a face at Telm. The older queen could only shrug in response.

"If you mean to find yourself someplace to live, there are a few estates which have fallen under the palace's care because they were abandoned by the lords who were to maintain them, or sold to those owed debt who then died without an heir. Surely there is one that the court would agree to sell to you."

"I don't think I could afford their price. It's not like I get paid to sit the throne."

Telm cleared her throat awkwardly, causing Aren to sigh loudly.

"It's not that you don't get paid, dear, it's that when there is a surplus in the treasury, you have free use of it," Telm said soothingly. "Lady Em drove us deeper into debt. With the North rejoining, we might see some small increase in taxes, which will allow us to pay off a debt or two, but you will be an old woman before there is coin for you to spend. Unless you can somehow unburden the palace of one of the three great loans, which total over a million coin each."

"A million is bigger than a thousand?" Aren asked.

"It is greater than a hundred thousand," Telm responded quietly.

"How did that happen? How are those houses not broken themselves?" Aren demanded.

"There were small amounts loaned over time by the three great lines. The Praisiers live on the southern border and dealt water to the South for centuries, amassing a huge fortune. The Liffers to the south-west deal in wine, which can only be grown in that climate, one which lords and ladies purchase because it is rare. They also deal in teas, again, which lords and ladies can afford."

"I had Liffer wine," Danya said. "It tasted like piss."

"How do you know what piss tastes like?" Telm asked.

Danya ignored the question and walked a little ways down the path instead.

"The lords and ladies pay for the wine and tea as a symbol of their wealth," Aren said quietly to Telm.

"Yes, that they do. The third line is that of Lord Chorval. His family has dealt with beef for so long that they have begun to be referred to as the Beef Barons. They do fine in this economy, but not as well as in days past. Their land borders that of the North. With the land rejoining palace lands, they may see an increase in sales, which will allow them to pay more taxes, which is how we repay our debt to them."

"Whatever they would pay us in taxes goes back to them to pay off the debt?" Aren asked.

"A fixed interest was agreed to at the borrowing of the first sum. Thus far we can barely pay the interest, let alone pay back what is owed."

Aren groaned and rubbed at her face. "I'm going to be stuck here forever."

"Not forever," Telm said with a shake of her head and a frown. "Such as, I hear you will be headed north to visit Castle Grey."

"I will be, something called a honeymoon," Aren said.

"I would advise you to draw the attention of as many warriors as possible," Telm said, motioning down the path towards Danya. Aren followed the motion and began walking with Telm at her side. "A queen cannot openly claim more than one warrior, not the way you claimed Av, anyhow. But you can win their hearts. The North has a great many warriors and very few queens. Much like palace lands, those queens or rank beside warrior that exist are located around Castle Grey."

"Just how many queens are there?" Aren asked.

"Sixteen, all belonging to the Marilton bloodline. Some few have mated into the line, but most of the warriors born to the Mariltons must make do with commoners or, those lucky enough, with healers. If a queen is found, she is directed to the baron's sons first. Any warrior or other rank who attempts to step in is killed. The North is not a place where disobedience is suffered from warriors.

"There are exceptions to this rule. If a queen chooses another, then her choice is accepted, but every effort must be made to direct her to a Marilton boy. Usually, the brothers sort out who will secede in childhood and the heir takes the first crack at all queens until he finds one willing to take him on. There has been more than once where the one who should have been heir was killed because he lacked a queen as his father took ill."

"You mean to imply that Url might be in danger?" Aren asked.

"By their traditions, yes. He's bedded a healer here. The two barely spoke to one another before he did so, which strongly implies that he will set eyes on no other that he might desire. He may be heir, but he has to become the baron for the title to be destroyed completely. He has several brothers, of whom three are rumoured to have dallied with multiple queens."

"But Url is the heir," Aren said, confused as Telm pulled to a stop once more. "And we've already said that he doesn't have to mate a queen to become baron."

The older queen sighed loudly. "How do I put this so that you might understand? You rule palace lands, but not all the lords and ladies want you to. So it is with all lands."

"There will be those that are against the North rejoining palace lands," Danya said as she rejoined them.

"It is my understanding, from conversations with the baron and through the various visitors, that the baron is only part of the hierarchy which rules," Telm said quietly. "Trainers are held in high regard, and when Ervam lived in the North, he had the ability to overrule his father's judgements and commands. I've heard mention of elders not liking various things, including bowing to an unblooded chit."

"Why do people keep saying that?" Aren demanded, upset and confused at the same time.

"Chit?" Telm asked.

"Unblooded," Aren countered.

"It would be easier to explain what a chit is," Telm muttered.

"A girl who reminds the speaker of a squirrel who chitters from a tree about everything," Aren said with a growl. "I'm not completely unaware."

"You have to recall it is warriors who keep saying unblooded," Danya said to Aren. "I think it just means untried. Url hasn't mentioned anything about queens having to kill to prove their worth, nor as Olea."

"Queens can be just as violent as warriors, and if that were the case, then it would be said that Aren has been tried by the barons and she nearly put Van through the floor for disobedience," Telm countered quickly. "No, this blooding thing must be a barony idea, but I haven't any clue what it means. Something about this blooding makes you worthy in the eyes of the people of those lands. The trouble is, what one land finds worthy, another may not."

Aren swore and looked around them. There were no servants or visitors in the gardens around them. No one to spy, no one to interrupt.

"I can't even go on holiday without being told to watch my every move!" she protested finally.

"You aren't going on holiday, that's not what a honeymoon is," Telm said sternly.

The two stared at one another for a long moment, expecting the other to look away.

A honeymoon had been put forward to Aren as a type of holiday for those who were newly mated. Obviously, she had been lied to, but that didn't mean that she would simply accept her fate and give up on getting a holiday, one way or another.

"A honeymoon is where mates settle their disputes out of the public eye. It's not uncommon for them to end up physically fighting. And then having sex by way of apology."

"Fighting, that reminds me," Aren muttered. "The captain of the guard will be furious that I'm heading north instead of training."

"You could speak with Url," Danya offered.

"He will place you with the young warriors," Telm said, motioning about stomach level. "And I do mean the young ones. The ones who they know are warriors but haven't begun the changes yet. Try not to seem insulted by it. You're safer with them than with the boys who have begun the changes or full-grown warriors, who, despite rumour, do not appreciate queens learning alongside them. The queens up north are free to do as they like, even free to learn to fight, but only from their mate, not in public where any man might strike her."

"That's ridiculous," Aren protested.

"It's smart," Telm countered. "If Av stood around watching you train and witnessed another man strike you, there isn't a warrior on palace grounds who would fault him for killing the one who struck you. It is well within his rights, here *and* there, to kill anyone who touches someone he claimed. Up there he's allowed to kill those who touch another warrior who he has claimed. The insults that might pass here will end in bloodshed up there. There are many warriors to go around and not one of them is going to complain at the loss of competition for the blood of a queen."

"What if one of them tries to kill Av?" Aren asked.

"Being mated to a queen typically stops that thought in its track. These warriors aren't looking to breed you specifically, but want to get close enough to you that they can push their sons on your daughters. If one of them thinks Av has crossed a line, raped you, beat you, anything of that sort, they will not hesitate to take him out and replace him with themselves, or their brothers, or their close friends."

"Because even if they don't end up mating me, they still have access to the blood," Aren muttered. "Does anyone care what I want?"

"They do, which is why you would have the choice of the conquering warrior's friends and family," Telm said quickly. "But Av won't go over that line. The only thing I would caution you on is making it clear that you want him at your side and that there is no open invitation for better blood to come along. The North has heard of Av and Jer's growth, but have never met them. To the North, the Marilton boys are untried and unblooded.

"When it comes to choice, a queen in the North has a great deal of choice, she only needs to voice it and it will be given to her. Do not take advantage of that, however, lest you be viewed as spoiled. Any queen who goes north will be pampered and will find warriors who call to her. How many and how strong they are depends on the queen herself. Olea has a guard of fifty men who would fall on their own blades for her, along with some two hundred men ready to mobilize at a moment's notice to protect Er in battle to keep her happy."

"But Olea is a great queen, so everyone tells me," Aren said glumly. "Compared to her, I am nothing more than a mote of dust."

"Olea has had decades to build her group of warriors," Telm said sternly, shaking a finger at Aren. "You've barely been public about being a queen for a year, not even a year yet. If you had begun as a child, as a queen is supposed to, you'd have no problems now. We could practically ride to war tomorrow."

Aren sighed again. "Is there anything that will get me killed? Besides killing the baron, of course."

"Killing Olea would get you killed. Questioning a warrior might if he gets at you before Av can intervene. Besides that, it is my understanding that there is little a queen could do. The traditions of the North were built upon protecting the queens, not destroying them."

"Meanwhile you all will be down here doing what, exactly?"

"Preparing for war—what else would we be doing?" Telm asked, sounding confused and mildly insulted.

Chapter Five

After speaking with Nae and making certain she would stay out of sight until Av left the palace, Url headed back towards his rooms.

It wasn't that he wanted Nae not to pass on whatever it was that she saw when she touched Aren, it was that he didn't want her near Av just then. Best to give both time to calm down and settle a little more before Av was given a reason to go looking for Lord and Lady Bilgern, who would be leaving very soon.

Hopefully, Url's anonymous letter to them would send them on their way the very next morning, before Av had time to recall that Nae, and the Bilgerns, existed.

In the middle of the hallway, Url came to a halt and stayed perfectly still. He sniffed the air, suddenly aware that he was being followed. Turning slightly, he studied the hallway behind him but saw nothing. Url frowned and continued, but whoever was shadowing him had made a mistake, and now Url knew the male was behind him.

He paused to study a painting, moving slowly and as naturally as he could. Whoever it was managed to hide in time, but his keen ears picked up the intake of breath and the too young voice that almost yelped.

Mie was stalking Url.

It was the only explanation he could come up with, as the other warriors at court had their parents to keep close eyes on them. They had one another to hunt and pretend to follow. They would play games with one another across the hallways and would not have slunk about in the shadows.

A lone, little warrior, however, would have to slink in the shadows and stalk his prey if he wanted to survive beyond adolescence.

What Url didn't understand was why Mie was stalking him instead of playing with the other children. He was new blood that no one had attempted to claim yet. Van's daughters should have been chasing after Mie as they did so many other new warriors. Lerd's children had joined the small flock of palace children without any trouble, yet Mie was still slinking about.

Stalking Url.

Unless this wasn't stalking.

Url glanced behind him and wondered if the young boy was an early bloomer. Most didn't start dominance challenges until their voices began to crack. Url still recalled the day when he had decided that his father had to die. Some foolish argument over a bedtime had set Url off, and he had tried his damnedest to take down the larger warrior.

Once he had calmed down, he hadn't understood it. He loved his father, and his father loved him. It had been that love that had kept Er from beating Url as he had so many challengers before.

Url also distinctly remembered the feeling of almost getting the upper hand, only to have his father force him to submit.

He tried to recall how the fight had happened. What had he taken away from that show of force? A young warrior was impressionable. If Url made a wrong move, Mie might take the wrong lesson from the fight. The boy wasn't very well trained as it was, years behind his peers to the north. Url knew he had to take that into account, but he felt as if he were about to fight a babe. He didn't want to hurt Mie, simply begin to lay the foundation for the awakening instincts.

Url paused at another painting and stared up at it, wondering how far away from his father he was. Er had raised several boys of his own and had helped raise numerous other young warriors who were wards of Castle Grey. He would know how to handle Mie.

Frustrated, and aware that Mie would pick up on that frustration, Url turned from the painting and continued down the hallway towards his rooms. He didn't share his rooms with his parents, thankfully, but that also meant that he would have to change direction and that would no doubt alert Mie to the fact that Url knew he was being followed.

He heard a sound behind him.

Then something collided with his back.

It took a moment for Url to turn and flick the something off of him, another moment for him to understand what it had been.

Mie had flung himself at Url and had latched on, only to be tossed back down the hallway. Url stared at Mie, puzzled, and wondered what doddering fool had taught him to leap upon a bigger form. As Url contemplated that, Mie lunged at him once more.

Url was caught off guard but still moved with the smaller body. He hit the floor and batted at Mie ineffectually, on purpose. It wasn't until the boy bit him that Url growled and turned the tables. Hands and feet were fine, he'd even put up with some clawing, but teeth could still draw blood, even if two warriors were fighting.

He flung Mie down the hallway and almost got to his feet when the boy lunged at him again.

Where had the boy learned to fight? From street rats? From dogs?

Url took hold of Mie's throat and slammed the boy into the floor with half his strength. If he had done that to a commoner child, Url would have been put to death. To Mie, it showed several things. One was that he didn't break when another warrior tossed him about, but it still hurt. The other was a show of strength. Url had decades of training over Mie, and the boy needed to learn that attacking a fully trained warrior was a good way to get oneself killed.

He simply held Mie by the throat as the boy struggled.

Ah yes, that was what this lesson was. Mie would remember how hard he had fought and how easily Url had taken him down, when he chose to do so. It taught restraint to young warriors, but also showed them what it was like for a commoner, or even a queen, attacking a warrior physically.

Fully trained, a commoner could hold their own against a weaker warrior, but Url's blood, Mie's blood, had never been weak.

Mie struggled and tried to reach Url, but his arms were too short. When he tried to beat at Url's arm, he found it solid as stone. The boy panted with his effort to get away but didn't stop struggling, as he should have.

Had no one taught Mie to submit?

"Url?" Aren squeaked out.

The horror in her voice was evident.

He looked up at the queen and saw the pale white colour of her skin. How long had she been standing there, that her skin was that colour? How long had it taken her to regain her voice?

Url glanced at Telm, a step behind Aren, who made an obvious motion.

Aren had witnessed Url slamming Mie into the floor.

"Hm?" he said in response.

"What are you doing?" Aren shouted back at him.

"Warrior things," he responded and gave her a toothy grin.

Except she was not impressed with the fact that he had pinned Mie without hurting the boy or breaking any of the furniture. She seemed more upset by his response than she should have been.

"Url?" His mother walked around the corner, glanced at Aren, then cocked her head and jabbed it towards Aren as if asking what was going on.

She must have followed a trail of something, must have felt Aren's surprise and horror.

Url could only shrug in response as Mie tried to claw his eyes out. He wasn't doing anything wrong. If he had been, Ervam would have shown up and thrown him across the hall, probably breaking his face in the process.

"Aren, is something the matter?" his mother asked the queen.

Aren turned to Olea and jabbed a finger at Url. "He slammed Mie into the floor!"

"Oh dear," Olea reached out and took Aren's hand. "Come with me. Telm, you should know better."

"Know better?" Telm asked, turning to follow the two younger queens. "It's not my fault we stumbled in on that."

Alone in the hallway once more, Url looked down at Mie and squeezed the boy's throat gently. Mie's arms dropped to the floor, his breathing ragged. For being so young, he had a great deal of energy to put towards a fight. The only reason Url could come up with for why Mie hadn't submitted sooner was the fact that Aren had arrived in the hallway.

Url held Mie a moment longer so that the boy would know that this was not just a game, and then let him up. He left the boy in the hallway and went around the corner, to where he had seen the queens go. His mother was whispering very quickly to Aren, who stood with her back to Url, tension in every line of her body.

"If Mie was older, *what* could happen?" Aren demanded loudly.

"Thank you, for making that less awkward," he snarled at his mother.

"I'm just saying it's a possibility," Olea protested. "Not that it will happen when he's older. If you catch a warrior when he's older than Mie is, it can happen. It has in the past when the warrior was old enough for the one but too old for the other. Mie should have been introduced to this years ago with Jer and Av at least going through the motions in front of him so that he knew what to expect."

Aren turned to Url, her teeth and hands clenched as she looked him up and down.

"It is completely natural for a boy to attack a grown man if they are both warriors," Url said calmly. "I'd suggest you ask Ervam if you want another opinion on the matter. That way if he has a problem with me putting his son to the floor, he can find me and sort it out with me before I leave for the North."

"But you just slammed him into the floor. He probably needs a healer!" Aren protested.

"No, he's fine," Url responded, holding up his hands to try to soothe Aren. "Pride might be a little bruised, but sometimes you have to bruise a warrior's ego to get through to him. It will happen several times before Mie is grown and then he will begin starting real fights, either with commoners or other warriors, the type of fights that he needs to know how and when to submit to.”

“Happens all the time?”

“I didn't say all the time, but when you have as many warriors in one place as we do at Castle Grey, I suppose that is a good way to put it.”

“Av walks into Castle Grey—”

“Someone is going to put him into the ground,” Url said before Aren could finish.

He should have let her finish. The queen looked as if she might swoon. She took in several small breaths and looked away from Url.

“No,” she said firmly.

“I'm not the one who would be doing it,” Url responded quietly. “I have no control over those who would be doing it. Likely a youth who wants to earn a place above anyone at all. We all start at nothing and need to climb through the hierarchy, even me. Even my father had to.”

“It's harder for them though,” his mother said quickly from behind Aren. “With other warriors, the challenge doesn't have to be physical, but when you're the heir to the North, every warrior, even visiting warriors, try to best you physically. It's why only the strongest is named heir.”

“What is the point of that?” Aren demanded of Url.

He honestly had no idea. Some ladies in the palace had asked just that question to be rude or to attempt to show Url that he was wrong in his ways. Aren simply didn't understand.

“Submission,” he blurted out, if only so that she wouldn't think he had no idea what he was doing. “It teaches a boy what it's like to be driven into the ground by a warrior. A lesson he's not soon to forget. He learns what it's like for a commoner to fight against a warrior and why they submit, in the process learning how to submit himself. If it's not done at a young age, he could fall.”

“Go mad, you mean?” Aren asked.

“Take to the fields,” Telm said quietly.

Aren turned to Telm, who met Aren's eyes then looked away.

"It's when a warrior stops feeling," Url said, drawing Aren's attention back to him. "Queens are supposed to go through something similar, but not in the same physical manner. If you don't feel, you don't submit to a stronger body, you end up either destroying yourself or others. Normally the problem with falling, or taking to the fields as Telm called it, is that when a warrior is in that place he doesn't hold back, but the rest of us do. We die, commoners die, our queens die.

"So yes, I have no problem slamming a boy into the floor. He's not physically hurt, he won't need a healer and him attacking me means his instincts are beginning to awaken."

"You can't do that in the hallway!" Aren shouted.

"I don't choose the place," Url responded with a shake of his head. "I was trying to do it in my rooms."

"Because walking in on you over top of Mie in the privacy of your room would have been so much better," Aren said.

It took far too long for Url to make the connection and realize what Aren meant. When he did, he took a step back and turned his eyes to the floor.

"That is disgusting," he said, making certain to keep his face turned away from Aren.

"You can't do that in the hallways."

"Once again,"—he dared to look back to Aren as he spoke—"I do not choose where it happens, and at Castle Grey, Lady Aren, it will happen in the hallways, at dinner, and sometimes in your very rooms because there will be boys who challenge the newcomer, thinking him an easy target."

"He's not a target!"

"He needs to make that clear to them. Shouting at me isn't going to change that fact!" Url shouted, matching his volume with Aren's.

"And no one is doing that in my rooms," Aren said sternly.

"They're boys. You'll be lucky if they wear clothing around you," Url growled in response.

"Young warriors express rebellion by running the hallways naked as the day they were born," Olea grumbled from behind Aren. "If you tell them they can't, it's a challenge to do so."

"You're telling me that your children run around naked?" Aren asked, turning to Olea. "And that your men beat on them mercilessly and you're fine with that happening?"

"I once watched my mother pick up a boy by his foot and use him as a bat against his father," Olea responded steadily. "They were both warriors, it happened on palace grounds, and the boy had decided that my mother was a target."

Telm smiled and chuckled quietly. "He's afraid of me to this day."

Chapter Six

Two days later, Aren was still mulling over the event from the hallway. Even Ervam had said that such an event was completely normal and healthy for a young warrior to experience.

Sitting atop a horse, almost ready to leave, she was still turning it over in her mind. She had witnessed a grown man slam a boy into the ground, and not in a gentle fashion as Url seemed to protest when Aren had dragged him to Ervam for an explanation. Mie was fine, sitting alongside Ervam with a smile on his face and everything.

"It's normal," Av grumbled at her.

"Shut up," she responded sternly.

Which earned them both looks from the other members of their party.

There was a great ado about Aren leaving palace grounds, lords and ladies well wishing and bestowing gifts on Er and Olea. The ladies whined loudly about how Olea and Aren were being made to ride a horse as if they were men. The lords eyed Aren's boots, then her legs, with an eagerness that made Av growl at them.

By the time they set off, the sun was high in the sky.

The only clothing they brought with them were those necessary to get to Castle Grey. It was a long journey and taking trunks of clothing, of which Aren still only owned a few dresses, would only slow them down. Olea swore on her honour that she would provide Aren with clothing for the court-like functions that happened at Castle Grey.

The older queen had also made a comment about making Av go naked, something about how it would help his case with the people.

The journey itself was tedious. By the third day, Aren was bored by the surroundings. There was conversation nearly constantly as they rode, but it was mainly between Url and Er and was, at times, in another language. The new language caught Aren's attention, but the men didn't offer to teach it to her, and she couldn't follow it, though it did seem to share some words with the language she spoke.

It seemed, from watching them, that Er was giving Url instructions of some sort and Url appeared to be asking questions to clarify his instructions.

On the fourth day, Url said something to Er in that language of theirs and turned to Av to say, "neh?"

Av responded in the language and motioned about them. When Aren finally caught his eye, he frowned at her and shrugged, as if asking her why she had a problem with him responding. He pushed his horse on ahead to join the conversation as Olea sighed and slipped back, allowing the men to have their talk as the queens lagged behind.

"Av likely learned the language before he left the North. Children are sponges," Olea said to Aren. "I've learned a bit of it, but it's difficult for an adult to learn, I think. Url struggles with it sometimes because his father spoke it in private, but I never did, so he doesn't have the conversational down so well."

"Why did he look at me like I was stupid?" Aren asked.

Olea shrugged, then called out, "Av, how many languages do you speak?"

"One," Av called back over his shoulder. "Why would you ask that?"

To which the older queen responded in the other language, and Av shifted on his horse to stare back at her. The look held confusion and a bit of amusement as if he was certain there was a joke being played on him but didn't want to ask what the joke was.

Olea waited until Av returned to the conversation before she looked at Aren. "I told him he is a man of many mysteries."

"He must not have used the language in three decades," Aren protested.

"Unless his parents wove it into their private lives," Olea offered. "The moment those two are in private, they start talking, at least they have the past couple of years. To the point where sometimes Url forgets which he's speaking in. As I said, I don't speak it so well, makes it difficult to understand how his day has been."

The men continued their conversation throughout the trek, never bothering to include Aren. Though in the case of Url and Er, the two likely knew that Aren hadn't learned the language. But Av never even bothered to try to include her, which didn't make the trip seem any better.

Each night when they stopped to set up camp, Url would pull Aren aside and lead her through some exercises. The others set up the camp, and when Aren protested that she wasn't helping, Olea sternly told her to go back to training, unless she wanted to end up with the toddlers.

At least while she trained with Url, she could talk about something besides lady things, which was all Olea wanted to talk about. What was expected of ladies at Castle Grey, how she was expected to act by the others, not that she had to act that way if she didn't want to, it was completely up to Aren how she chose to act.

It was so annoying.

Url was patient in showing her how to move just the way he wanted her to, but the way he told her to move was not how she had been learning on palace grounds. He showed her why he wanted to teach her a different way to move as well, by whacking her when she moved the wrong way.

Which, he explained, was because the North had learned to fight palace warriors. By learning how to move around them, he could easily take out the guards and kill her in her sleep.

So he said in a calm, quiet manner as if he were commenting on the weather.

The last night, Er pushed them on even after it became dark. The moon was not out, leaving Aren wondering how Er found the way. In the forest around them, she could hear something moving, which caused her horse to make an agitated sound.

"What's that?" she asked.

Av responded in the other language, causing Url to call back to Aren, "Wolves. The castle will have released the hounds, though. They're headed our way. If you listen close you may hear them call out."

"You'll certainly hear Er call them to us," Olea muttered.

"What do you mean, call them to us?" Aren asked.

A howl came from directly in front of them. Because of the darkness, Aren had a hard time pinpointing where the creature was, it almost sounding as if it were level to a horse's back.

"Call them," Olea said quietly to Aren. "They hunt wolves, some of them are half-breeds. It's not safe to camp this close to the castle, we don't hunt the wolves down this way, good guard dogs. But if you want to visit, you need something to scare them off so you can get to the castle and lighting the way would simply encourage visitors, or so I'm told."

"But what if your people want to visit?" Aren asked.

Olea laughed as a dog barked nearby. "Castle Grey is south of all Northerners. We stand against palace lands. Our people come to us from the roads on the other side. Those we light."

"What sort of dogs hunt wolves?" she asked in response.

"If you want to hunt a wolf, you get a hound," Olea responded. "We have a hunting dog, yes, but it's intelligent and, thanks to the wolf that accidentally mixed in, is large as well. They don't hunt the wolves. They just drive them off. If a wolf kills a dog, Er will go hunting tomorrow with the hounds for a few pelts. He does love his dogs."

"They aren't just dogs," Er said sternly. "You women get up here with us, in case the wolves get bold and come to the road."

"They aren't going to come to the road," Olea muttered with a sigh. "All you need is his dogs or a queen who knows how to send fear into a creature, and I can do that."

There was a yelping to the right of them. Er growled from atop his horse.

"That's not one of ours," Url said quickly. "They must be getting bold, lean spring I suppose."

"Or they smell weakness," Olea huffed out.

"I am not weak," Aren muttered.

"My horse is, we should have selected better," Olea said steadily. "Up here, we're going to round a corner, and then the lights will come on."

"Lights out this far?" Aren asked.

"I am a queen of some skill," Olea responded as the night lit up.

To the side of the roads were poles with orbs atop them. The orbs did not feel like light orbs from the palace, which knew they were lights and responded eagerly to magic.

Aren turned to Olea to ask her what they were.

"They are light orbs, but they are solid glass balls," Olea said to Aren's silent question. "You see, pipes are difficult to relearn, even ours are so old that no one recalls how to link it to actual water. But light orbs look like glass balls and, as it turns out, once were. They have simply been used by queens for so long that they simply light up when a queen's magic touches them. These here have yet to be trained, and so cannot be lit by just any queen. Even my daughters have difficulty with them."

Arriving at Castle Grey was nothing like coming to the palace. There was no one waiting for them, and they tended their horses, placing each in a stall before Er gathered them together and pulled them into the palace.

Aren only regretted not being able to see Castle Grey in the daylight.

"This isn't my palace," she said sternly to Url, even though she didn't know why she would say such a thing. "You can keep it."

"Look..." Url pulled Aren to the side. "Aren, there are things we must discuss, but not right now. Just behave carefully, please."

Aren blinked up at Url, wondering why he had chosen then, of all moments, to bring up trouble. She looked down what she assumed was the greeting hall and met eyes with an elderly woman who was waiting for them. The woman seemed to dismiss Aren and glared at Url instead.

Perhaps Url hadn't counted on who would be greeting them in the hall?

"Lord Url, I'm not going to stub my toes just because I'm tired," she said without bothering to lower her voice.

Let the woman think that Url was concerned about Aren being weary from the travels. Either way, her words spoken were true; she had plenty of warning from Telm to watch how she behaved, even if Url didn't know of that conversation.

She moved away from Url, towards Av, as more people filtered into the hall. A few Aren recognized as rank, though there were several men present whom she couldn't pin down as being either commoner or warrior. While she was better at seeing rank, she still needed work. She assumed the men were warriors.

Aren took Av's hand in her own, hoping that was all the display that those present needed. She didn't want anyone fighting anyone else over a question of whether or not she was mated.

A young man approached them and smiled at her. "Hello, greetings, welcome to Castle Grey. Might you be interested in mingling your blood with mine?"

"I am mated."

The man waved to Av dismissively. Not as if he meant nothing, but as if he meant that Av needed to leave and let the stranger try to have his way with Aren. Av made a face at the young man as if he didn't believe what he had just seen. Aren almost giggled at the scrunched-up look.

Which drew the eyes of everyone in the hall to her.

The desire to giggle vanished and she looked down at the floor, knowing it was too late to hide. Taking a breath, she looked back up at the young man.

"I am mated."

"I will kill him, and then you will be available."

They were a violent people, that was what Aren told herself as she slid forward to the stranger, releasing Av's hand. She stood almost on his toes and looked up into his eyes as he smirked down at her.

"I am mated," she said.

"I can still kill him and make you available."

"Let me try that again."

She kneed him in the groin and, as he groaned and sank to the ground, yanked his blade from its sheath and placed it against his throat as she stepped behind him and jerked his head back by grabbing a handful of hair with her free hand.

Did everyone carry blades on them in the North?

Aren pressed the blade tight against his throat and met his eyes. She saw the flash of fear there and smiled slowly at him.

"I am mated," she said.

"As you say, lady."

She tugged on his hair and gave him a look.

"I will not try to kill him to make you available," he said quickly.

"You'd best not because I don't need a blade to kill you."

She tossed the blade to the side and moved back to Av's side. He met her eyes, but only for a brief moment before he turned his attention to Er.

"No weapons," the elderly woman, the one who had glared at Url, said as she approached them. "She is not allowed to carry a weapon while on Northern soil. It would give her an unfair advantage."

"She demands to be trained," Url said respectfully to the woman.

Meaning that this older woman was probably one of the elders that Telm had heard about. Perhaps even had a rank similar to Telm's. One that others revered and respected because she had a reputation that could not be explained in a few short sentences.

"Then she may have a training sword or stick for those moments only," the woman responded steadily. "That much we might allow. You had best find him a blade, however, if that's how his woman fights."

"As you wish," Er said dismissively.

Almost as if he were giving in to an adviser, but Aren had the distinct feeling that he had very little say over the matter.

"I have made certain that all know that they are to have access to public areas as well as set up a tour for them. There are three lords who wish to dine with you to discuss opening trade routes. Oh, and your bitch birthed wolves again."

Er swore loudly. "How did she escape this time?"

"Dug a hole out of the kennel and then jumped the fence," the woman responded.

To which Url and Er both swore.

"Are the pups still alive?" Er asked.

"They are, awaiting your judgement. Those lords that came to beg audience have also offered great sums if only you'd be willing to part with a precious Marl."

"So they can breed it to death," Er muttered. "Is that all the news you have for me?"

"Your niece is here," the woman said in a bland tone, one that Aren almost understood, but not quite.

"What's she done this time?" Er asked.

"Got herself pregnant and then miscarried the child after her beloved flung her down a flight of stairs."

"After she..." Er asked in the tone of a man who had heard such things before.

"Killed the dog you gifted him, stabbed his father, and lit his estate on fire," the woman responded with a small smile. "In his defence, he was trying to get her away from the flames and didn't know she was pregnant. Boy's been by as well. I sent him to your sister for safekeeping until you could deal with the girl."

Aren looked up at Av, who looked back at her in an awkward fashion. Even he wasn't certain what was going on. It was good to know, at the very least, that his days of talking in another language hadn't given him an upper hand somehow.

"Uh, if you don't mind," she said quietly. "We rode for a long time."

"And?" the woman asked.

She opened her mouth and almost said it, then closed her mouth again, unable to express the sudden desire to relieve herself. Perhaps it had been dealing with the stranger, who was still kneeling where he had fallen, or perhaps it was simply late, and she was tired.

"I have to piss," Av said. "He wouldn't even stop to let me piss."

"Ah, of course, I will show you to your rooms, and you might relieve yourselves," the woman said, motioning to the pair of them.

Av leaned down to whisper to Aren. "They don't understand tired, but they believe not relieving oneself in time might damage something inside and it will get you out of almost anything."

"Good to know," she muttered in response.

Chapter Seven

Aren stared at the toilet and pushed the button again. Nothing. Happened.

"Problem?" Av asked, walking into the bathing room.

"What if I had been going still?" she demanded of him.

"I can hear you jabbing the button, so what's wrong?" he asked, reaching around her to stab at it. "Oh. Right. Uhm, Aren, you need to flush the toilet."

"I tried that!" she shouted in response, jabbing at the button several times.

"No, I mean, you're responsible for the water in these rooms. I'm... I'm kind of surprised the lights work."

And the lights went out.

Aren gritted her teeth, set her weight and turned to him as they flickered back to life. "Kindly take a flying leap off the nearest cliff, of which I'm told there are many around here!"

"On the plus side, you can work the lights without any problem," Av said, then motioned to the toilet.

"I don't know how to work water. I've had to light things before, in the village, it was the only way I could see because I had a light orb."

"That's..." Av looked Aren up and down. "I don't need you to explain every small detail. I trust that you worked lights before."

He reached over and put the cover of the toilet down and gave her an apologetic look.

"Just in case. So, tell it to flush."

"Tell it to flush?" she asked him.

"The way you'd tell a light to work."

"Oh," she said slowly and then looked at the toilet.

She tried to focus her magic on the toilet and then tried to command it to flush. The water gurgled in a way that did not sound healthy at all.

"And that is why I put the toilet cover down," Av said expertly. "Try again." When Aren frowned at the toilet, Av made a sound. "Oh, wait." He reached out and jabbed the button, and there was the distinct sound of the toilet draining.

As Aren felt a different sort of drain.

"That doesn't feel right," she said.

"That's fine, we don't have to flush every time," he said quickly, taking hold of her as if she had wavered. "From what Er said, it's something you get used to. Olea's been doing it for years and probably doesn't think about it anymore."

"Which is probably why she didn't think to mention it," Aren grumbled, moving to the sink to wash her hands.

She turned on the water and washed. Then shut the water off and heard a gurgling coming from the sink itself. She looked down at the drain and frowned.

There was another gurgle, and she closed her eyes to grimace, only to be splattered in the face with something.

Something that smelled like...

Aren screamed.

"Close your mouth and stop screaming," Av said as he wiped at her face.

She closed her mouth, but that didn't stop the tears from pouring out of her still closed eyes. When most of it was gone, he pulled away, and she opened her eyes, sniffling all the while.

"I smell like shit."

He laughed.

The bastard *laughed*.

"Yes, you do."

"Hullo?" a voice called from the other room.

"We have visitors, and I smell like shit." Aren wept.

"Oh, it's not a funny thing that you said that." Av grimaced and left the bathing room quickly.

He returned a moment later with Olea, who blinked at Aren in surprise and then looked at the sink. The sudden fury on the older queen's face was momentary before it vanished and she looked at Aren with pity.

"It's not your fault, my dear." Olea waved a hand dismissively. "There, she's gone from the room. It's now yours. You worked the pipes quite well. It wasn't until you accessed the water that I recalled I should have told you about that and I came to make certain you did know and didn't just do it by accident. There's the bath, that's a shower."

"What's a shower?" Aren asked.

"Falling water," Av said with a gasp. "They work here? Em, well, she couldn't make a shower work near the end, and Aren doesn't know what it is so it just didn't start working."

"Yes, the showers can work." Olea watched Av walk to the shower excitedly. "Lord Av."

"What?" he asked mournfully.

Something about the older queen's tone pulled him to a stop and made him scuff his foot on the bathing room's floor. He looked at the shower and then to Olea before he looked at Aren.

"Oh, right," he said slowly.

"You're a bastard," Aren said in response.

"At least I don't smell like shit," he said with a chuckle.

"That's why you're a bastard," Olea snapped angrily at Av. "Get out of the bathing room this instant, you idiot!"

Av looked startled but did as he was commanded.

Aren sniffled again, inadvertently drawing the smell into her nose. She burst into a fresh bout of tears.

"He's excited, he doesn't mean it," Olea said quickly, approaching Aren as she did so. "Once it settles in a bit he'll take action. Come on, over to the shower."

"I don't want a shower!" Aren wept.

"Trust me, you do. The water falls from that there, almost like rain, and rinses everything clean. You won't be sitting in water that smells like whatever it was that hit you in the face. You can take a bath in the morning, or after you shower for all I care. But a shower would be the best course of action after that. There are two taps here. They're mainly for the men to adjust the temperature. This one is for heat. This one is for cold. Just like so."

Aren's tears came to a stop as curiosity took over. Olea turned the knobs and water fell, just as she said it would. Aren held a hand in the stream and felt the warm water falling, surprised at the entire idea of a shower. She had never thought of such a thing.

"A hot shower after going hunting is a marvellous thing. Instead of cooling water, the heat is constant."

"You just hold the temperature of the water as it runs out the tap. This is wonderful, though."

Olea hesitated, then said, "Good, I'll leave you to it, then. Strip and hop in. There are clothes in the other room for you. Soap is already in there, towel there. Drop your clothing in that basket there and then in the morning set the basket outside your door if you want the staff to wash them. They aren't servants here. They are staff. Though from what the servants told me, you won't have a difficult time adjusting to that idea. What am I forgetting? Oh, yes, Url will fetch you in the morning to take you to training.

"If your sink explodes again, you'll have to deal with it on your own."

"But I don't know who did it."

"Er's niece did it."

"Why?" Aren asked.

Olea blinked at Aren quickly. "It's a long story."

"Will you introduce me to her? I can't stab someone I don't know."

"Trace the magic back."

"You say to the person who didn't know how to shut off the lights when you met her," Aren said pointedly.

The older queen growled and made a face. She looked away and then to Aren and away again. There was a long silence.

"Fine!" Olea said. "I'll have bloody tea with that girl and invite you. If only so I don't have to break tradition and interfere again."

"Good," Aren said, looking at the shower. She watched the falling water for a moment, then turned back to Olea. "Is it possible to have this meeting outside?"

Olea frowned ever so slowly.

"Why?" the queen asked with all the command she could muster, even though it had no effect on Aren.

"No reason, just asking."

"Are you going to make a bird poop on her head?" Olea asked. "Because if you can do that, you have got to teach me that trick."

"I was just going to re-route the gutters. You do have those, don't you?"

The wicked grin that spread on Olea's lips was all the answer Aren needed. Olea patted Aren on the arm.

"You'll do just fine in the North."

Once Olea left the bathing room, Aren stripped off all her clothing and stepped into the shower. It was startling to have water raining down on her head, but there was something to be said for the constant stream of clean, hot water.

Stepping out of the shower clean, Aren found her mood had calmed quite a bit. She was also weary from a day's travel and using her magic in a different sort of way. Getting the water to work took quite a bit of thought, which meant she would need to stay awake while Av showered, least he run out of water halfway through.

And of course, he would insist on a shower.

She walked into the outer room with the towel wrapped around her and grabbed her clothing before moving back to the bathing room to change.

"You that mad at me?" Av asked as she walked out once more.

"Pardon?" she asked.

"I've seen every inch of you, you've changed in front of me dozens of times," Av said, motioning to the bathing room door. "But today you change in the bathing room, out of sight."

"I'm not upset, I just did it without thinking," Aren responded.

"Are you sure that you're not upset?"

"Go wash," she protested. "I can't sleep until you're done."

"Oh, suppose that would be true," he muttered, heading for the bathing room.

Aren waited until the water turned on before she dropped face first onto the bed and groaned. She was exhausted to her very core, something that she was fairly certain had more to do with the magic use rather than a long day of travel. She dragged herself the rest of the way onto the bed and lifted her head slightly, listening to the water still running in the bathing room.

With another groan, she dropped her face back into the bedspread.

When she heard the water stop, she sat up and climbed under the covers but stayed sitting up as she ran her fingers through her still drying hair to set things to rights.

Why was her hair still wet? She asked herself the question and held up a lock of hair, smiling as it dried itself. Not a trick she liked using often, but she knew how to and would use it when necessary. That night was not the night to roll over into a wet pillow because her hair hadn't had enough time to dry before bed.

She looked to the bathing room door as Av stepped out in absolutely nothing.

"I told you before how I like sleeping," he growled at her surprised look.

"I'm not surprised you're naked. I'm surprised you have the energy for that," she said, motioning to his crotch.

Av looked down, then looked back up, going just slightly red. "That was, uh, a little unplanned. It's fine though. We're both tired, and we should go to sleep. Url will be by at dawn to wake you for training and then I need to report to the arms master, possibly to get beat up for your display in the greeting hall."

"You should have just stepped in yourself," she said.

"Which is no doubt why I will be beaten," Av muttered as he climbed into bed. "I'm not blaming you, but the rules are different here, and I don't know them, and no one seems intent on explaining. You, however, you walk in and just do, and everyone seems damned impressed with you."

"Except Er's niece, who rigged the sink to spray me with whatever that was," Aren said with a disgusted shudder.

"Now that seems something that I should keep out of," Av responded. "At least until you give it a shot yourself. If that doesn't work, I'll bend the girl over my knee."

"She's old enough to get pregnant, which means you can't bend her over your knee."

"Says who?" Av asked.

"Says my mother," Aren responded sternly.

"Why?"

"Because it gives the girl the wrong idea and might be seen as an invitation."

Av frowned at Aren. The frown deepened after a moment, and he looked away from her.

"No," he said finally with a shake of his head. "The reason you don't bend a girl over and give her a swatting is because once she reaches a certain age, you'll hurt her pride more than her backside, which is why grown men will sometimes threaten to bend ladies over and give them a smack for misbehaving."

"I thought you only wanted to bend ladies over for that one little reason."

"I may not be the largest I've come across, but I would not call that little," Av said pointedly.

Aren simply looked at Av.

"What?" he groaned.

"Well, that seems an odd thing to say to a woman who has seen so few," she countered.

Once more Av frowned. "Damn it. I was supposed to see Nae before I left the palace."

That was an oddly suspicious thing to say after her comment. Aren wondered what Av was thinking, if she had to have a talk with someone about something that she didn't want to talk about.

"Why?" Aren asked.

"Url hid her on me, on purpose?"

"Av," Aren said through gritted teeth, "why would Url hide your healer friend from you?"

The way Av flinched away from Aren said it all. The man stared back at her for a long time before he responded.

"She's probably pregnant, and he's worried we'd fight."

"If I find out there's another reason for you wanting to see Nae before we left the palace, I will beat you to within an inch of your life."

"What other reason?" Av asked. "I'm not sleeping with her."

"I don't think you're sleeping with her, I think you're snooping where you shouldn't be snooping!"

"Oh, that," he said, not even trying to deny it.

Aren stared at Av expectantly, but he only rolled over and shut off the light beside him.

"Av..."

"Goodnight, Aren."

"Av, so help me."

"An inch of my life, I got it. We're both tired. It's affecting our moods. How about we talk about this in the morning?"

Chapter Eight

Jer had just sat down to breakfast when there was a knock on the door. Laeder, who had also just sat down, sighed and stood to answer it. It wasn't that Jer expected Laeder to answer the door, but it simply seemed the roles they took on. When there was a knock, Laeder answered and took messages or sent lords away who wanted to see Jer.

Somehow it worked. Jer hadn't been bothered in his rooms in nearly four days and the last lord to even try was two days before.

Laeder closed the door and returned with an opened missive, which he handed to Jer.

He wiped his mouth and then his hands and accepted the missive.

"I'm to attend or he'll what?" Jer asked, almost choking as he turned to Laeder.

"Will send me home to my father," Laeder said quietly. "Would he?"

The missive was signed with the signet seal of the master. A seal that sat in the master's house and was rarely used. The last time he had seen the seal was when Ervam had stepped down as master. It was a sign that he was very serious.

"Yes, and he has the power to do it," Jer said, setting the missive to the side.

He ate another mouthful of food as Laeder watched him. Knowing that the look on Laeder's face was the scribe's attempt to hide a hurt, Jer swallowed the food and looked at the missive, then to Laeder.

"He didn't say immediately, I can finish my meal first," Jer said.

"The servant said it was urgent."

"I didn't hear that part," Jer responded, standing.

He knew that if it were urgent, Ervam would have commanded he attend now. The missive had simply said to attend, giving Jer enough time to finish up his meal, which Ervam would have known that Jer had just sat down to eat.

He couldn't help being a creature of habit.

But Jer knew that something had been jumbled along the way, and if he remained in the rooms or tried to tell Laeder otherwise, his love would assume that Jer didn't care enough about him. To keep Laeder happy, who still didn't know Ervam well enough, Jer would skip breakfast.

"I will go and sort this out," Jer said, pausing to kiss Laeder on the temple. "You stay here, and don't open the door for anyone but me. If you hear war cries, get in the bathing room because one of us is coming through the door and not by turning the knob."

"You're going to end up fighting?" Laeder squeaked out.

"Only if he tries to send you back to your father, which I highly doubt, but it's always good to give a warning for the just-in-case scenarios."

Jer left the rooms and closed the door behind him. He waited on the other side until he heard the click of the lock sliding into place.

Annoyed, he left the palace, went across palace grounds and was rewarded when he found Ervam just sipping his morning cup of tea. The trainer looked startled to see Jer. Ervam looked to his tea, up to Jer, then back at his tea and swore.

"I did tell her it was urgent, but I meant urgent that she not get sidetracked," Ervam muttered, motioning to the chairs he had placed on the porch after taking over the master's home in the spring. "Take a seat."

"You'll do what with my mate?" Jer asked.

"I only sent that because I needed you to understand that what I need you to do is a very serious matter," Ervam said with a growl as he took a seat, lifting his mug to sip his hot tea. Then the tea lowered ever so slowly, and Ervam's head cocked to the side. "Your *what?*"

"Mate."

"Now yeh've a choice. We discuss you not inviting family to the ceremony, or going gently into the task."

Jer wanted to be rebellious. He wanted to deny everything and perhaps even start a fight. He had mated Laeder for a year and invited no one but an officiant. But he had just found out that his father wasn't really his father and... his entire world had been upside down. What else could he have done? It was only a year. Laeder didn't even consider it mating, he considered it handfasting. So, it wasn't really that big of a deal.

But obviously it was a big deal to Ervam. And either which way, whatever the trainer's problem with them mating, Jer had to find it out before he brought Laeder around again because he wasn't going to bring his mate into a possible hostile situation.

To get there, though, he'd play nicely, because he knew Ervam and knew the trainer wouldn't respond to anything else. The only time Ervam used 'yeh' in place of 'you' was when he was about to attack.

"Such a serious matter to discuss that I don't get offered tea?" Jer asked, sitting beside the trainer.

"And give you something to throw at me?" Ervam countered.

Playing by Ervam's rules, that meant Jer would want to throw something at him for the original reason of his being called. Jer tried not to assume that Ervam knew it was a delicate topic, Jer's being mated to Laeder.

The palace might preach equality, but the lords still ruled, and those lords had a problem with men mating other men. Women mating women, well, that was encouraged because at some point the lords assumed they would be invited in.

"Where are you sending me?" Jer demanded.

"South."

Jer swore loudly. "Why? We're at war with the South."

"Not that far south, just to the vineyard," Ervam said, sipping his tea again.

"You may be right. I might have flung the tea at you," Jer grumbled. "And why, oh wise one, am I going to Bilgern Vineyard while Aren and Av are up north...?" He trailed off as his father smiled at him. "Because you want me to go hunting."

Ervam nodded. "One of you at the very least had to go, preferably both of you to retrieve who needs to be brought back. But Av would have gotten in the way with his questions and nagging. I need you to do what you do best."

"I hunt ranks," Jer said sternly.

"And from what Av told me, you turned that on and missed Aren."

Jer gritted his teeth together and looked over the yard. "Sort of. You know how I get when I'm like that. He just asked me to find out who was bleeding."

"And you can sniff out blood that's been cleaned away," Ervam said gently.

Which made Jer groan. "No, no. I don't want to do that. That's not what the hunting is for."

"It's exactly what that is for," Ervam corrected. "Warriors like you help warriors like Av by destroying those who have done harm in the past, before he can find them because him destroying them will leave a mark on their relationship. You at least know to leave them alive. We need to know the damage."

"Nae knows the damage."

"Nae knows the physical damage and won't speak of it to anyone but the mate to the throne. Her words."

Jer swore again.

"If we want to know beyond the physical damage, we need to go there," Ervam said steadily. "However, Para was not exactly one to strike a child."

"Are you talking about the weeping at the insinuation that she might die sad and alone?" Jer asked.

"Basically, some wounds aren't physical, and it's more difficult for them to heal. A healer can't exactly ease the scar tissue. We can't recommend a hot bath to relax sore muscles or medicine for painful joints."

"The healers must have something for wounds that aren't physical," Jer protested.

"Warriors are how they solve those problems," Ervam said, then growled loudly and sipped his tea. "Or Danya, from the sounds of it. Have you spoken to that woman?"

"No, I can't say I have had one of these conversations with her, why?" Jer asked, looking at his father, who went red in the cheeks and played with the handle of his cup.

"I somehow volunteered to take tea with some widows."

"Somehow?" Jer asked.

"It wasn't anything she said. She barely said anything at all. Just asked about your mother and how long it had been."

"So why is Danya here and not in the North with Aren?" Jer demanded.

"I started the conversation with Danya about Aren. It seems that Danya is aware that Aren is holding things back. They keep hitting walls because either Aren doesn't remember, or is too afraid to speak up."

"But if she's afraid of her parents, how did she send them away?" Jer asked.

"I have no idea, but it probably took a great deal of strength to do that."

Jer considered the information. He closed his eyes as he recalled fights with Em. Some days he would manage to say what was bothering him, but for days afterwards no matter what she said, it hurt.

"She's raw, that's why she started crying," Jer said quietly, opening his eyes slowly. "We just sent her north, and she's unstable. Everything will be the end of the world for her."

"What are you talking about?" Ervam asked. "Aren doesn't follow that pattern."

"Because she blocks it out like she does anger and pain and all the other emotions. She stood up to her parents and forced them out of her life, and now she's alone just like they predicted. Mated to a man she doesn't love and who doesn't know that he loves her... She's fragile, and we should have caught it. *I* should have caught it."

"They're both stupid. They do love each other. They just haven't had the time for their minds to catch up to their bodies yet."

"That doesn't change the fact that Aren is amongst your relatives."

"She'll be fine, Olea will look after her."

"You once told me that if I had trouble with Em, I'd never have been able to handle a queen of the North."

"I... more of said that hoping you'd get your head out of the clouds," Ervam grumbled. "I certainly didn't expect you to remember it, given the fact that you were twelve years old and drunk."

"Yes, speaking of things you've said that will stick with a person..." Jer said. "You've upset my lover."

"Oh, he's your lover now?" Ervam asked, sounding surprised. "Last I heard, in this family, you bring your lovers to dine with your father."

Jer was just thankful that sentence hadn't involved the word 'mate' and that perhaps Ervam was going to let it slide without much of a fight.

"My father's dead."

"So is mine. Don't be smart with me, Jer."

The two of them looked to one another at the same time. The awkward silence that followed was laden with unspoken things. Neither had come right out and said it before, even though Ervam had been driven to that point over the winter. Ervam certainly hadn't known that Jer had known.

"If I bring him to dinner, I want the right to take him public," Jer said.

"Why are you negotiating that?" Ervam asked. "For starters, I'm the master. I represent equality."

"A good son provides children for his parents to find joy in."

"That's from a story!" Ervam shouted at Jer.

The trainer made a face and glared at his yard. The mug turned several times on the arm of the chair as Ervam considered whatever it was that was bothering him.

"I've *never* felt disgraced by your desires, Jer. I tried to separate you and Em because she was bad for you, because her damned mother was whispering those disgusting things in your ear. She was the one who told you the myth of the barony of the North, where yes, one such as yourself was forced to choose breeding over love in order to continue the tradition. This is not the North and you're not a damned baron."

"It's also, somehow, the belief of the court at the moment," Jer said.

Ervam glanced at Jer. "Just to be clear, you've never thought that—"

"Even if I did, I'd have a few choice words for a master who told a warrior under his care that he couldn't love another man."

"I was under the impression that you stayed with Em because you believed you had to be with a woman," Ervam said quietly.

"I stayed with her because she made me believe that if I left her, I would die sad and alone because no one else in this world could love me and I was blessed that she put up with me," Jer said.

"You're not going to fall under Para's influence, are you?"

"No, that woman? I knew her when she had spots on her face and still stuttered."

"I'm serious, Jer."

"So am I," Jer responded. "Em and Para may have taught one another a trick or two, but Para took a baby and frightened it, changing everything to take complete control. Em just made me think that no other woman could ever want me and as it turns out, that's fine. I don't need a woman."

"Are we in agreement then?" Ervam asked.

"As to what?" Jer asked in response.

"You and Laeder will come to dinner here tonight, then tomorrow morning you'll head for the vineyard."

Jer groaned. "Can't I take him with me?"

"To Para and Cerlot?"

No, that was not a good idea. The pair of them wouldn't take kindly to Laeder visiting their estate after the events of the previous fall.

"Can I take anyone with me, to help keep me sane?"

"There's an excuse for you to go," Ervam said sternly. "As steward to the court, you are the only one they would trust to take in the accounts of a ward estate, which is what Bilgern now is. You go in, say you're there for an assessment, and they are required to give you the full run of the estate."

"The steward always goes alone on such tasks as a sign of the trust of the throne," Jer said quietly.

"Unless the warded estate put up some sort of fight, which they did not," Ervam countered. "If the steward position had been filled by someone else, then yes, I would be sending a warrior or two down. I think you will suffice to keep them in place."

"But the war effort could keep us busy for months," Jer said, grasping at any excuse not to go.

He didn't want to. He found the whole idea of a vineyard boring. Not to mention the fact that visiting Bilgern would be uncomfortable to start with, given the history between them and the newly formed court.

"We've sent all our letters and our messages. All we have to do now is wait for responses, most of which will take ten days to reach us. What is it, again, three days' ride? Three down, four there, three back up, and you'd still arrive before the missives."

"You thought this all out well ahead of time."

"Yes, I know you quite well. I don't necessarily blame you for not going, but this is the type of thing that warriors are required to do, Jer."

"You raised me, I'm allowed to whine and moan," Jer said.

"Not if you keep saying that your father is dead, you don't."

Jer was quiet because he knew he deserved that jab. He thought about how he had addressed Ervam recently—when was the last time he had called the man Father or even affectionately? Too long, surely.

After learning the truth, it was difficult to look at Ervam and not feel something about it. What had happened wasn't Ervam's fault, he had done the best he could with what he had. The trainer had taken a bastard child, born of rape, and raised the child as his own, all while daring anyone to claim otherwise.

"It slipped out, I'm sorry."

"Have you told anyone else?" Ervam asked.

"Av is aware. Aren likely knows because Url said something."

Jer felt the fury of a trainer and thought about fleeing the porch. There was something cold and sharp about Ervam's anger as the man turned to him.

"Said something to you?"

"You're the moron who went ranting about queens walking with the spirits," Jer said pointedly.

"Which wouldn't have made any sense if you didn't already know, the child might have died. We might have put it up for adoption. I might have flung it from Castle Grey, all things which have happened in the past."

"I've always felt out of place, but I assumed that was because I was the youngest and hadn't really lived in the North at all."

"You were never out of place. You were right where you belonged."

"So, I'm stronger than Uncle Er?" Jer asked.

"As is Av," Ervam said pointedly. "I love you both, but Av could rip you apart. If you were both in a rage, I'd hide behind him. You'd put up a good fight, but you'd end up dying, and he's not going to turn on someone who hides behind him. Which gives you an edge, I'll admit, but warrior to warrior, he's the stronger."

"Wait, you decide who is strongest by who you would hide behind?" Jer asked.

"Same principle as a queen: who wouldn't you want to upset and, were they to be upset, who would you hide behind. Whoever would cause you to hide behind a queen is the strongest."

"Aren asked me that question in the fall. I struggled to explain it to her," Jer muttered.

"It is an explanation that one in the rank itself cannot give."

"How do you tell which trainer is stronger?" Jer asked.

"What's the name of a trainer?" Ervam asked.

Certain he was walking into a trap, Jer responded slowly. "Ervam…"

"Is the strongest trainer," Ervam filled in. "Healers are who can do the best, but if you want to know who is the strongest, stab yourself somewhere vital and walk into the healer hall. Whoever you move towards is usually the most capable at your wound, making her the strongest. Normally, anyhow."

"What about the unranked ones?" Jer asked.

"They do not exist in this era, and so we do not speak of them," Ervam said, quoting the archivist. "No idea, but you won't run into any of them on the vineyard. If they do live in this era, they hide very well. Just don't stab anyone."

"Not even Para?" Jer asked.

"Especially not Para. Need her alive. If there are other ranks there, however, just recall to ask yourself whom you want to run from. Even if you don't know them very well, your instincts will rarely lead you astray."

Chapter Nine

Aren wandered the hallways, lost. After morning training, Url had sent her on her way. She hadn't protested at the time because she had been fairly certain that she knew the way back to the rooms.

Apparently, she was wrong.

Castle Grey had many windows. The hallways had them, rooms that didn't line outer walls had glass ceilings in places. The roughly carved rocks that made up the walls were a grey colour, but she was fairly certain that her initial assumption was correct.

This was not the palace. There was no magic in those stones. Aren wasn't in awe over the age of the blocks. They were newer than the palace was said to have been, even if one took into account the protective magic that had saturated everything that resided in the palace.

Hearing water, she walked towards it. Running water surely meant people.

But around the bend, she found a small stone fountain, trickling water in the middle of a round room. The ceiling of the room was made up of glass, letting in the morning sun. There were twelve alcoves built into the wall of the round room, each with a stone sitting on the floor. Each stone was almost black in colour.

Around the stones, even on shelves above them, were growing plants in pots. The plants reached towards the ceiling for their light. They were probably even watered from the fountain.

One way in, one way out. The room was a sanctuary, and Aren didn't feel right being there.

"Are you in trouble?" a small voice asked from the other side of the fountain.

Aren jumped in place and turned towards the voice.

A woman walked around the fountain. She was dressed in red and gold, though the few women Aren had seen in Castle Grey had all dressed in bright, happy colours. Her black hair hung down, in palace lands style, and hardly moved as she seemed to glide towards Aren. The woman's eyes drew Aren's attention, for they seemed an odd colour, a brown that was an almost red.

Perhaps that was why the woman chose such a deep shade of red to drape herself in.

Women at Castle Grey all had their hair up in various styles, all except Olea. While born of Northern and palace lands bloodlines, Olea had chosen to let her hair hang loose, as it had been all her life.

Which would mean that this woman was also from palace lands, though Aren hadn't been told that those from palace lands visited Castel Grey at all.

"I seem to be lost," Aren said.

"Aren't we all?" The woman chuckled to herself and turned to the fountain. "You would be the one who sits the throne? I didn't catch your name."

For some reason, Aren wanted to say that behaviour suited a queen. What other rank would speak to the one who sat the throne with such assured disregard?

"Aren, Aren Argnern. No, sorry, Aren Marilton—I just mated the baron's nephew."

"Aren?" The woman sighed out the name and stiffened. She turned towards Aren, and those almost red eyes roved down, then back up. "Of course you would be."

"You know me?" Aren asked.

"I know the name," the woman said quietly. "No doubt there are many with names just like yours, headed towards the palace as we speak."

"Why...?" Aren asked.

"A message, for those of us who know how to read it," the woman said quietly. Suddenly she gave herself a shake and blinked at Aren. "My apologies, where are my manners? My name is Raven. I'm a queen. I didn't mean to be rude as if I'm better than you. I just forget sometimes that people still need a name to go by."

"Raven, like the bird?" Aren asked.

Raven smiled, a wicked sort of thing. "Yes, like the bird."

Did they now share a secret? One that Aren didn't know she was sharing? Did no one else know Raven's name?

And what sort of damned message was being sent by *her* name?

"The throne chose my name, didn't it?" Aren asked.

"No doubt had one close to it suggesed the name to your mother, it would have told her it's good luck to name a child as rank before the child is born," Raven said steadily. "That name has only appeared a few times through history, and if what Mirmae Hue said is true, the lands are in for as much trouble from you as they were from your namesakes of the past."

"I'm sorry, I'm...?" Aren trailed off.

"You are not the reborn spirit of those Arens, no. It used to be a family name for the unranked ones, which you are not. Queen, through and through. Isn't that delightfully different?"

"Well, the throne did make me, and I don't think it's capable of making unranked ones."

"It led your parents together to breed when otherwise they wouldn't have. The throne didn't make anything. It simply used the magic of a queen to alter the perception of the intended breeders. It's a very common thing and queens used to do it all the time, though their mark was a great deal less obvious and typically the romps would only last until the woman was pregnant, and then everyone just seemed to forget that anything happened at all. Which complicated things when bastards were seen as bad instead of good."

"Are you a history keeper?" Aren asked.

"You could say that. I do know a great deal of history," Raven said with a smile.

"Where's my palace?" Aren demanded.

To which Raven laughed, and Aren swore it grew a little brighter in the room. The other queen placed two fingers over her lips and quieted, but still smiled widely at Aren.

"Castle Grey, despite how the North speaks of it, is only built with some hundred stones from the old palace," Raven said. "Of those hundred stones, many have been removed since. They don't speak well with the other stones and keep insisting that they are part of a library, or the kitchen, when in fact they are part of a hallway or Er's little throne room. The few that remain are in this room and hold no structural value at all. These stones are called foundation stones."

"The important bits," Aren muttered.

She looked over the stones in the alcoves, then back to Raven, who still smiled back at her.

"Not important in the way that Er believes them to be important, but still very important, to the right people. And back then, it was *very* important that they bring the stones here rather than allow commoners to destroy them. These stones, Northern myth says, must always be filled with magic. The queens who mate the barons all work with their daughters to fill a stone during their lifetime. If ever the stones fall silent, Castle Grey will fall from its cliff-side and kill everyone inside."

"That's a little gruesome," Aren said.

"Gruesome, but necessary. The need for these stones was so important that they wrote it over and over again, and then lost the real reason why the stones were important. Here— this one here is almost empty. It will be safe for you to touch."

Aren blinked at the stone, and the dying plants atop it, then turned to Raven. She pointed to the plants in a questioning manner.

"Yes, they are an indication that the stone is about to empty. Url, bless his little heart, has no mate when he should by now. Olea and her daughters cannot fill another rock, but bless them as well, theirs is filled to brimming and will last fourteen generations."

"Are these like the throne?" Aren asked.

"No, these strictly..." Raven trailed off. "It's difficult to explain the metaphysical data you would be required to consume to understand even the wrong concept of what these rocks contain and are for."

"I'm going to go with some sort of landscape magic," Aren muttered, frowning at the stone. "Is this all of it, though—the entire magic?"

"The important bits, yes."

"I asked you if this was all of it," Aren countered sternly.

"No, Lady Aren. This is not all of it. The magic is capable of tracing back to origin but something happened between there and here, or with the magic, and it's never made the leap back, as it was supposed to."

"What do you mean by that?"

Raven motioned to the fountain. "The fountain is relatively new, compared to the rest of the room. Do you see the black stone under it?"

Aren looked down. Sure enough, there was a ring of black stone under the fountain. The stone had the same shade to it as the rocks in the alcoves.

"Those don't have to be filled?" Aren asked.

"They would, if they worked," Raven responded bitterly. "Part of, but not entirely, the purpose of these stones was to link back to the palace. It's my understanding that only a queen could use it because the stones in the middle cannot hold magic, they are an anchoring point. The queen steps on and flits from here to there."

"What would be the point of that?" Aren grumbled. "Lone queen popping into the palace. Especially since they don't believe in training their women up here either, like I was told they do."

"You've been training?" Raven asked as if she didn't believe her.

At least the older queen could be caught off guard, Aren told herself silently.

"Yes, all I wanted was a quiet life out in the country somewhere, and people were pushy, and Lord Av insisted everyone train so I decided that if I knew how to fight, I could protect myself and then I wouldn't have to worry about hiding."

"But on palace lands, women aren't told those myths," Raven said quietly. "Only the East speaks of women standing for themselves."

"Someone said something about women joining their men in battle," Aren said with a shrug.

"No, you don't understand, women on palace lands are discouraged from picking up a blade, from fighting or training. Where is Av?"

"I'm lost, how would I know?" Aren demanded.

"Right," Raven muttered.

"He probably got the idea when he was almost kidnapped along with his brother, and his mother was attacked in the process but unable to defend herself because she didn't know how."

"She was damaged in the process, wasn't she?" Raven asked. "Mirmae should have had at least six children before she threatened Ervam with a blunt instrument and even then she'd probably have three more."

"Whatever happened, she only ever had two."

Raven swore. "Such a waste of good blood."

"She had two sons," Aren protested.

"But no daughters," Raven countered. "Queens in the North, as you no doubt know, are very rare. They're raised from birth being told that if they don't at least try to have one of their rank, they are failing the people. Mirmae must have been devastated. I'm devastated. Er would have surely brought the girl back to Castle Grey, and then there'd be none of this nonsense now."

"What nonsense?" Aren asked.

"The stones!" Raven shouted. "You think I want to go tumbling down a cliff?"

"But you said that was a myth," Aren said slowly.

"The magic in those stones may not be the throne, but it is a thinking magic. After so long by itself and very, very clear instructions on how to care for it and the consequences of not providing the magic, you don't think it won't just rage and quit and kill you all?"

"You said almost gone, it's not going to kill me in the least," Aren said quietly.

Raven glared at her. Aren smiled slowly.

"I do see the frustration," Aren said.

She turned back to the stone and studied it, then walked slightly to the side and studied it some more. Even trying, she couldn't feel any magic in the stone. Looking to the others, she still couldn't feel any magic, but there was something.

"I don't feel any magic," she said.

"It's an old magic, the queens simply put wood to its fire," Raven responded as she sat on the edge of the fountain.

"But shouldn't I still be able to sense something?" Aren asked.

"You do know how to use magic, don't you?"

"I know how to shut off the lights at the palace," Aren said. "And I learned how to use the pipes here, but not before they exploded brown sludge on me because Er's niece has some problem with me despite the fact that we've never met."

Raven arched an eyebrow at Aren. "The girl is strong in magic but weak in every other aspect. Touch the stone, Aren."

"Don't give me commands like you're above me," Aren said with a grumble.

"Why are you protesting if you do it anyway?" Raven asked, motioning to the stone.

Aren turned her head and frowned at her hand on the stone. She didn't recall touching it, and it wasn't until she laid eyes on her hand that she felt the cold stone under her fingers.

And the icy hole that wanted to drag her down into an eternal darkness.

Aren snatched her hand away and stumbled backwards, over someone. She nearly hit the floor before a set of strong hands dragged her to her feet.

"If you were *anyone* else, I'd think you'd done that on purpose," Er snarled at her.

"Did what?" Aren asked faintly, feeling a numbing almost-warmth coming over her. "When did you get here? Where'd she go?"

"Where did who go?" Er asked.

"Raven, she was just here, said the… what happened?"

Er lifted Aren right off the floor, causing her to squeak in surprise. The baron growled again, but this time Aren didn't think he was growling at her, he was facing the entrance, and there was definite frustration.

"You touched something that shouldn't have acted like that unless you knew how to use magic and did something very stupid," Er said sternly.

"Is that why I feel floaty?" Aren asked, setting her head against him to stop the room from spinning.

"Probably, I don't know much about magic beyond what I'm told," Er responded. "I'm taking you to your mate."

"That's fine," Aren whispered.

"And I'm telling him what you did," Er said, putting an edge to his voice.

"Is fine," Aren mumbled.

She almost fell asleep but pulled herself out of her daze at a thought. She dragged her head up and blinked up at Er.

"Where's Raven?" Aren asked.

"Lady Aren, there's no one in Castle Grey named Raven."

"Palace-born queen, of course, she's here."

"There are only two palace-born queens in the whole of the North—yourself and Olea," Er said, the frustration returning.

"Maybe she calls herself something else," Aren sighed, recalling the secretive smile. "She'd be hard to miss, eyes are almost red."

"I'll keep that in mind when I speak with the elders."

"Hair dark as the bird she was named after."

"Of course, Aren."

"Where did she go, I wonder…"

Chapter Ten

Av looked up when Er entered the room carrying Aren. He frowned as the baron marched around him and set Aren ever so gently on the bed. There was a furtive motion, and then Er was headed out the door again.

Glancing at Aren, obviously fast asleep, Av frowned and left the room, closing the door as gently as he could behind him.

"What's going on?" Av asked.

"Come with me."

"Will she be safe in there?" Av countered, motioning to the door.

Er stiffened and turned his full attention to Av. It wasn't until that moment that Av truly understood what it was to be a dominant warrior. There was a fury in Er, at even being asked that question, and the barely restrained threat that now seeped into the hallway because Av had been stupid enough to voice a concern.

"In my home, you ask that of me?" Er asked in response.

"Last night another queen used magic to splatter her with something, and now you're bringing her to me unconscious. Yes, I dare ask a question that obviously needs to be asked," Av said sternly. "You know I would not have asked that, had you brought her to me awake. Though, to be fair, my question at that point would be if you were certain she'd stay there just because you said so. What's she done, anyhow?"

"That's why you need to come with me," Er said, heading off down the hallway.

Without answering the question, as if the complete disregard for a question of safety was, in itself, the answer.

Trying not to growl, because he was fairly certain it would be taken as a challenge, Av followed Er. They moved silently through the hallways and deeper into the castle. Finally, they pulled to a stop in a circular room.

Av breathed in and knew immediately what the problem was.

"But how did it end up like this?" Av asked.

"She touched a stone," Olea said, motioning to one of the alcoves. "It's true then. You can't feel the magic of the other queens who have anchored here?"

"No, just Aren," Av said, frowning around the room. "Though I'm not certain how I know that feeling is Aren, I've never felt it this strongly before, and I've gone looking for her by trying to search that out. I like it."

"I can still feel the other magic," Olea insisted. "She didn't destroy it, just told my magic it was hers, and then it converted."

"Stone?" Av asked Er.

"No, there was a fountain there," Er said, motioning to the middle of the room.

Av stared at the empty spot, looked at Er, then back at the spot. "No, I meant do you think it happened because she's infected?"

"Oh," both Er and Olea said as one.

"How big was the fountain?" Av asked.

"Large," Olea said.

"And sealed to the floor," Er said in a tone that drew Av's eyes to him. "She also asked where Raven was."

"The palace?" Av asked.

"A woman with red eyes and black hair," Er said cautiously.

Av swore. "I knew she was unstable, but I didn't think it was that bad, or that the madness would start so soon. I thought we'd have years at least."

"You assume it's madness?" Olea asked. "Why not the throne speaking to her in a different manner? I mean, Raven, a woman represented in black and red? It could be a bid to take the palace back."

"This was not the workings of the throne," Av insisted.

"How do you know?" the queen demanded.

"Because I know, damn it!"

"Can we argue that?" Er asked Olea.

Olea was quiet as she studied the room. "They can't very well put demands on her because of this, she's not Northern-born or mated, she sits the throne."

"Who are 'they'?" Av asked.

"But we can, Olea," Er said as if Av hadn't spoken at all. "Which is why I asked you. What's this going to cost us?"

"I don't know," Olea said, sounding flustered. "Who can even do this? Changing magic, reclaiming what was laid out by others before herself? And then there's the fountain. That will cost us. We'll have to replace it at the very least."

An elderly woman walked past Av, giving him a swat to the backside as she did. The swat caused him to leap to the side as several more elders walked into the room. The women amongst them smiled at Av in an almost inviting fashion.

"I'm mated," Av said to their looks.

"Leave him," the first elder said to the others. "That's a warning, and they will act upon it."

"Oh, but my granddaughter is looking for a breeder," one of the women grumbled almost too quietly for Av to hear it.

Av gave Er a questioning look and was answered with the look that he thought only his father was capable of.

He was to stay put and keep his mouth shut, or else.

"We gave you time to figure this out, do you know what has happened?" the leader of the elders asked Olea.

"She converted the magic into something she can use," Olea said. "As Er reported to us all when he returned from the South last fall, she is infected with the living stone. With queen's stone. When this happens, there are changes to magic, to behaviour, even to her ability to find trouble. We should not have let her wander the hallways by herself, but we cannot very well put her with someone at all times. We have lives of our own, and it would seem as if we do not trust her."

"Trusting the one who sits the throne is foolish."

"So foolish to trust the one who found the only part of the palace that is still accessible," Er said sternly. "Very foolish indeed, that she should find her way here past the guards because somehow she knew to take the family hallway. Stranger still, that she was touching the stone which Url's mate would have added to, somehow knowing, despite the fact that this girl can barely heat her own rooms, that this stone had the least magic in it.

"Yes, what she did is strange and creepy, but it's saved us a great deal of trouble. With the magic from the stones unified, it's—what did you say it's done, Olea?"

"It's begun to reproduce itself," Olea said quietly. "The magic is working together, and the older magic is converting purely to Aren's desires, but by doing so, somehow it is stretching."

"Stretching magic?" the lead elder demanded. "However would a girl who cannot heat her rooms be able to stretch magic?"

"I don't know," Olea responded.

"How can a girl with no capability to use her own magic convert that of others?" the elder demanded.

"I don't know," Olea said again.

"The throne," Av said and flinched when every person in the room focused on him. "It's an old magic. Each queen who takes over doesn't destroy the magic that came before her, she simply takes it over, and it becomes hers. Aren probably didn't do it on purpose and learned how to do it from the throne when she took over from Em."

"That wouldn't surprise me," one of the elders said, though Av wasn't certain which one.

"And what happened to the fountain?" the leader demanded. "My father placed that fountain here sixty years ago. It's irreplaceable now."

"I don't know," Olea said to the floor.

"You don't know. A whole fountain up and disappears, and you don't know what happened to it? All that knowledge you claim to have brought with you from the palace, and yet still you're as stupid as a child. What use are you, exactly?"

"I have use as a breeder," Olea protested, but barely.

What kind of insanity was going on? Er was the baron, Olea his mate. Neither of them was well known for being submissive in the least. More than once, news had reached the palace of them beating a man at dinner for questioning their *menu* choices.

"And if you've only use as a breeder, you keep your damned tongue silent," the leader said before she spun on Av. "You wake her and bring her to dinner."

Av swore at the woman, then he smiled at the fury that played over her face.

"I may be a Marilton, but I am mate to the throne and you have no reach over me. If Aren is awake and if my uncle extends an invitation to dinner, then we will gladly attend. However—and let me be very clear on this—if you ever use that tone of voice on my mate or call her stupid, let alone imply that her only use is as a breeder, no amount of reputation or protection offered to you by the warriors of Castle Grey will stop me from slitting your throat."

"I see there's a warrior somewhere in you, but in this land? We listen to our elders."

"My blood is from this land, my *family* is south, and they include the likes of Ervam and Jer, so don't you be ordering me around."

"Obey."

"No." Av batted a hand at the air and then frowned over his shoulder as he felt something brush by him. Growling, he turned back to the woman. "Did you just try to issue a command to me? Do I look like Er? Do I look like Url? Wait, no, we're closely related, so I suppose I do."

"You will come to heel, one way or another."

Av made a very rude sound. "You can go now."

"I beg your pardon?"

"As mate to the throne, I need to have a discussion with Baron Er," Av said, and then he focused pointedly on his uncle.

The women hissed at him, but he didn't think that was a bad thing. None of them would be looking to breed him with their daughters if he couldn't even listen to their commands while in private. The elders left, muttering amongst themselves.

"By the spirits, what is that?" Av asked once he was certain they were out of earshot.

"They uphold tradition, which will no longer be in effect once the last of them passes," Olea said quietly.

"I have a knife," Av offered.

The queen giggled behind a hand. "No, Av. Doing that would incite others, and then they'd insist the elders remain. They already are, and we're trying to steer away."

"They uphold the traditions of the North," Er said to both of them, not just Av. He was also correcting his mate at the same time. "More than once they have done just that."

"Then this is not their place, this is not tradition," Av said.

"It is tradition," Er and Olea said as one. Olea sighed and then continued. "The baron's mate and her daughters put their magic into a stone, if you don't or if a stone loses all magic, Castle Grey will fall from the cliff."

"But it's built into the cliff," Av said.

"Not really," Er said. "I'll take you hunting tomorrow, and then you'll see the truth of the matter. Van might brag about how his queens hold up their homes, but Castle Grey is held by the magic from the stones that were brought from the old palace. I think."

"Fine, how do we think this happened?" Av asked. "Because Aren's going to have questions and I am not going to be able to just dismiss it all."

"Well there are those who do not wish us to rejoin palace lands," Olea said hesitantly, glancing to Er.

The baron grimaced. "She is correct, but a majority of those who voice against the alliance were in that group there, and none of them expected to live to see the day."

"And this Raven that Aren claims she saw?" Av asked.

"There is no one here by that description," Er responded. "No palace blood beside Aren and Olea. Raven isn't even a name for a person."

Av chewed his bottom lip. "Could it have been another queen setting a trap for us?"

"Absolutely, though the choices in colour are strange, to say the least," Olea responded. "Red eyes?"

"A mistake, perhaps," Er said quickly. "Tried for something else, hit a red instead. Now we just have to account for the queens; whoever isn't accounted for is the one who we lay this blame on."

"If they did it," Av said.

"The other explanation is that Aren has lost her mind and teleported a fountain out of here and probably onto the head of some poor unsuspecting fool," Olea said.

"Which is a great deal simpler than if a rival did it and then… made the fountain invisible?" Av asked.

"True," Olea muttered.

Av walked forwards and kicked the air a bit where they had said the fountain was supposed to be. He studied the stones and stopped in the middle of the room and looked down. There was a small hole in the floor. He motioned to the hole and looked at Er.

"Pipe," Er said.

Av looked back down and wondered if he had ever seen an actual pipe before. The taps, certainly, but not a pipe. He poked the pipe with his toe and frowned back at Er.

"I was under the impression that if you broke a pipe, it would spray water all over," Av said, turning his attention to Olea, the one who had control over the water.

She could only shrug in response. "I can explain that about as well as I can explain what she did with the fountain in the first place. Or who Raven is, or what's going on with the stones, or how Aren did any of this at all, given the fact that she can't even shut off the lights at the palace."

"Wait," Av said. "What?"

"You didn't notice that?" Er asked.

"The lights stayed on where I was," Av responded, then jabbed a finger at Olea. "What happens when she tries to do that herself?"

"She'll probably pull it off," Olea said with a growl and a motion around her. "Besides which, I will be spending time with her while you spend time with Er learning about military things. Between myself and my daughters, we will figure out a way to teach this woman, even if we have to throw her off the highest tower just to show her how to fly."

"Flying is impossible, you will not experiment with Aren," Er said sternly.

"Don't experiment with flying," Av said, then sighed. "But I get the feeling that she'll be experimenting on me so go ahead and blow her eyebrows off. Just don't push about this. If she asks, then she asks, and we'll make something up, I guess."

"If she's going mad, we should tell her now," Olea said.

"No, she already sees sitting on the throne as a terrible end to her life, so I'm not going to tell her that her life is going to be even shorter through no fault of her own."

"We can't make promises for the elders," Er said.

"Er, you can't be serious, we need to tell her that she's seeing things," Olea protested.

"Not until we know for certain that she *has* been seeing things," Er said quickly. "If we find out that she is going mad, then and only then will we tell her. But you do need to get her to dinner if you can. I don't need them getting uppity, they will say something stupid."

"And then I'll stab them."

"Someplace that can be healed."

"I promise nothing," Av said with a growl. "Being violent helps fight off the..." He trailed off and glanced at Olea, wondering if his aunt had been told about his predicament. Meeting Er's eyes, he received a small nod of understanding. "I will stab whatever comes near me, or her."

Chapter Eleven

Between preparing the court for his absence, and sending the messenger ahead of him to alert the vineyard, dinner approached quickly. Ervam had been clear.

They were to attend dinner, then Jer was to leave for Bilgern Vineyards the next morning.

Jer was exhausted just walking into Ervam's home. He didn't have the energy to protest as Ervam hugged Laeder as a father-by-mating might. He knew that he should have protested, but he didn't.

Not because Ervam wasn't Laeder's father-by-mating, but because it was that ever-constant fight that seemed to have begun. Everyone assumed that Laeder was in the role of the woman. Those roles didn't exist; neither of them was the woman, which meant that Ervam shouldn't have greeted Laeder as if he were Laeder's father-by-mating.

"Say the words out loud, next time," Ervam said as he walked towards the hearth. "Rather than make the motions and growl. I hugged the boy because it is my right. If I had a daughter, I'd hug her mate as well, does that settle the matter?"

Jer grumbled to himself, but didn't quite answer the trainer as he slunk to the dining table and sat where he always sat. Ervam turned with a spoon in his hand and made a face at Jer.

It was the same look his mother used to get on her face when she had asked a question and one of her boys grumbled instead of answering.

"We're equals. It's an equal relationship!" Jer barked out.

Ervam hesitated, then motioned to Laeder with the spoon. "Behind you there's a bottle of wine in that cupboard. Do pull it out."

"We can drink now?" Jer asked.

"Is Aren somehow involved?"

"No."

The trainer shrugged and turned back to the hearth. "Maybe make yourself useful and set the table."

Jer stood and went through the motions of setting the table. By the time he was finished, dinner was cooked. They all sat down to a grain and pheasant meal with a side of spring greens. He almost made a face at the meal, but picked up his fork and ate a little.

"I think the fatty foods of court make men slow," Ervam said to Laeder. "The sugars and fat used to make them taste in such a way to make warriors foggy and stupid. In the North, we were raised on meats and starches. The fatty bits were reserved for winners of dominance fights, or those returning from skirmishes."

"Feed a blooded warrior fatty foods to weigh him down," Laeder said. "That makes sense. There are entire books on how to feed a warrior properly in the archives."

Ervam made a small sound at the back of his throat. They ate in silence for a bit, then Laeder cleared his throat and sat back.

"Why did you invite me to dinner, if you have a problem with this—with us?"

There was the sound of dropped cutlery striking the plate. It took Jer a moment to get over his shock and realise that he had been the one to drop his fork. He fumbled to pick it back up again, ducking his head when Ervam turned his attention to Jer.

"What did you tell him?" Ervam demanded.

"Not that," Jer protested.

"I asked a question!"

Ervam and Jer both turned ever so slowly to Laeder. Afraid to move, afraid to comment because they had no idea what they were dealing with. Laeder had never been so outspoken before.

"I believe in equality," Ervam said carefully, in the tone he used when talking to children.

That tone annoyed Jer, but at the same time, he saw the rationality of using it. Neither of them knew what had put that edge on Laeder, but they also didn't want to blunt the sharpness. Laeder wasn't just some meek follower. He had been made that way after years of living under his father. He might have just been testing the waters, and Jer wanted to encourage his mate to bite people.

"Equality is not the same thing as equal rights in marriage," Laeder said.

"Mating," Jer said quietly. "And our mating is different from your marriage."

"While you are correct, Laeder, one may believe in equality but be against those who like their own, I do not. I have never expressed anything against the couples who share genders. I never will. While I may not understand that my son, Jer, might have come to that conclusion, it was an incorrect one, so why do you think I have a problem with you bending my son over and having your way with him?"

"When I visited in the winter, you separated us."

"Oh, that."

Ervam looked a little uncomfortable as he picked up his cup and sipped the wine. Laeder shot Jer a look, then focused on Ervam again.

"Oh?" Laeder asked. "That?"

It was said with about as much acid as a rank who had just found someone chewing on their lover. Jer ducked his head again and put a forkful of food in his mouth, if only to get out of talking about that topic.

"Laeder… that has nothing to do with gender. My boys are not allowed to have someone sleep in the same room as them who is not their mate or a blood relative. It's always been a rule."

"That's rather Southern traditional of you."

"It's not about tradition. I couldn't care less if they sleep with everyone, if they were prostitutes. But it's not happening under my roof, because one day Av dared me and I took him up on that dare. I banned all of it. Once you tell a young warrior where the line is, you cannot simply move it."

"Oh," Laeder said.

"That," Ervam said with a small nod. "It has nothing to do with who should have sex under my roof. I drew a line in the sand. Now I must continue to enforce that line. It's a part of their foundation, of their core. They know in my home, this is how the rules work. This is their comfort."

"No, I understand it now," Laeder said, poking at his plate, all fight gone out of him.

"Good, because I don't appreciate someone coming into my home and accusing me of such a terrible thing."

"I'm sorry, I can't sleep beside my man because one time, twenty years ago, you got mad at *Av*?"

"I may have told people I set down the rule to separate you and Em."

"Ervam!"

The trainer sipped his wine, watching Jer over the cup. Annoyed, Jer looked away.

"Struggle with the idea all you like, I'm still your father and I can still bend you over my knee. Laeder, has Jer told you the dirty family secret yet?"

"Dirty as in naughty, or the reason for you two looking at each other like that?" Laeder asked. "Do I want to know?"

"Father, please," Jer pleaded.

"You mated my son without witness," Ervam said to Laeder, jabbing a finger at the scribe. "I might forgive you, because you don't know our customs. But he does. And the only way to get through to a warrior is to hurt his mate, you understand me?"

"Uh… if we mate for ten years without you there, you'll kill me?" Laeder managed to get out.

"No, I'll bend you over my knee," Ervam said sternly. "It's a hurt of the heart, that I wasn't invited. He didn't invite me to his matings with Em either."

"That has nothing to do with you not being invited to this," Jer said.

"Then what was it?"

Jer slowly let out his breath. "Av and Aren were to be mated, and we didn't want to steal their light by announcing our intent at the same time. And no, I wasn't going to wait for all the things to settle down. We all know what Aren's being infected means. There will never be a quiet or calm time. And if there is, it's going to end with one of us dying."

"Av is going to smack him and kill you."

"No, he's *not*."

Ervam sucked in a breath and sat back in his chair. "Really?"

"Really, Father."

He watched his father scratch his nose, then consider Laeder for a very long moment. The trainer made a small sound, then gave a little nod.

"Welcome to the family, Laeder."

"I'm so confused right now," Laeder said. "You two realise that you sound like crazy people, right? He's growling, you're growling. He threatens to tell Av and have me beaten and that somehow solves the problem? What is going on?"

Jer rubbed at his chin. "Family dynamic. You'll catch on."

"Basically, Jer was in trouble for not bringing you home. My boys, they hide a lover when they think I won't approve. Jer never brought Em home. Aren was the only one Av brought home. But they both know that you don't mate a body without bringing them home to Father."

"I think I got that," Laeder said quietly. "That doesn't mean I'm not confused. Jer is headed to the vineyard. No one has mentioned that yet."

"We waited until we knew they were in the North," Ervam said with a small nod. "In case the steward had to head that way to do what Jer would do to those who touched his sister. He'll be gone a couple of days and back again. Nothing overly complicated."

"I'm not having children," Laeder said. "Just putting it out there. Women are not my thing. At all."

For a moment, Jer was rankled. It was that annoyed sort of feeling that he had gotten when Em had said she wasn't ready to carry another child. She had continued to say that for over a decade before he had given up.

Then he clamped down on it and just nodded.

"It's what you want, Laeder. Different lands put pressure on ranks to carry children because rank is more likely to produce rank, but palace lands at the end of the day believe everyone should keep their opinions to themselves on the matter. Yes, there is that pressure, and, for example, Aren will be expected to have a child. There will be a pressure. But if, at any point, Jer pressures you into bedding a woman, you come see me. I'll take his balls."

"Father!" Jer shouted.

"Jer's nurturing instincts have been surrogated for the court and now onto Aren. But at some point he will want another child. Adoption is a good option. Unless, I'm sorry, are you not wanting a child at all?"

"Sh-should I even be thinking about that? I'm not that old," Laeder said. "Commoners in the South of my age are worrying about their legacies, but not their blood or children."

"Where we go is not a conversation for the family," Jer said. "It's me and him. We decide where we go in our relationship."

"A child would do you good," Ervam said.

There was no judgement in his tone, just the master giving advice to a warrior under his care. Jer knew how it went from that comment. There would be subtle hints towards surrogates, because Jer could perform in such a way. There would be young children suddenly stumbling in his path, perhaps even a sudden influx of orphans in the palace.

Then one day, when he least expected it, Jer would find himself bringing an orphan home like they were a stray kitten or something. Then he'd just wake up one day to a bed full of children and Laeder at his side.

Jer gritted his teeth and growled, jabbing a finger at his father, who smiled in response and picked up his fork.

"There may not be orphans at the palace, but there are plenty of wards, young girls who need a guiding hand. Not much of a commitment, but certainly something to keep your attention until Laeder decides if he wants children at all. And of the sort that he won't become jealous, thinking that you are chasing after a woman."

At the thought of waking to a bed full of young wards, Jer's mind skittered to a halt. For a moment, he was disgusted by his own reaction. Then he revisited the image and realised that with none of them was there a sexual hunger.

In his mind's eye, he simply woke to a bed full of young women who were under his care and trusted him enough to sleep in his bed and know that he would never cross that line. *That* was what he wanted—not necessarily the bed full of women, but the trust and understanding.

"And… I hate you more," Jer said.

"Naked women?" Ervam asked.

"No, they were clothed; it's a feeling I want, not a body," Jer said. "Well, I suppose that it's lots of bodies, not a body. But yes, I see your point. The nurturing instinct is there and I would like it if Laeder was a part of that."

"Male, or female?"

"Female, but male would just assume," Jer said.

Ervam made a little sound and sipped his wine. The trainer considered the table and took in a long breath before he looked at Laeder.

"Hope you like a big family."

"My family was kind of bad."

"They've declared war on us," Jer said.

"You can still declare war and only be kind of bad," Laeder said with a shrug.

He almost said it, but he managed to hold back. Instead, Jer looked at Ervam, who blinked back at him and was clearly biting his bottom lip. Ervam was also holding back a comment.

There was a very high probability, given the few messages that had been back and forth, that Merkat intended to raze palace lands to the ground and build a new empire in his own image. He had no intention of keeping anything alive. Jer doubted that even Laeder would survive the battle over palace grounds.

But as a warrior, that was his burden to carry. He did not tell a commoner that their family was attempting to murder everything. He did not force them to see that truth.

"Family in the South is blood," he said finally. "Here, the palace recognizes that blood will betray a body. Family is that which we choose to surround ourselves with, whose connection is too deep to describe as friend. It's not friendship that binds us, it's something beyond us. Just like a family, we might not talk or we might have our fights, but we will protect each other from the end of the world itself."

"Blood is bred family," Laeder said slowly. "One day, I'll get it down, I will."

"For the South, they're one and the same," Ervam said. "That's why there's such a negativity around those who like their own. There's no way to mingle the bloodlines if neither have the necessary parts. Palace lands, however, are supposed to stand for equality of all. That means those who like their own, for men and women, and those few who are born in the wrong body."

"Wait, what?" Laeder asked. "Like a male queen?"

"While very rare, it has happened," Ervam said. "But a queen can be male and be in the right body. A person who is born in the wrong body may express differences from their peers. We only really know from their word. The healers can see no difference but oftentime ranks can see a sadness in them, because they just never feel in place. Palace lands are supposed to represent them and keep them safe."

"I'm not like that, are you trying to figure out if I'm like that?" Laeder asked so quickly that it took Jer a moment to figure out what the scribe had said. "I'm male, and just because I prefer my bedpartners to have penises instead of vaginas, it doesn't mean that I was born in the wrong body."

"He's even bold enough to use the term penis and vagina. Aren blushed at the idea and then dared to chastise me."

Jer, with a sip of wine in his mouth, choked at the words. He had to put a hand over his mouth to stop from coughing wine all over Laeder.

"What's wrong with calling it a penis?" Laeder asked. "That's what it is."

"I believe dear Aren's sexual maturity is quite a bit lower than her peers," Ervam said. "Para didn't exactly teach her children the facts of life. Aren thought it rained because ranks serve after death by providing magic to the world, I think is what Av told me."

"She has a ways to go with her education," Jer said, then he shrugged. "But we knew that."

"And we've a scribe in the family who isn't afraid to say the word penis," Ervam added.

"Testicles, boobs, cunt," Laeder said. "Does that somehow make me a better teacher than most?"

"What's a cunt?" Jer asked.

"It's what prostitutes call their vaginas," Ervam said.

"Oh, having never used one, I didn't know."

"Having a father who thought I just hadn't met the right cunt, I *do* know," Laeder said, then turned to Ervam with a dark look. "I will not be breeding."

"I would not suggest it, you made your wishes clear. But if you change your mind… uh, come see me. Better to ask forgiveness with this one and if you show up with a babe of yours? You could be forgiven for a great deal more than sleeping with a woman."

Chapter Twelve

Aren tried not to grimace as a plate of food was placed before her. She wasn't hungry, but she knew she had to eat, and she knew she had to be polite to the other dinner guests.

She glanced around, assessing her chances of making it through dinner. There were those dressed in richer clothing. Obviously lords and ladies, intermixed with several older folk who all wore a grey that was almost the colour of the stones of the castle. Then there were the more worn folk who looking nothing like a lord or even a servant from down below.

They looked like the downtrodden whom Er had invited to dinner to fill his table.

"Charity," Av said quietly to Aren. "Visitors, especially those who don't look to have had a good meal, are offered clean water, reprieve, and an invitation to dinner. You may or may not speak their language, but they will try to question you."

She almost asked why, but then she realized they were all staring at her. They knew she was different from them. Aren focused on her plate.

The dress that Olea had given her to wear almost fit properly and had been cut in the Northern style. The neckline was very square, though it came above anything Aren had covered at the palace. In the chilly hallways, she had been grateful for the extra coverage.

Av had insisted on braiding her hair, to keep it out of the way. The braid was nearly identical to the one that Olea and all her daughters wore to dinner. Aren had yet to be introduced to the children of Olea and Er, and it was difficult to pick them out.

Castle Grey was filled with people who could claim the Marilton bloodline, though many were second or third cousins to the baron. Nearly everyone besides Olea and one of her daughters had the same grey eyes.

Aren glanced at the other end of the table, to the visitors, and realized that there was a palace lands' lord sitting there, poking away at the plate before him with a grimace.

The man was wealthy by the look of his hair and skin, almost flawless. He obviously had the coin to pay for whatever he might need and to pamper himself, but there was a harder edge to that clean look as if he were not a stranger to a hard day's work. His clothing was well made and fit him, meaning that he had brought that clothing with him. The only piece of jewelry he wore was a ring on his little finger of black and white wound together, almost as if they had been braided.

Aren stared at that ring for a very long time before she looked up and found the lord staring back at her. She had a flustered moment, for she had been caught staring and she hadn't meant to, before the lord dropped his hand under the table and held her gaze.

She looked to her plate and used the fork to spear a piece of vegetable she had never seen before.

"Aunt Olea, I seem to be forgetting how Northern dinners go," Av said suddenly.

"Ah yes, see, we begin with a light vegetable course," Olea explained. "Here in the North, our healers are constantly concerned about us getting things like vegetables and fruit. We keep a large greenhouse to help with this."

"And trade with Gamen," Er said quietly, then grumbled. "And with some palace lands' lords, but they always overcharge us. The damned treaty says we have to have some trade with the lands. It didn't protect us from being robbed blind."

"We weren't robbed blind, dear," Olea chimed in.

Aren glanced at the palace lands' lord and saw the man flush a slight white colour.

"No, we knew it was happening all the while," Er growled.

"Is there no growing season at all?" Av asked.

"Yes, of course, there's a growing season," Olea said. "We've maintained the belief that Castle Grey is locked by snow, but as you saw there is none now. It's simply a different area, the snow lasts longer and can come earlier, but the main differences are during the winter itself. One day is fall, the next is as if it is the middle of winter on palace lands.

"The healers' main concern is during the winter months. When left to themselves, warriors will eat nothing but meat and bread, it seems. So all year round we set a good example for the winter months."

"I see," Av said, eyeing Aren's empty plate.

She set her fork down gently, aware that everyone else still had some food left. It hadn't been a very large serving size, only one piece of each vegetable, really.

"The next course is a small meat course, to keep the men from complaining, then there is a soup course to warm us up, the main course in all its glory and a light dessert. We don't believe in those heavy creams and four cookies per person that the palace does. Not even for our special visitors."

"You need to be used to that food, or else it comes back up," Av responded calmly.

And so a conversation began around foods of the two lands as the plates were removed and replaced with even smaller portions of meat. There were four little pieces, none of which Aren was certain on. Her stomach turned over and threatened to expel the meagre first course.

She swallowed hard and picked up a fork to at least pretend she was eating. Instead, she poked at the meat until she managed to pull a small part off and put it in her mouth, instantly regretting it, but unable to spit it out.

Av's hand set on her leg, drawing her attention to him. He gave her a look that questioned what was going on.

"I'm fine," she said, and set her fork down.

She didn't feel well at all.

Av stood, giving her a pat on the shoulder and left for a moment. Aren turned, horrified that he would get up in the middle of a formal dinner. As he approached a table along the wall, something prodded her.

Aren spun to face whoever had done it, only to realize that there was no one close enough *to* prod her. She stared at the old woman across from her, who stared back coldly. It was a look that Aren was beginning to recognize as an annoyed queen.

"Where is the fountain?" the woman asked.

"What fountain?" Aren managed to get out.

"The fountain my father placed in the anchor room, and you stole," an elder to Aren's right snarled.

Aren glanced over the table and spotted the other elders as they ducked their heads.

"Don't look at them, look at me when you babble out your excuses, or do they breed stupid ones all across palace lands? I thought it was only the half-breeds."

"Mother," Er said quickly.

"Er?" she demanded.

Av sat down beside Aren and cleared his throat as he looked over the table. Down one side, then the other. The warrior looked confused as if he had just been distracted by a conversation and wasn't quite certain what he had just heard going on at the main table.

The plates were removed as Aren tried to eat once more, but it was too late.

Formal dinners meant she had to eat a bit of everything brought to her. She could feel the prickling at the back of her eyes, felt her chest constrict.

She was going to get hurt.

Except Para wasn't there.

Aren dragged in a breath as a plate of vegetables was set before her and a bowl of soup to everyone else. The soup was more of a stew and smelled strongly of meat, a smell that Aren was very certain she didn't like at all.

"Bear," Olea announced. "I do apologize. Er apparently wrestled it and would like to tell the story now."

"You wrestled my dinner to the ground?" Av asked, sounding quite impressed.

"It wasn't no cub, either."

And so the conversation then turned towards the tale, and Aren tried to smile and pretend to be interested. At the back of her mind was the nagging thought of what the woman had said. It was hard to shake loose.

That she was stupid? She wasn't stupid and she wasn't daft or any other version of the word. People from palace lands shouldn't have all been viewed as stupid just because she had no idea what the woman was talking about. As if she could make an entire fountain disappear?

Stupid, sullen child.

A little tomato flew off Aren's plate as she tried to spear it. It shot across the table and missed the lord across from Av by the breadth of a finger.

The lord blinked in surprise, then he laughed. "You need to work on your aim, girl!"

Aren mumbled an apology and ducked her head down, poking at the remaining vegetables.

"Now she's throwing food. And they call *us* barbarians," the elder spat out.

It was suddenly difficult to breathe. Aren dragged in a breath and set her fork down.

"Aren, are you all right?" Av whispered.

Which only made the tears sting her eyes. "I-I can't, I have to—"

Aren stood up and was out of reach before Av managed to get to his feet. Leaving the dining hall, she almost burst into tears, but there was a servant standing near the door, wide-eyed as she rushed past him.

She could not cry in front of the servants just because someone called her stupid. And why was she crying because of that, of all things? How often had lords and ladies said something very similar at court?

By the time she made it to the rooms, she was crying despite trying not to. Aren wiped at her eyes and tore the dress off, tossing it to the side. She was furious with herself for breaking down into tears, furious that she had no control over it.

And that just made her cry more.

Aren swore and went to the bathing room to wash her face and pull on the robe.

Stupid, sullen child.

She tied the robe and left the bathing room, only to be jerked to a halt. Aren looked down at her left wrist, which was angled towards the bathing room doorway. She was stuck.

Again.

She almost burst into a fresh set of tears, but Av marched into the room, absolutely furious. Aren gulped down the sob and tried to meet his eyes as he stomped towards her and pulled to a stop just out of arm's reach.

"What was that?" he demanded.

"I wasn't feeling well," Aren said, keeping her eyes on the floor.

"Weren't feeling well?" he asked. "Aren, why won't you look at me?"

Gritting her teeth, Aren forced herself to look up and meet his eyes. His fury increased. Av turned away and swore, clenching his hands into fists.

This was it, this was where everything went horribly, horribly wrong and she was back where she started—except now with someone who could actually hurt her.

Av turned back to her and reached out. Aren stiffened as he took hold of her shoulder and tried to draw her close. When she wouldn't budge, because her wrist was still attached to the doorframe, he stepped up to her and wrapped his arms around her.

"I'm not angry at you, I'm just angry," he said, hugging her. "Come on, let's get you into bed."

"Oh, I thought I'd just..." Aren swallowed and knew it was a terrible excuse even as the words spilled out of her mouth. "...Stand for a bit."

Av pulled away slightly and met her eyes, then followed her left arm down to the wrist, then to the door.

"I see," he said quietly. "Look, Aren, the elder who spoke to you is Er's mother. I didn't know that until dinner tonight."

"And your father killed her mate," Aren said as the pieces began falling into place.

"And then palace lands knowingly hid and even protected him, his mate, and her two sons," Av said with a grimace. "She's never liked palace lands, from what I understand. I watched her call Olea stupid today. Olea, stupid? If it weren't for some insane tradition of keeping the elders alive, Olea would have skinned the woman then and there, probably with a bit of stone she punched off a wall. She's neither stupid nor weak, but the elders have some say above the baron."

"Because they all have rank and know tricks that others don't because they don't teach others," Aren said quietly.

"Yes."

"What's this about a fountain going missing?" Aren asked.

"See, earlier today, that whole thing?" Av asked and waited as Aren nodded. Of course, she remembered the event. "The fountain in the middle of that room is now gone, and we think you may have teleported it somewhere, and she, Er's mother, holds you responsible. Apparently, her father placed the fountain there, and it was precious and cannot be replaced because the craftsman didn't pass on his knowledge before he died."

"Oh," Aren said.

"So if you can think of a way to bring the fountain back or make it visible, or whatever it is that ended up happening—not that I'm saying you know what happened—that would probably calm her down quite a bit."

"No," Aren said and walked around Av.

"No?" Av asked, following her to the bed.

She turned back to face him, and his eyes were on the wrist once more. Av slowly met Aren's eyes, and she was afraid she saw an understanding there. Like he knew what was going on but wasn't certain about it.

She prayed he couldn't make the connection. Something like that could very well be used against her to hold her places when he thought it inconvenient for her to leave.

"No, she can't have it back," Aren said.

Av blinked at Aren, chewed his bottom lip and then said slowly, "Do you know where it went?"

"To the palace," Aren responded, taking off the robe to climb into bed.

"And why won't you give it back, because she will ask?"

"She knows why," Aren said. "And because it's mine now. If she would like to come and try to take it from me, by all means."

"Which would put her on palace lands," Av said with a smile.

"What does that mean to you?" Aren countered.

"It would also put her in the position of trying to take something that is yours and on palace lands," Av said pointedly. "That means I can stab her in a violent manner!"

"There's a nonviolent manner to stabbing a person?"

"Yes, you do it gently," Av said quickly, turning his head towards the door, then back to Aren. "You should sleep, you look weary.

Chapter Thirteen

Av shouldn't have let Aren attend dinner. When she started poking at the meat, he assumed it was because bear and boar were on the plate. Both tended to be acquired tastes. He had gone to request that she be fed something else so that she would at least eat.

The servant had kept her head down, black bangs in her eyes. Just when Av was going to say something rude, to make the woman look up without him touching her, he caught what was being said at the table.

He returned, and the conversation had shifted as the plates were replaced. Aren received another plate of vegetables and began picking away at them, but she was obviously upset.

Av had tried not to focus on that. He tried to focus on the tale his uncle was telling about wrestling a bear. It was interesting for several reasons, the first being that, the way Er told it, this was not the first time he had wrestled a bear and then brought it home for dinner. The other reason being that Av couldn't figure out when, or how, Er had slipped out of Castle Grey to go hunting.

Av had gone to training with the young men, men who were almost ten years younger than himself, that morning. He understood that the placement had to do with the fact that he was unfamiliar with how those in the North fought. He knew some of it, certainly, but his father had made certain that Av had learned how to fight the way palace warriors fought.

The young men had gotten in a few shots, but Av had more experience and had taken part in real fights before. He adapted quickly as any warrior must, and had made his sparring partners work for the bruises they tried to give him.

Perhaps it was during that training time that Er had gone hunting, though that did imply that Er hunted nearby, or that a bear had wandered onto Castle Grey's lawns.

After the events of the morning, he had spent the remainder of the day with Aren in the rooms. While she had napped on and off, he had struggled through reading a book on military tactics of an era past.

Sitting beside Aren through the soup course had been painful. Even being 'ignorant' as others like to say, Av could feel how uncomfortable the queen was. The whole table could feel it.

When the tomato flew across the table, he thought perhaps the tension would break. The warrior who was almost struck certainly thought it funny, but his comment made Aren flee.

Whatever the look on Av's face, the man across the table turned an ashen grey. Av stood, casually picking up the sharp-edged knife that sat beside his bowl. He walked down two chairs and slipped the blade in the elder's arm and back out before she turned to him, looking confused.

It wasn't about being violent. It was about keeping a promise. He had promised not to kill the elders if he could control himself.

Av leaned over and set the bloody tipped knife across the elder's soup bowl. Her eyes fell on the blade as confusion, and then pain, played over her features. The room swirled with the conflicting emotions of several queens as he bent to whisper to her.

"Next time, it's going into your heart."

He had left the dining hall and met eyes with the servant who stood outside the door.

"She went that way," the servant said and motioned down a hallway.

"Make yourself scarce," Av said.

The man nodded and left, but didn't flee. Obviously, the servants at Castle Grey would have no problem handling an angry warrior.

Av turned back to the dining room as Url stepped out. Av arched an eyebrow in question at his cousin.

"It's a formal dinner," Url said sternly. "Of course my father can't leave the head of the table before the main course is served, Mother would beat him then and there."

"Am I in trouble?" Av asked.

"You're a warrior who just followed through on a threat, of course you aren't in trouble," Url growled. "If you apologize for it, you will be. Unless Vivlia dies and you didn't mean for that, then you should probably apologize for killing my grandmother."

"Well, perhaps your family should be better behaved," Av countered.

"I have little control over my blood, Av, a fact you should well remember. She's an elder and has claimed the dominant spot amongst all the elders. They have to listen to her."

"I need to go check on Aren."

"I'll have food sent to the rooms," Url said quietly. "But, um, how did you do that?"

"Do what?" Av asked.

"You…" Url struggled.

"I stabbed her gently," Av said sternly. "I promised I wouldn't kill her and if I was violent about it, I might have. So I did it gently."

"You're supposed to use a blunt item and jab a person when you stab them gently."

"That's not stabbing, it's jabbing," Av growled. "I need to check on Aren."

"And I will have food sent to the rooms," Url repeated and bowed his head slightly before he turned to rejoin the dinner.

Av moved through the halls, trying to control his irritation. His mother had often warned him about his temper. Not because she wanted him to curb it, but because queens could pick up on his anger. If he was upset and she was upset, she might think that his anger was directed at her and that wasn't the case at all.

He had slipped into the room and spoken with Aren for a few minutes before there was a knock on the door. Assuming it was food, and not wanting anyone to deal with Aren directly, Av slipped back out and closed the door behind him.

Outside of the rooms, there were two men waiting. Av bared his teeth and growled. The one was the warrior who had sat across from Aren. The warrior bared his teeth in response and almost growled but ducked his head instead. Reacting to instinct when he didn't want to, then controlling the action so that Av didn't think it was a challenge.

Turning to the second man, Av growled again. The man had grey in his hair, which only seemed to draw attention to the grey Marilton eyes.

It was said many people of the North had those grey eyes, but Av had only ever seen them in his blood.

The second man, also a warrior, held up his hands to stop Av from reacting violently. Not quite a surrender, just a begging for a moment to explain.

"We elders are supposed to take on the role of trainer because there are no trainers," the elder said quickly and quietly. "The men rule the warriors, the women the queens. The one you stabbed leads us and makes us submit to her will, but few of the elders wish to hold on to the old ways. We knew your mother. We helped raise you when you were young enough to swat. When you still thought clothing was for weak-willed commoners. You will lead us to good things. The warriors, we know this. The queens fear that rejoining the palace will remove them from power."

"Aren will only ever recognize Olea," Av said. "Yes, she can submit to another queen, but not some elder who calls her stupid, calls Olea stupid."

"It's personal for her."

"As a queen, it's her duty to step outside of personal and act like a rank, not some spoiled child."

"Your queen fled a formal dinner crying over someone being mean to her," the elder said sternly.

"That's not a spoiled child, that's a broken one," Av countered.

"If you want this to work, truly work, Aren needs to show her strength. The warriors know it must be there. Otherwise one of your skill would not be drawn to her."

"She's been having some trouble adjusting," Av muttered, running his hands through his hair. "But that doesn't mean I'm not going to stab people who are rude to her!"

"Let her stand on her own," the elder said.

"That would make her think that she stands alone," Av said with a shake of his head. "I would never isolate her more."

"What do you mean more?" the elder asked.

"Her parents were not kind people."

"What sort of unkind?"

"The unkind that should allow me to slaughter them and their entire bloodlines, but I'm not allowed to because her choice of punishment must be accepted. She banished them from court and made them change from the bloodline that they claimed to her father's so that she could keep the one she had been given as a child."

"When was this?" the elder asked quietly.

"Almost a month ago."

The elder was quiet a moment and glanced to the other warrior, who looked between the two as if they had just demanded he give them an answer.

"I just came to apologize," the other warrior said quickly.

"I will be sure that Aren knows of your apology," Av said.

The other warrior nodded and took his leave, likely grateful for the dismissal.

Av turned his attention back to the elder. "I need to check on Aren."

"She will see your anger as being angry with her. That will cause more problems," the elder said quietly.

He didn't want to think about the fear in her eyes when he had approached her. There had been a resigned sort of defeat to her as he had pulled her into his arms, as if she was waiting for the day when he hit her.

That only made him angrier.

"I know that, my mother taught me that."

"And I do believe you were correct, in saying that making her stand for herself could be detrimental. How far gone was she?"

"I don't know, we don't know. We just know that she couldn't feel before, but could put on the face of emotions. She vanished over the winter, came back with a friend and now feels on and off."

"Feels on and off," the elder said faintly, paling. "No wonder her behaviour is erratic, if she's used to not dealing with it and now must face it full on. This other, was she a queen?"

"No, a healer," Av said.

"Are you certain she was a healer?"

Av shrugged. "Ask Olea. She's Danya's sister."

"I see."

The words were said in a tone that did not settle Av's mind in the least. He glared at the elder, who jumped in place when he realized that Av was watching him still.

"Some queens can make others… stop from hiding from themselves," the elder said slowly. "They have to be raised differently. Bastards used to be given over to those who were like that, to raise more of themselves. There has been talk amongst the elders of bringing back this old way and raising a queen in such a manner, but none of us is certain we can do it properly."

"Why would you want a queen like that?"

"She's always happy, always calm. When she does become angry, it's as if the life of the land has simply vanished and everyone knows, but they all protect her. She can take a broken child and put him back together like he was a toy, then send him on his way."

Av thought about the conversations he had had with Danya. He licked his lips slowly and met the elder's eyes.

"And when you talk to them, you start off angry, but end up calm," Av said quietly.

"Yes, I believe that may be what this Danya has done to Aren," the elder said quietly. "Which will not be a bad thing later on, but for now I suppose it is terrifying to be able to hide one day only to be dragged out the next and forced to face what has happened. But I brought that up for more than one reason."

Av dragged a breath in through clenched teeth. "She can do it too."

"But she ended up twisted somehow, her mate started on her once they were joined, she was a perfectly willing participant. Perhaps adults cannot learn to become that way. Perhaps it was him who broke something in the changes. She can do it, but it seems to do the opposite of what it should. It gives her great control."

"Wait, I thought she was dead?"

"The baron's mate at the time of his death, yes, she is dead. There was no love between Er's mother and father. They mated for a year to produce Er and then remained close friends, but not lovers. She never blamed your father for the old baron's death. He was doing what came naturally. She blamed your mother, and without her to take the anger now, it surely has been turned to Aren, who has scooped up what she once referred to as great blood. She had plans to mate you off, young as you were, with Cara, Er's niece on his mother's bloodline."

"If she can do that, and Danya's magic works on me, why doesn't her magic work on me?"

The elder simply stared at Av. "I've no idea. It works on everyone—Aren, Olea, all the queens here and through them, on the warriors."

Av's anger came boiling back up. He relished in the feeling because at least, with it, he knew he could keep himself safe. No one wanted to try an angry warrior, let alone the warrior stupid enough to harm an elder.

"This is the only time we can speak on this. She's already furious with Url."

"Why?" Av asked.

If his cousin was in danger, he had to put an end to the threat. Aren would not take kindly to Url being damaged or hurt simply because Av thought Url should stand up for himself.

"Because Url tried to warn Aren when you first arrived. Once she lays eyes on you, you are hers, and you may not recall, but she was the one to greet you two your first night. She saw what he was doing."

"Url is mine."

"Warriors typically don't say that, like that... about their blood."

"I don't know how else I can put it so that you all will understand," Av said, feeling frustration set in, which only made the anger worse. "If anyone hurts him for speaking to Aren, there will be trouble. And if anyone does anything undue towards him, they will hurt in different and more spectacular ways."

"I cannot make the promise that others will listen to me."

"But you are an elder. You can tell the other elders that Url is mine."

"You don't understand—"

"He's mine, what is not to understand?"

"You don't understand her temper, nor her in the least. You have only seen her demand obedience. You've yet to see the rest. If you fight her over Url, she will break him. If you wish to keep him, you must make careful plans around it."

"You're talking about the cage of silk and lace that my father likes to refer to."

"Here it is not spoken of, they can all see, and there are too few of them and too much need. If she is upset, she will end the magic we can use."

"I could just slit her throat, that would uncomplicate my life awfully quick."

"Again..." The elder trailed off. "Olea could explain better, but they watch her constantly. If she utters anything about it, they will end her, which will end us all. The last Marilton who flew into the rage was just over rape, but outright murder? Castle Grey will be awash with blood. Not just the guilty—the innocent, his children, Url. It is a sharp edge we dance upon. I wish you to blunt it."

"I can't blunt it with my mate on a different sort of edge," Av purred out, considering the idea.

He might be able to draw blood, might even be encouraged to do so. Cause a ruckus, destroy some things.

His whole world settled into place, but the anger remained. Anger was a strong tool. It was one that could be used to keep a queen out of one's mind.

"I can speak with Olea about blunting her edge. She's raised several queens." The elder's head cocked slightly to the side. He frowned at Av, and it looked as if he were listening to something far off even as he continued speaking. "She will know how to calm your mate so that she might be presentable to the public. Once she is calmer, she should present herself to the elders and apologize for destroying the anchor room."

There was a forcefulness to the elder's tone that made Av's eyebrows rise. Then the hair on his arms did the same as he realized what was going on.

Something that those who couldn't use that particular brand of magic called the all-seeing eye. Those with magic could use that magic to see things that they were not physically present for. He had heard of it before, he had heard Mie and even Mar mentioning being able to see things, but he had never really put much thought into how dangerous such a magic could be.

His anger turned to a brittle rage as he struggled to control himself enough to answer the elder.

"I will see if my mate is willing to do such a thing, but can make no promise as to the outcome given the fact that I told that woman not to hurt my mate and she did. If that's what you really mean, that she needs to be apologized to because it was her father's fountain."

"That is what I mean. She is a great woman. She has led us through tough times and many years."

"You know, Telm, the head of house at the palace, once told me something that I truly believe the North needs to learn."

"And what is that?"

"Tradition says follow. Honour asks why? But it was Er who told me that a man has to answer to the spirits for the choices he made for the sake of religion. How about you, Elder? How many things would the spirits judge you guilty for because you followed tradition, followed the woman who has led for years, just because she has always been there?"

"She is what is best for the North."

"This is no longer the North. This is palace lands, now. It's time to change tradition."

Chapter Fourteen

Jer sat atop his horse and looked out over the valley that Bilgern Vineyard resided within. Green, lush, the land felt as if a queen had resided on it for years. There was a brightness to it that the road between the estate and the palace had lacked. After living on palace grounds, and then seeing the stark contrast, it was easy to pick out.

This was Aren's land.

He sniffed the air, opening his senses as he adjusted on the horse. There was an undercurrent of Anue and another queen, though the other queen was muted, obscured by something.

He felt...

With a grimace, Jer closed his senses. There was something wrong with the vineyard, very wrong. Over the fields of grapevines there was a disgusting feeling, but then also in the building itself.

Senses closed, he looked again and found a gorgeous piece of land, one that shouldn't have been a ward of the throne. That led him to believe that it was purely management that was the problem. As steward to the throne, it was Jer's duty to look over the estate and keep it for the heir. If that meant placing someone in the estate to run it and making Cerlot a figurehead until his son came of age, then so be it.

He spurred the horse down the road and breathed in through his nose, then his mouth.

The land was healthy, but the fields had that feeling that reminded Jer of bitterness. Yes, like the bitterness Bilgern wine had taken on, which had led to its downfall after over a century of being the most sought-after wine in all palace lands.

It was no wonder. The land was rich, even without a queen's influence. It was perfect land for a vineyard.

At least he assumed, with what little reading he and Laeder had gotten in before he had left for the estate. He was determined to get the visit done and over with so that he could return to the palace and claim Laeder publicly. From there, if the relationship went well, he could...

But that was a thought for another day.

He focused on the road and tried to look like a warrior. There were people working the yard, commoners all of them, who stopped to look at him, but none dared to approach. He had no weapon, but that was because he was a warrior. Travelling with no weapon might have meant a fool, but the worn travelling clothing with the well-bred horse tended to tell people what he was.

The raven's head clasp on the grey cloak he wore told those he passed that he belonged to the court. The small black pack with the golden raven's head closure was the mark of his title, steward.

Stopping at the stable, Jer looked around for the stable master but only found a boy, thin and dressed in rags. He swung off the horse and approached the boy, who flinched away from him.

"I need you to care for my horse during my time here, do you know how to do that?" Jer asked as calmly as he could.

"I will take good care of the horse, sir, very good care. Food, water, cleaning. No one will touch your horse, sir."

All this was said very quickly as the boy stared at the ground between their feet.

"If you do well, I may have a place at the palace for you," Jer murmured in response.

His heart broke when he saw the intake of breath, the hope with a sudden dash of despair. The boy fully expected Jer to leave him there, thought Jer was saying what he had said to have the horse taken care of, not because he would act upon his promise.

Jer clenched his teeth and left the horse in the boy's care.

Entering the estate, he realized that he had a major problem.

Every servant he saw, he wanted to save. He couldn't save them all. He couldn't take them all out of there, and placing a manager would only make things more awkward. The staff had to be dismissed, split up, and sent to other estates to work, where they could recover amongst happy people.

He ran straight into Para, drunk and swaying as she snarled at him and stumbled away. Jer watched her go, wondering what the woman was saying under her breath as she stumbled around the corner.

It put a chill through him because he swore she was muttering about not being a broodmare.

Given the fact that Jer knew that Para had produced at least two ranks, and the fact that she was still well within the age of having more children, he could make the leaping conclusion.

The Cerlot Jer had met, however, was not capable of commanding his mate to breed more.

Jer turned and came face to face with Cerlot and realized his mistake. While this was the same man who had come to the palace, it was a completely different expression. Gone was the daft and dazed look, Cerlot was back in his territory and hadn't expected Jer to show up that early.

He had pushed through the night, and changed horses, to make it there as early as he could.

If Para came to him and said anything about her comments, Jer could kill Cerlot, and there wasn't a thing anyone could say about it, not even Aren. As the idea occurred to Jer, that this could end very well for him, Cerlot's expression changed to one very similar to what Jer had seen at the palace, but was also a bit of what he had just seen.

"I'm here as steward to the throne," Jer said.

"To assess the estate that my mate lost being the woman that she is," Cerlot snapped back at Jer, then sucked a breath through his teeth. "My apologies, Lord Jer, but you must understand my annoyance and predicament at being forced to live as a warded estate simply because of my mate's childish actions."

"You're the child!" Para shouted with a definite slur a moment before an apple struck the wall behind Cerlot.

The man looked at Jer with all the annoyance of someone who wanted to swat his mate, and Jer couldn't really blame the man.

"First off," Jer said quietly, "the estate has been failing under your control. Either through conditions or the fact that you were not raised as heir and thus did not know how to handle a vineyard and produce a profit. Secondly, Lady Aren has, technically, only removed your mate's bloodline from the estate, bringing back the Bilgern bloodline, for your son will inherit, and he will be taught how to do what the Bilgern line has done for many generations: create wine.

"Thirdly and most importantly, you should know that if you ever, and I mean ever, see my brother again, you had best run in the other direction and pray to the spirits that you find Aren before he catches you. Because he will rend you limb from limb—and you and he and I all know exactly why. The only reason you are still alive is because she suffers you to live, so pick your damned jaw off the floor and open this estate to my command or, so help me, I will end you here and now and risk both their wraths. Hers because I killed you, and his because I denied him the pleasure of doing it himself."

"I did nothing—"

"Recall to whom you speak," Para said from off on the side, suddenly straight. "Lie to me, and nothing happens, lie to him, and the spirits and the throne and all the rest can hear your filth. Bare your spirit to the world, and perhaps you will live long enough to redeem yourself."

That was creepy.

Especially given the fact that Para was no longer slurring her words and there was the utter hatred of a commoner. The type of hatred that Jer had felt from women who were given a chance to confront their abuser after they had healed.

Except he had heard that the abuse went the other way, that Para was abusive to Cerlot, not the other way around.

Neither should have ever had the chance to raise children. Have children, certainly, but not raise them.

"You're drunk, woman," Cerlot said sternly to his mate.

"The throne boils and roils, and she calls from the North. You couldn't keep them apart forever, and Aren, your precious little gem? She will bring them together, and the world will scream out its pain as they shatter everything you have ever been."

"Go to bed!" Cerlot shouted.

"One queen, two queens, will there be any more queens? Likely not, but if I'm lucky I might produce another, perhaps then you'd leave me alone."

Para pushed off the wall and wobbled. The woman swallowed hard and frowned as she swayed.

"Para, darling, you should go to bed and sleep it off."

"I... I should," she said weakly and stumbled off.

"Does she do that often?" Jer asked.

"More and more. When Aren was behaving strangely, I thought perhaps it was the Argnern bloodline," Cerlot said to Jer. "And I'm not talking... that."

"You noticed behaviour changes outside of that?" Jer asked, realizing that Cerlot had just admitted to abusing Aren.

For a brief moment, Jer entertained the idea of killing Cerlot and just being done with it, but he found himself swallowing the lump in his throat as he realized that he had to leave this man alive and well. Aren commanded it because she didn't feel like she could live in a world where her actions had caused her parents to be killed. She'd never be able to forgive herself, let alone the one who did it.

"For a queen, she has little emotion," Cerlot said. "But besides that, she would say one thing, Para another, and the servants yet another. She would say she did her tutoring—because I did teach my daughters to read and write, I insisted on it even though Para demanded they remain ignorant of all that ones of their status should know—but it wouldn't be there, and the servants would say she was reading a book or off in the corner sitting quietly."

Miscommunication was all that was.

"I will need to speak to the servants," Jer said quietly.

Already he had an image built in his mind of Aren's time at the estate. She did things, the servants were aware, he knew that from his time over the winter with Anue. The servants must have caught Aren doing something and had told Cerlot a tale that a lady would not be troubled over.

Reading a book, sitting quietly. No doubt once or twice the servants said that Aren was embroidering and even produced a piece she had worked on.

"Why would you need to speak to them?" Cerlot asked, sounding confused.

"Call that abuse of power, if you please," Jer murmured and smiled when Cerlot went a red colour. "You housed my queen on this estate and you will tell me one part. Your mate will tell me another. But I've yet to meet a servant who didn't know exactly what was going on in the house at all times and could relate to me her education, her flirtations, and any strange events that I might need to know about to ensure that she is stable enough to rule a long while."

That was right. There was another reason to keep Cerlot and Para alive. With Aren on the throne, there was a chance that she would begin to go mad as the magic was drained off of her. If at any time she began failing, Jer could send for Cerlot and Para. They would come to the palace and their mere presence would keep Aren alive for years to come.

He latched on to that idea, reminding himself of it.

Then again, Cerlot could live without many things. Such as his toes. His fingers. His nose.

Jer shivered in delight at the thought and smiled at Cerlot. "Please show me to my room."

Cerlot frowned, but turned and motioned. "You didn't bring much with you."

"I don't plan on being here longer than I need to be. You might have heard of the war that is about to start because you and Para thought it'd be best if Aren mated the Southern baron's son."

"It was a good move politically."

"That wasn't a complaint, Cerlot," Jer grumbled as they walked through the estate. "Not only did I get a lover out of the mess, but I get to go to war. My complaint is that I have to arrange the army portion of the war because my brother has no idea how to do that. I get to go to war. I get to kill people.”

“And that is why commoners will never understand ranks.”

“You raped your daughter. You don’t get to be judgemental of me.”

Cerlot pulled to a stop and stared at Jer. The lord frowned.

“She went to the palace a virgin. If Av found her in any other state, you should find another scapegoat.”

“If you had done that kind of rape, he would have killed you without thought or understanding, upon meeting you. You’re damned well lucky that Aren is so secretive about her childhood, else—” Jer hesitated and wondered what was coming out of his mouth. These were not his words, he knew too much, and for a moment he almost saw it. Taking hold of Cerlot, he slammed the lord into the wall and was rewarded with a frightened squeak. “I could end you here and now. Break you apart, bit by bit. But I want it to be very clear that the *only* thing keeping you alive is Aren’s word. Everything else wants you dead. And if you *ever* touch her or hurt her, or any other child, I will risk my queen’s rage to put an end to you, do I make myself clear?”

The man was too frightened to respond. Jer tried to growl, but when he breathed in to get the air to do so, his nose, and then his mouth was filled with the smell of piss. He grimaced and pulled away.

“Sir?” a quiet voice asked.

Jer turned down the hallway, towards the voice.

A boy of no more than fifteen stood there, his hair far too long. Tall and lean, the boy had inherited Para’s height and a combination of both his parents’ features. The brown eyes were almost a mirror of Aren’s.

What had she said? That he wasn’t a bad person, but she couldn’t be comfortable living under him?

There was something dangerous behind those eyes, but the expression seemed honest. The boy looked to Cerlot, then back to Jer, frowning just slightly.

Did the boy know nothing of what had happened in his home?

Was it Jer's place to correct that?

He realized suddenly that this was probably the boy's first interaction with a warrior. Jer swallowed his rage and tried to calm himself down.

"I apologize. Adult problems," Jer said, trying to keep his voice steady.

He didn't need this boy to be soured towards ranks because the boy didn't know what his father had done to his sister.

"Who are you?" the boy asked.

"My name is Jer Hue, steward to the throne," Jer said.

"Here to audit the estate to hold it as ward?" the boy asked.

Why could he pick nothing up from the boy? The emotion was curious, but Jer couldn't tell if the boy was happy or upset by the fact that the estate might be held in trust for him.

"Yes," Jer said, watching as the boy walked around him.

"This way," the boy said.

No name? No introduction?

Jer thought back and wondered when Aren had first told them her name. He frowned as he tried to recall but couldn't. Telm had told Av her name, and then Av had told Jer her name...

Aren had never introduced herself.

Jer followed the boy, now curious. "And you are?" he managed to ask, but only because he believed they should be on even ground.

"Eln Arg—" The boy stopped mid-word to curse. "Eln Bilgern."

"That's a good, strong, warrior name," Jer said.

"Is it?" Eln asked.

"It is," Jer said carefully.

Both looked at one another sternly. Eln suddenly turned and continued.

If Eln was a warrior, he was a quiet one, a calm one. If Eln wasn't a rank, which was what Jer was feeling, then he was what Ervam would refer to as a strong commoner. Eln wouldn't have any problem standing up to a rank. These were the sort of commoners Jer was to look for and encourage to mate and breed.

Strong commoners made more strong commoners. They were also more likely to create ranks, the likes of which could rival those born of queens and warriors.

Which meant new blood to create even stronger queens, or stronger warriors, to breed with Jer's children, and the idea of that excited Jer in a way that made him want to find an available woman.

He had to remind himself that he had a daughter who was expecting her first child. He did not need to breed.

Though, tackling Laeder was definitely going to have to happen before he felt comfortable in his own skin again. It was difficult to overcome generations of instinct. He understood that if he had enjoyed only one gender, then he would not have been conflicted. Liking both meant that he quite desperately wanted to breed even as he wanted to jump into bed with Laeder.

And Aren's brother created that conflict because Jer wanted to breed to keep his blood available to cross with this boy's blood.

Jer wondered if he knew an available woman whom he could toss at Eln.

"I said this is where you will be staying," Eln said loudly and slowly.

"I'm not stupid, just distracted," Jer said in a similar tone.

The two of them glared at one another for a very long moment.

"By what?" Eln asked. Suddenly curious and almost kitten-like, the boy's head cocked to the side.

"How old are you?" Jer asked.

"Fifteen," Eln said, then frowned. "Why?"

"I want to breed you," Jer muttered, then caught himself as he realized exactly what he had said and what it sounded like. "I like the idea of your having children. I was wondering how old you are compared to how long I would have to wait before I could toss available women at you."

"How long is that?" Eln asked, sounding a little strangled.

Jer thought back to that age and realized that Eln wouldn't recall his odd wording. All Eln would recall was that a man said something about knowing many women who might be interested in sex. Jer did know quite a few ladies who could introduce Eln to sex, he also knew a few that might make for good breeding, but the only one he knew comfortably enough to maybe offer as a mate was Wena.

Was he trying to pair off Eln, or Wena? Why was he thinking about Wena suddenly?

"At sixteen, I can legally offer my friends as your partner, if they're willing," Jer said quietly, assuming that Eln knew as much as Aren. "But if you were to find someone willing to bed you, you could have begun such as soon as you were able to think as much. Palace lands recognize the ability to mate for a year at the age of fourteen, which is actually when I accidentally became a father. That, yeah, they're right, that age limit should be raised."

"Why?" Eln asked.

"I became a father before I was your age," Jer responded.

"But sex."

"Sex did not follow."

Eln frowned at Jer. "I'm confused. First, you want to breed me, then you say you regret being a father."

"Maybe if I were able to raise her, it would have been different," Jer said quietly.

"Can... can we focus on the sex portion of your interest in me and not in the breeding?" Eln asked.

Jer tried to talk, but a strangled sound came out. He cleared his throat and looked up.

"Oh look, my room!"

Chapter Fifteen

Aren sank deeper into the hot water. She wore a small shirt and a pair of shorts. Others in the large, public bath were Olea and her daughters, all dressed in a similar fashion. The hot water was unlike anything she had experienced before.

Olea was heating the water to that special temperature.

"Aren, meet Cara, Er's niece, and my daughters Ula, Erma, Ulfa, and Alya," Olea said, finally introducing most of the others. "Then there are my nieces, Alta, Olina, Yela, Ayel."

"I'm named after my grandmother," Alya said with a bright smile. "On my mother's side."

"How many children did you have?" Aren asked Olea.

There were too many names. She wouldn't remember them all. Though she was noticing a pattern in the names she was given. Children seemed to be named after their parents in a way. She hadn't even noticed that Url and Er were very similar.

A warning to strangers, whose blood you meddle with.

She turned her head towards the whisper, which had come from near Olea. There was no one crouching there, whispering in her ear, of course. She could only say that, perhaps, the throne was being more obvious about its instructions to her.

"Twelve: nine survived birth, and one died at the age of six."

"I'm so sorry," Aren responded.

"Why?" Alya asked. "Women miscarry, it happens all the time and Mother probably lost more before she knew she was pregnant. I know it will be a terrible feeling for me, and it is horrible to carry a life and lose it, but it passed before it was birthed because it wouldn't have survived otherwise. It happens more often than women talk about and it should be talked about."

"She's about to be mated," Olea said to Aren. "And I am trying to teach my daughters not to grieve too long."

"I lost one," Aren said, feeling tears prickling her eyes even though she didn't know why she teared up.

When she had learned that bit of information she hadn't cared so much about it, why then?

"When?" Cara demanded.

The girl was haughty to say the least, but it may have had something to do with her unique look. Cara had bright blonde hair, as if sunshine had come down and been captured by her head. Her eyes were a startling blue, and she had features that were undeniably beautiful. She was likely used to men fighting over her, ranks and commoners alike.

"Last fall when I went out to a village. I lost a child then, it had barely taken hold."

"That's terrible to know," Olea said.

"Av's a true warrior, as the archivist calls him," Aren said calmly in response.

"No," Olea responded. "What's terrible is that someone was such an asshole as to tell you that you had lost a child before you knew!"

"Oh, yes, but then Av killed him," Aren said.

"Av's a what?" Cara demanded.

"True warrior," five voices called out before Aren could open her mouth.

Olea sighed loudly and looked at Cara. "A true warrior will only breed ranks. If he finds himself with a woman who is incapable of carrying a rank, it will appear she is barren. Oh my, Aren, it's just occurred to me."

"The archivist told me what a true warrior was," Aren said quietly. "Which I suppose means I lost a little queen or warrior."

"You're only eighteen," Olea countered.

"How old were you?" Alya demanded.

Aren looked between Alya and Olea. Then she looked back again and tried to recall. Aren scratched at her chin and turned back to Olea.

"Is she your firstborn?" Aren asked.

"I was not eighteen!" Olea bellowed.

There was an awkward silence afterwards as they all sat in the water. Aren noticed the way Olea's daughters seemed to engage in washing her nieces. She turned to Olea.

"You left the South at sixteen, didn't you?"

"I did," Olea said quietly. "Er is a wonderful man, and we waited several years before we tried for a child. I had three that I ended before they began."

"W-wait. You can do that?" Aren demanded.

"You..." Olea frowned and then made a face as if she remembered to whom she was talking. "Yes, Aren, you can do that, but it is a very personal choice. I chose that because of the situations of the time. If I had carried those children to term, I would have suffered greatly. The land may have fractured. I chose the lives of many people over the life of one. And... and then I cried my eyes out for several months. Because I wanted them, but it would have been such a terrible thing for hundreds and hundreds."

"I ended one because of a drunken night," Ula said quietly.

"Cara's supposedly lost three now," Alya said with a huff.

"He shoved me down a set of stairs!" Cara shouted.

There was a brittle quiet over the bath as Aren looked over the women present. She understood that there was a long history between them all and that she was a bit of an intruder.

"But you're the one who splattered me with brown stuff," Aren said to Cara.

Cara scoffed loudly. "Not my fault you're so we—"

The queen was yanked under the water.

Aren looked at Olea, who seemed to give her a look in response. Aren shook her head and made a questioning look.

"Let her up for air!" Olea shouted.

"What—I'm doing that?" Aren asked.

Cara popped up, gasping for air. The woman, who was the same age as Aren, surely, dragged in breath after breath as she turned to Aren with an accusing look.

Realizing that she had done that accidentally, Aren tried to look relaxed as she said, "Don't do it again, or I'll have to make a public example of you."

"Are you threatening me?" Cara demanded.

Aren looked past Cara, to Raven walking into the room with an armful of towels. Raven blinked at Aren and seemed to convey a plea not to mention her presence.

"I will cut you."

"With what, water?" Olea asked with a laugh.

Then each of her daughters started laughing, then her nieces. Aren watched each of them start laughing and realized, as each one joined in, that they weren't laughing *at* her, they were laughing to try to ease the tension.

"As if you would be stupid enough," Cara responded.

Aren blinked at Cara as Raven reached down with a knife and cut the other queen's arm.

Which begged the question of why Raven was in a servant role and where she had gotten the knife.

As Cara screamed, it also brought to question why no one turned to Raven but instead looked to Aren as if she possessed a magic she shouldn't have known. The cut was little more than a nick on Cara's arm, but Cara acted as if Aren had just chopped her limb off.

"What?" Aren asked.

Raven placed a single finger over her lips and smiled at Aren before leaving the public bathing room silently.

"Now," Ulfa said, the youngest of Olea's daughters and barely fourteen, "I'm not making an accusation. I'd just really, really, *really* like to know how you did that."

"All the knowledge we have suggests a queen has to touch a person to be able to use her hands as weapons," Olea said to Aren. "And we've tried, we have, but we can't figure out how that works."

Aren shifted towards Olea and took her right hand, her dominant hand, and held it just away from the other queen's neck. Olea stiffened against the approach as Aren trembled.

"I don't know how I knew that," Aren said.

Olea whimpered. "Did anyone catch that?"

"I did," Erma said quietly.

Aren and Olea both looked to the young woman, who was approximately Aren's age and shared Olea's eyes and her father's hair. The queen had a distant look as she waded across the bath to her mother.

"I'm not familiar with what happened, but she sits the throne, I assume it spoke through her," Erma said in her soft voice, then lifted her left hand. "Dominant hand. It's a weapon."

"It's not that—" Olea lifted her hand and stared at it as if it had grown a head.

"There you go," Erma said with a smile. "But Lady Aren's other hand—" Erma took Aren's left hand in her own and lifted it above the water. The young woman traced a line between Aren's mating ring and the black manacle. "Mother, if she ever lifts this hand to you, it will be your end."

Aren peered around Erma, to Olea.

"She is very good," Olea said. "Not strong, but nearly perfect control and can stretch a drop of magic into what you or I would use in a day."

Aren blinked at Olea, not understanding.

"She takes nothing and makes it into something," Alya said in a tone that strongly implied she had explained this more than once in the past.

"Can we..." Aren trailed off as she moved away from Olea.

"Of course," Olea said. "What were you wondering?"

Aren blinked at Olea, wondering how Olea knew what Aren wanted to ask. Olea simply smiled in response without actually responding.

"When your mate is twice your age, how do you bring up children?" Aren asked. "I know they're going to happen. We *will* have children. But in the meantime, I don't know how to even talk about that. He's older than I am, and at his age, his father had two children. You probably had nine."

"A warrior wants children the way any person wants water," Olea said quietly. "He craves to nurture and protect, so the more children you give him, the calmer he will become because his attention is spread across several people."

"But I'm eighteen, and I have my whole life ahead of me."

"Jer had a child at fourteen," Cara said sternly.

"You're my age, and you've lost three on purpose," Aren countered.

"You lost one because you're just not capable," Cara snapped back.

"No!" Olea snapped at Cara. "Never say that! That is so rude! You have no idea why she lost the child. You have no idea what happened! You don't get to say that she lost a child because she's not capable. Never say that again!"

"If... if I weren't capable, I wouldn't have been pregnant in the first place," Aren said meekly.

She said it that way because Olea was getting angry in a way that Aren was certain would make the men come looking at any moment.

"I don't care if you are capable! It is rude to say that to another woman!"

"But I can get pregnant, so what she says doesn't matter," Aren said to Olea.

"She is being—"

"Olea," Aren said.

The two of them met eyes and Olea clenched her teeth. There was a low growl from Olea before the older queen drew in a long breath and made a visible attempt to try to relax.

"What I asked was how to talk to him about it," Aren said.

"Contraceptives only work so well. You can have the talk all you like," Olea said. "Unless you befriend a healer and she is willing to make the special something for you, you're very likely going to have an unplanned child."

"Why don't healers do that for anyone, anyhow?" Aren asked.

"Well, it takes magic, which could pull from their ability to help those who are hurt. It also causes this expectation that healers will create our contraceptives for us."

"There's already the expectation that they heal people, and the expectation that we will give our magic to commoners," Aren said.

Olea smiled. "True, but in the past healers have been blamed for a queen being poisoned because it was believed that the contraceptive was the reason. If you make your own, you can't be poisoned by healers, but you also take responsibility for your bed play."

"You still haven't told me *how* I talk about it," Aren said sternly.

"Be honest?" Olea asked with a shrug.

"That's not really helpful," Aren muttered.

"Sometimes others can't tell you what you need to say or do, you just have to do it and figure it out for yourself," Olea said.

"And now you sound like Telm," Aren grumbled as she sank lower into the water. "Meanwhile Av gets to leave the castle and go hunting."

"Maybe they'll get a deer," Alya said with a smile. "Bear is getting boring."

"This is Av's first time hunting with your father," Olea said sternly. "There's probably not going to be meat coming back with them. And Aren, you aren't a prisoner, you can go outside anytime you please."

"You just need a guardian," Cara said with a sigh. "So that you don't destroy any more priceless historical artifacts."

"I didn't do it on purpose."

"Like you didn't yank me under the water on purpose or cut me?" Cara demanded, motioning to her arm. "Look at this. I could bleed to death!"

"It barely grazed your skin and has already stopped bleeding," Aren countered.

She almost blurted out about Raven but kept it to herself. Suddenly she wondered if Raven was a part of the madness that had claimed all the short-lived queens before her.

No one else could see Raven. That was why Er had been surprised, why everyone blamed Aren for moving a fountain and breaking something.

"Aren, are you all right?" Olea asked.

Which meant that if Raven was invisible, she wasn't real, and it also meant that it had been Aren's magic that had caused all that trouble, that had yanked Cara under the water and cut the other queen.

"Is using magic like imagining an invisible person is going around and doing things for you?" Aren asked, turning her attention to Olea. "Because I think that might be what it's like for me."

"That's... an interesting way of seeing it," Olea said.

"Most of us just use it to heat things and work the lights," Erma said.

"It does take a great deal of magic, though recently it has seemed less," Olea murmured. The queen adjusted in the water and frowned. "Almost nothing since the day in the anchor room."

"Why do you think that is?" Aren asked.

"I don't know. Whatever you did to the anchors was creating its own magic and stretching."

"Like stretching dough to make bread?" Aren asked.

"Somewhat, or more like how you let the bread rise," Olea said. "But it shouldn't be affecting the amount of magic it takes me to heat Castle Grey. I should probably look into that. We've collected a small library, it's not as impressive as that of the palace, but all the information pertains to the running of Castle Grey."

"Magic has been around since the dawn of time, why does no one simply know what I've done?" Aren demanded. "Everyone has opinions on me, on my childhood, on my moods, on my not being able to feel properly. Everyone wants to stand around talking for hours and hours about everything in my life, but when it comes to magic, everyone scratches their head and acts like I'm the first person in the world to move a fountain from here to there.

"The damned thing is at the palace, and she isn't getting it back. And as for the anchor stones… Did you ever think that maybe, since those anchor stones are from the palace, they're used to having the magic of one queen, of the one sitting the throne, flowing through them? Maybe they are part of a landscape magic that got trashed, and that's why we have short-lived queens because the old palace just did that and the new one is plaster and should be burned to the ground, did anyone ever consider *that*?"

"Are you suggesting that you activated a magic that has lain dormant hundreds of years?" Olea asked. "One which has been made to create more of itself to fuel the throne?"

"I suppose that is what I said."

Olea stared at Aren, her mouth falling open.

"Yes, because an idiotic, palace-land queen without any training whatsoever can really pinpoint the reason for the short-lived queens when no one else in the past six hundred years has been able to figure it out," Cara snarled.

"Call me idiotic one more time."

"Idiotic moron."

Chapter Sixteen

Jer stepped into the room and felt a weary nothingness. He opened his senses but found nothing out of the ordinary.

The bed was small, in the corner, and was made as if waiting for Aren to return. Atop the bed were blankets and a pillow, but they were more what a servant might have, not a young woman from a wealthy estate, let alone the heir to a vineyard.

He turned slowly and looked at the desk, which was beaten and old.

Laying a hand on the top of the desk, he considered what he had been told. That Aren had been moved to this room three years before heading to the palace, likely because Para couldn't stand having the young woman near her rooms.

The anger of a queen could make life very uncomfortable for commoners.

There were no trinkets, no notes or keepsakes. No ribbon or jewelry. If Jer had not been explicitly told that this was Aren's rooms, he would have thought that it had sat empty for years. There was too little of anything to it, so that not even a commoner could have stayed in that room.

"What are you doing here?" Eln asked from the doorway.

"I asked to see Aren's room. I was shown to this door."

"That's because no one will go to her room," Eln said, motioning down the hallway.

Jer left the room and looked to where Eln pointed. The idea of going farther down the hallway made Jer's stomach churn and roil. He looked back to Eln, but the boy simply stared at him.

"Why is she staying down a darkened hallway?" Jer asked. "There are no lamps down there. Looks like the door doesn't even close properly—I can see the thing is off its hinges."

"Mother said that if we were going to act sullen and bring darkness to the estate, we would live in such a place, because surely we would feel more at home there," Eln said quietly, looking down the hallway, then back to Jer. "You want to know things about her?"

"That is part of why I am here," Jer responded.

"Never tell her to smile," Eln said with a slow shake of his head.

"You grew up with her, and that's all you can tell me?" Jer asked.

Eln shrugged. "The rest doesn't really matter. Things happened, we grew up. She was distant. I'd ask her about stuff, and she'd not remember it at all, even though it just happened a few days before. She liked Anue, but everyone likes Anue, she's the complete opposite of Aren. But even Anue didn't go into Aren's room."

"I can see why."

"Do you know why?" Eln asked.

Jer thought about Van's destruction of the bed when they had met just under a month ago to discuss Aren's emotions. He recalled the tale of how Van's father was said to have punished the queen.

"I have a few guesses," Jer responded, leaving Eln in front of the first door.

Entering the room at the end of the hall, Jer felt disgusted. He closed the door, to keep hidden whatever he moved.

As soon as the door closed, the feeling changed, the light in the room changed from gloomy to bright. Even the air itself seemed to move. The stale, stuffy feeling was replaced very shortly by fresh air.

Jer approached the window and found it closed, nailed shut from the inside. The air movement was coming from the window, however. He reached out and put his hand through the glass pane, fully understanding that the glass should have stopped his hand. He leaned out the window and looked down, at the trellis up the side of the estate.

It hadn't been used in over a year, but he could pick the pathway down, the carefully selected places almost overgrown now.

He pulled his head back into the room and looked over the furniture. All old, all worn, but there was a tenderness around the furniture. Jer touched the desk and felt a reverberating anger. He frowned but kept his hand on the desk as he attempted to open his senses further.

The room darkened. A vile smell arose from the corner behind the desk, and something dangerous was standing behind him.

Knowing that the thing behind him wasn't real, Jer turned to face the empty room. This was how he had expected to find Aren's room, but what he had found instead was utterly baffling.

"Sanctuary," he said quietly to himself, moving back to the window.

It was now solid.

He rapped his knuckles against the glass and looked out over the yard.

Aren's room overlooked the stables and barn.

Which begged the question of where she had gone when she left her room by way of the trellis.

Jer turned to the wardrobe and opened it. Inside were a few sets of clothing, mainly boyish things that wouldn't fit Aren, at least not any longer. There was a formal dress, one that looked very much like something Para would wear to court.

He moved the clothing to the side and rapped his knuckles on the bottom of the wardrobe. Sure enough, the bottom was hollow. He reached under the wardrobe and probed for the latch. When it opened, he was disappointed by the spider that skittered across the empty and dusty space. If Aren had ever known about the hollow, she hadn't used it.

Jer closed the bottom of the wardrobe and stood, frustrated.

There were no papers here, no nicknacks, nothing physical to suggest that anyone had ever lived in the room, besides the clothing hanging in the wardrobe. The magic was the only indication that someone had lived in the room, and even that baffled him.

One moment glass was solid and the next not? The change in smell, the change to the lighting, even?

How had Para and Cerlot not noticed that Aren lit her room with magic? How had Aren not mentioned that before? She struggled with the most basic magic, yet somehow had created a sanctuary for herself.

Or perhaps the problem wasn't that Aren struggled with one thing and was excellent at another, but that she had accidentally created a sanctuary. She had brought light into her rooms without realizing what she had done and, once she was required to do so on command, couldn't recall how she had done what she had done before.

He searched the room, going through everything, lifting everything. It was not the first time he had had to search a room for an item, yet it was the first time he found absolutely nothing useful.

Frustrated, he left the room and closed the door.

Eln stood by the first door still, staring at him.

"Does she own nothing?" Jer asked.

"Mother burned her dolls when we moved here, and then found Anue had given her a stuffed animal right before she was placed in there. Aren was accused of stealing from Anue even though Anue said that she had given the toy to Aren."

"Do you know of anything Aren might have hidden from your mother?" Jer asked.

"We all keep things secret, that's why they're called secrets," Eln responded.

"I would like to be able to bring something back to Aren, something personal."

Eln shook his head. "If Aren had one of those, she kept it super secret, like... liking a servant, you don't say that to anyone and don't even look at them or think about it because if you do, Mother will know about it."

"Did she take to any dogs on the vineyard?"

"Mother said that if she caught Aren near the dogs again, she'd be housed with them since she seemed to prefer behaving like a bitch in heat."

Jer sucked in a breath through gritted teeth and reminded himself, once again, that he was not allowed to kill the Bilgerns.

"Did she actually like the dogs?"

"Like them like she should a man?" Eln asked, sounding confused.

"No, did she pet them and play with them?"

"Yes, that was Mother's problem. Dogs are here to help with hunting and guarding, not to be petted and played with, since it'll make them soft and us stupid."

Liked animals, was likely the case. But then, an animal had never beat her or starved her. The animals had probably suffered under similar abuses, allowing Aren to make a connection with the animals that she couldn't with another person. He would have to remember that.

Perhaps it would be something he could pass on to Av. Get her a puppy and she would be very happy indeed.

"She also went to the barn often," Eln said quietly.

There was a suddenly haunted look to the boy's eyes. Jer tried not to let his pity show, pity that this boy would spend years still under Para.

"What's in the barn, Eln?"

"You came to take him away, didn't you? Mother said he'd be leaving soon."

"Why is he in the barn?" Jer demanded.

Eln was talking about his brother, the one that had been described as a dimwit. Aren wanted him removed to the palace because the boy could not protect himself against Para's attacks.

"Because Aren wouldn't behave when he was around, so Mother moved him out there. She said he's not part of the family, that the midwife must have switched him at birth because she couldn't have birthed something like that."

"Then why keep him—" Jer saw the way Eln flinched and looked away.

The other brother was kept around because Para had used him to control Aren. The thought made Jer wonder what state he'd be finding Aren's brother in and just what was affecting him that made him a dimwit.

Aren's desire to have her brother at the palace, despite the fact that they might look alike or rumour, might circulate and the boy could be killed, made a great deal more sense. She wasn't putting him in any more danger than he was already in, but at least on palace grounds, the murderer could be brought to justice for his or her crimes.

"Have you ever been hurt?" Jer asked.

He had to know if Aren was making a mistake leaving Eln on the estate.

"Anue and I have kept our heads down," Eln said quietly, looking down in shame. "What Aren did to get into trouble, we didn't. There's a time or two where we got a slap for something or went to bed without dinner, but that was our mistake."

"Were you ever told what happened to Anue?" Jer asked.

"Mother said that Anue is being held against her will at the palace. That those who should uphold the laws are allowing it to happen because she has rank and therefore her desires are no longer considered because her parents have done their duty of birthing and raising her to breeding age. She's more angry than anything that she hasn't been compensated for Anue and that Father tells her it's their duty to have more children."

"I suppose you were questioned thoroughly when they returned home?" Jer asked.

"No," Eln said, shaking his head. "Mother did manage to speak with Anue before she left and Anue told her the truth of the matter. I have great potential, but I hold no rank."

Which meant that Jer had to speak to Anue. If she could feel the breeding capabilities of her blood, the instinct should be reinforced. Anue could be a grand matchmaker, with how easily she got along with everyone at the palace and the strength of her instincts.

"I think it's a mistake to leave you here without a guardian," Jer said quickly.

"Mother said that next spring I'm to go to be a ward of the throne," Eln said to Jer as if the warrior were an idiot. "I'm the one who helped Aren talk Mother into letting her go. Aren knows the ward laws. She knows that she cannot call an heir if he turned fifteen after the current court began.

Unless you find gross breach, something bordering treason, an heir must remain with his or her parents until the date of the court's convening in the spring on the year after he or she turns fifteen."

"I should get her to change that law."

"It's to protect parents from palace reach. Otherwise, girls of eleven would be taken because they hold rank. A girl of eleven can be bred to make more ranks. Which makes me wonder what you're doing with my baby sister."

Jer chuckled, then caught himself. "I'm sorry, that's not funny at all, but surely you know your sisters well enough to know their beliefs on breeding. They will not submit to anything of that sort. If they were so weak willed, my father and Telm, who are interim guardians of Anue and have both raised ranks, would put an end to the discussion and anyone stupid enough to bring it up."

"What rank are they?" Eln asked.

"Telm is a queen, Ervam is a trainer—do you know what that is?"

Eln relaxed visibly. The boy glanced down the hallway that led to the rest of the estate, then looked back to Jer.

"Talk to the kitchen staff. Aren didn't work down there, but they were the first ones who started acting differently."

"Do the dogs have a caretaker?"

"He won't speak to you," Eln said, shaking his head slowly. "He's the one who told Mother that Aren was visiting the dogs. But then..."

"But then?" Jer pressed.

"You might want to see *him* because there's... there's always been something over the fields my father has set aside as most the vineyard. And over the cellars. But ever since Mother killed the pack leader and made them all watch, and Aren too, they've not been the same. Even the new ones."

"Queens can control animals to a point," Jer said, repeating back what he already knew, but also giving Eln some information on why what had happened, happened.

"Like in the stories, where the warrior would go out to the forest and find a woman with a bird on her finger, singing as the animals came around to her?"

"That's a little extreme."

"Oh, you mean the *other* stories."

"What other stories?" Jer asked.

"The one Balya tells," Eln said. "She works in the kitchens. The way she tells it, the legends are stories that have always been told and have some small seed of truth to them. Myth is what was once history, but has been told so often that facts have changed.

"She stopped another servant who was telling a tale of two ranks coming together and said that it didn't happen like that at all and then she told a different version of the story. Except instead of being out in the forest, the queen was being held captive by her mother and had to work as a servant because she was a disobedient and willful child. And for a while that all worked, though the servants knew what was going on.

"One day a warrior comes on through, he's wandering the lands, see, just visiting everywhere. His being there causes things to start happening. The queen starts acting out and is almost caught by the warrior several times, but her mother doesn't want a rank to see the child she's ashamed of, so the queen is always hustled off before he arrives.

"He goes hunting one day, dogs and the men from the estate, and when they come back, the queen is running from her mother. Whatever's happened, the woman's in a fury and the queen's full of fear and she stops at the sight of the dogs. Looks over them and spots the warrior."

"And the whole world seemed to stop," Jer said with a tremble in his voice.

Like the day when Aren ran. She had taken Jer out easily, but when she spotted Av, Jer swore the whole world came to a standstill as the two stared at one another, summing up their opponent.

"The queen bolts in the other direction, and he's off his horse and after her. He captures her and does what warriors and queens do, and when they get back to the estate, they find out that the dogs have ripped apart her mother and several of the men."

"That definitely sounds closer to the truth," Jer said. "What does Balya look like?"

"Oh, you'll know her when you see her."

Rank, rank was the only thing that commoners could tell a stranger that about another person. Jer gathered his courage to face an unfamiliar, unknown rank.

"Would you show me to the kitchen, please?"

Chapter Seventeen

Url walked into his study, eyes on a report as he was trying to make sense of what he was reading. Trying to figure out if the damned thing had been sent to the heir, or to the high lord. It might have even been a mistake that the report had been sent to him, that the lords in question assumed that Url was now baron because of the announcement.

Or he was distracted in general. He had attempted to write to Nae, but each letter he wrote seemed insufficient. They sat in his desk, sealed in case he changed his mind, though he doubted he would send any of them. None of them quite said what he wanted to express to the healer.

The world shifted, and Url hit his desk as a hand pressed between his shoulder blades, holding him down as a hot body pressed tight against him.

"Finally alone."

He tried not to let his fear show. "Reld? What are you doing?"

"Stranger's got you pegged already?" Reld snarled.

"He's my cousin, get off of—" Url squeaked as Reld ground his hips against Url's backside.

That was not how things were done in the North. According to his father, warriors might end up paired off during gatherings if there weren't enough women offering themselves up, but they were taught to control their animalistic urges.

"It's my turn to be on top."

Reld meant the dominant warrior of Castle Grey, not that they had found themselves in such a position before. To try to take the position was ridiculous. Url had his supporters and had put Reld into the ground on more than one occasion.

"Elders say you don't know your place."

And there went half his supporters. Url tried to get up off the desk. Reld let him up only enough to slam him back down and knock the air out of him.

"She says that if I can bring you under control, I will rule and that you'll enjoy it. Since you don't enjoy the company of queens."

The panic was setting it. Url knew he had to fight back but couldn't seem to get his limbs to work. Was it magic at work?

Or was there some truth to the old tales and he wanted this to happen?

He thought of Nae and managed to swing his elbow back. All it met was empty air. He used the motion of his body to turn, a startled Reld moving back just slightly.

The struggle that ensued was brief, but Reld ended up on top of him again.

"You do want this, don't you? Don't worry, I'll be gentle with you. This time."

"Reld?" Er asked from the doorway.

There was amusement and surprise in Er's voice.

"Busy," Reld snapped back.

"Atop my son, Reld."

"Still busy."

"I'm not going to wait outside the door while you mount my son, Reld. Do it another time, either of your own free will or with two broken knees."

Reld swore and was off Url in an instant. "This isn't over."

Humiliated, Url dragged himself off the floor and straightened his clothing as his father closed the door to the study. Er played with the lock pointedly; it was broken, probably by Reld when he broke into the study.

"What was that?" Er asked.

"He thinks I need to be brought to heel," Url said.

"I meant, why didn't you fight back?"

"I tried."

"Hit me," Er said.

"What?" Url demanded.

"I want you to hit me so I can judge what's going on. Come on, you're not going to hurt me."

"Last time you said that we broke half the furniture in your rooms, and then Mother beat me until I cried my eyes out," Url said. "So no, thank you, I don't want to hit you. He said the elders think I'm out of line."

Er sucked in a breath. "Which means there's nothing wrong with you."

"Which means there's nothing wrong with me," Url said.

He gritted his teeth at the way his voice cracked when he spoke. He had to stop that. As baron, the breaking of his voice would be all the sign the others needed that it was time to revolt. They were in a delicate position when it came to rejoining the palace.

They knew what was at stake. No one else did, or at the very least, they didn't care.

If the elders wanted him in line, they had ways of keeping him from fighting. There had been a few times, very few, when those same elders had helped Url gain the upper hand to show him what they were capable of.

"What do I do?" Url asked.

Er was quiet for a long time, his eyes on the floor. Finally, the baron shook his head.

"I don't know," Er said, frustration in his voice as he looked around the study as if to find the answer there. "You could kill Reld, but two would likely take his place, and if you think one would be unpleasant, two is worse."

"The only other option is to…what? Let him mount me? To make the elders happy because they think I just need a romp since I don't take after queens?"

"The mounting is about domination, not romping. If it were about romping, you'd start the fight, he'd end it, and it would be on the training sands where the other warriors could watch and make certain that's what it actually was. We do not allow mounting here. You know that."

"And you're the baron!"

"You also know it has to happen before I can do anything about it. As your father, I could break his legs, but that would undermine your strength."

"I know that," Url said in annoyance.

"What did you do to upset them?" Er asked calmly. "Perhaps we can fix this another way."

"I tried to warn Aren."

Er sucked in a breath through clenched teeth. "You, son, have just built your own pyre. You can't warn them! She is the last word here. She has been the last word since I was born for a very good reason—she is strong. She knows how to use her magic in a way that no one else can. And when we need her, damn it, she's brought our broken fellows back from the brink so that we at least didn't lose them when something went wrong during the blooding."

"Speaking of blooding…" Url said. "Av's not been chasing ghosts."

If there was another way to calm a warrior down, another way to get back from that brink? Url wouldn't have to keep his grandmother around, he could just throw her out the nearest window.

"Not since the mating. He's been able to express himself how he pleases. His behaviour is borderline madness, however."

"Only borderline. She attacked *me*, recall, not him. I take that as meaning she's given up on him?"

"The men are protecting him, he is a warrior, he made himself very clear and then acted upon his threat when she did what he told her not to do. She might be frightened though, he whispered something to her, and now she has the feel of a queen who is shaken to her core."

"Didn't you two talk about it on your hunt?" Url demanded, frustrated and annoyed that he had been left home so that Av could join in.

"You know the rules of the hunt, Url," his father said sternly in response. "There has to be an even number, and when introducing someone new, the others have to be well acquainted with it. As it is I had to throw him in a damned river."

"Surely you mean the hot spring," Url responded.

"No, the river. Broke the ice with his back and dunked him a few times for good measure. He thought hunting was hunting."

"As in for food?" Url said, not believing what he was hearing.

"Yes, still didn't hesitate when we found the poor bastard."

"He murdered a child, why would you think he's a poor bastard?"

"Let's just say your cousin isn't going to have to try very hard to make the warriors believe he's violent when pushed," Er grumbled, then shifted uncomfortably. "He tried to gut me with an arm bone because I suggested the others should have a go. He believed, quite rightly, that if we got close enough, we'd put the criminal out of his misery."

"We knew it could happen, that's why we do the hunts."

"Better a criminal slated for execution than a warrior within the walls of Castle Grey, but we expected hesitance, revulsion even. Palace lands still execute with a noose. It's what happened to that fellow who tried to murder Aren."

"When did you tell him what you were hunting?" Url asked.

"At the stables," Er said. "He went still and gave me that look, that one there. He wanted to hunt. He needed it. And yes, I took his damned weapon from him. If I hadn't, who knows how many of us would have come back sliced up because the one didn't slate his thirst."

"Well, we can't make people break the law," Url said, then grumbled out a low growl to himself. "And the lords are petitioning to do their own executions now. They have plenty of warriors and don't understand why bringing the criminals to us is best for everyone's health."

"It'll never be granted."

"Unless of course the elders unseat me and have me rule while Reld tells me how it's going to be," Url snarled in response. "Because she knows I like hunting."

"She also knows what happens when a warrior isn't given an outlet for his rage."

"Olerna never should have gone south with that man."

"He was her mate, and none of us knew how bad it was. We thought they were just fighting. We didn't realize it was because he needed to hunt and was a bad man. Point being, no one is going to stop the hunts. The warriors here do need to restrain themselves when they want to kill an idiotic lord or an elder who is interfering."

"Av isn't exactly suffering, and they will try to argue that."

"They wouldn't if they saw what he did to our prey. Or the black eye he gave your brother."

Url stilled. "I'm sorry, he did what?"

"It can happen, and yes, we know what it's a sign of. That was actually why I came to see you."

"No way am I getting in a fight with a warrior who is to the point of bruising another warrior."

"I'm not allowed to go to war. Your mother calls that going to war. Which means my heir has to. He's got to be resettled and, as you pointed out, we have no criminals. At least none to be executed. It has to be done soon, otherwise—"

Er and Url stiffened at the same time. Url didn't know how to describe it, but he knew what it was.

"Where did you send Av after you got back?"

"To the baths, the women are in there, and you know how delightful it is to soak in water and listen to women giggle after you've killed the bad guy."

Url was out of the study as his father finished speaking. Er would follow behind, but at a slower pace than Url could run.

Startled servants jumped out of his way, and Url almost ran straight into his grandmother, who had a smirking expression on her face. He was tempted to run directly into her, but habit made him bound around her and the corner as she called out some question or demand.

He stumbled into Av just outside the baths, realizing as he touched his cousin that this was not anger or fury.

Blinking at Av as the other warrior turned slowly to him, Url looked past the larger man.

On the floor of the bathing room, Aren and Cara struggled. Sopping wet, in linen clothing. Url squeaked out a sound and turned his eyes to the ceiling when Av growled at him.

Av wasn't angry because something was going on, he was aroused because he was watching his woman fight, and win, against another queen. The wet clothing was just that extra incentive, but also reason enough for Av to turn his fury on a warrior stupid enough to look for too long.

Url turned to the hallway and saw warriors coming towards them from both directions. He lifted a hand, and they came to a stop.

Except for Reld, who approached them and shoved his way into the bathing room.

"Enough of that!" Reld shouted. "Break it up! Why are you women just sitting there? Stop them!"

"Cara challenged Aren, Reld, and if you interfere I will bend you over my knee and give you a spanking the likes of which you will never forget, and then I'll hand you over to Av," Olea shouted back.

Av's focus moved from the women to Reld. Av sniffed the air slightly, head turning towards Url.

How good was Av's sense of smell? And why would he be taking that sort of interest in Url's bodily condition?

Av motioned with his head, and Reld left the bathing room, leaving the women struggling. He bent ever so slightly towards Url.

"Can we throw more water on them? I think they're drying out."

"Aren's already won, you could just separate them, since that's not really the struggle for domination anymore," Url squeaked out, glancing at the queens.

"Then what's it a struggle for?" Av asked.

"Let's just say that if this were not a public area and you planned correctly, you could be having a threesome tonight," Url responded.

"Queens do that?"

"If warriors do it, queens do it."

Av glanced casually over his shoulder at the other warriors. "Does Cara need a warrior to resettle her?"

"Loser doesn't get anything," Url countered.

"Fair enough."

Url watched his cousin enter the bathing room and pick up a hissing and kicking Aren. Av dragged Aren away from Cara, moving her almost to the door and then let her go on purpose. She lunged back at Cara as Av smiled ever so slightly and moved to Aren, only to pluck her up and give her a little slap on the backside as a reminder to behave.

Av carried his prize away, obviously proud of himself, and perhaps of her as well. The gathering warriors parted, each with a smirk on their faces.

Then he turned to Url hopefully, but he shook his head.

If it had been any other queen, he would let them offer themselves to the loser and see if she found any of them acceptable. But Cara had a reputation, and there was no point giving them hope that she might let one of them claim her. There was also no point in starting a rivalry with Av over what his mate had done to Cara.

He looked to his mother, who had an angry glint in her eye.

"I apologize for the intrusion, Lady Olea," he said quietly and ducked his head in deference.

"Don't apologize, Url, I'm not angry with you," Olea said sternly in response.

He nodded and left the bathing room, looking to Reld, who smiled slowly at him. Url crossed the distance between himself and Reld, who stood at the front of the one group of warriors.

"If I were you, Reld, I would stay out of Lady Olea's way. And I would pray that Av is too taken by his mate to recall that you were stupid enough to interfere."

"Please, we're all feeling a little out of sorts," Reld purred out, reaching out to touch Url's jaw. "Why don't we all just forget about the bathing room and have a bit of sparring practice?"

"Not interested," Url said, brushing past Reld.

He hadn't known before just how intense Reld could be, or how interested the other warrior had been in him. Obviously this was not just about being the dominant warrior or pleasing the elders. Reld wanted Url in ways that he shouldn't.

Perhaps it was a desire that Url had accidentally led Reld to believe might be mutual.

Either way, it was going to end in a fight and whether Url won or lost was dependent on the elders. Gritting his teeth, Url went in search of his grandmother.

Chapter Eighteen

Jer walked into the kitchen, and the staff came to a stop. The head cook came around the counter as he turned pointedly and closed the door.

"No, don't—"

He clicked it shut and turned back to the head cook as the lighting changed, as the light orbs lit up in the kitchen and air circulated. The stuffiness that most kitchens had, the smell of food, and the pail meant for the midden heap, all seemed to disappear.

"My name is Jer Hue. I am steward to the throne. Do you know who sits the throne?"

"Lady Aren Argnern," the head cook said.

"She chose me and is now mated to my brother. We are both warriors, do you know what that means?"

"It means you are here to question us about her life here, to know what sort of things one might need to control Lady Aren. But we won't do it. We won't be giving you any information. Go ahead and tell Lady Para about this, about whatever you please. Kill me where I stand, it will make no difference."

Jer looked over the head cook, who wasn't the matronly woman who usually took up residence in an estate after years of training. She was not yet middle-aged.

To Eln's children, she would be older, perhaps have a few children of her own.

"How long have you been working here?" Jer asked.

"Five years."

Five years past, Aren would have been almost fourteen. Her magic would have been strong enough to do all sorts of things.

"How far away did you live from here?" Jer asked.

"I came for Lady Anue, not Lady Aren," the woman countered. "I lived on the coast, at the village they once lived at. I came because I didn't want what happened to my sister to happen to them. I knew she could hide, but that was because we taught her how."

Comforts of the East, where queens learned how to use magic for everything but lights and heat. Jer looked the cook up and down.

"Are you a rank?" he asked.

If she was, he was impressed with how well she hid it. The woman's nose went in the air. She shifted just slightly to the side.

"My rank is commoner."

"And you hand-selected each of those working in your kitchen?" Jer asked. "Trained many of them, given their ages?"

"I did, yes."

"This is good. This is a family, families work well together. Who, though, does all this?"

"We can't say."

Jer sighed out. "What do you mean, you can't say?"

"Saying their name draws their attention," the head cook said. "And I just don't want to."

"You mean to tell me that you saying her name would be a betrayal of her trust, and this would end?" Jer asked. "That would make this a spell. No one knows how to do spells."

"This one does."

Not Aren, maybe Anue. How they shielded themselves might be considered a type of spell, magic that worked until such a time as someone brushed it aside.

Spells were linked to witches by commoners. What witches were said to do was say words, draw shapes, and mix strange things like eye of newt and baby liver.

What queens did was weave magic into something either real or noticeable. A spell was a bit of magic that had to be activated. The throne was a spell, the palace was a spell, but they were called landscape magic, to keep it as separate as possible from the word that had been linked to witches.

He looked over the kitchen again and focused on the head cook.

"I will need to ask you about your inventory, parties, wine, and the like. All for my audit, you understand. Bilgern has been placed as a warded estate, to be held for the heir of the Bilgern line, Eln."

"Oh no," the head cook gasped out. "No, no. Lady Aren inherits this estate. She is the eldest."

"She is Lady Aren Argnern. The lord and lady here are Para and Cerlot Bilgern and their heir, Eln Bilgern."

"But a lord cannot mate a servant," one of the others said in despair.

Confused, Jer tried to pick out who had spoken, but everyone was staring at the head cook. The woman made a face at Jer.

"The boy is taken by Balya, and she is taken by him."

"First off, who said a servant can't mate a lord?" Jer asked.

"Those with title can only mate those with title, as per Lady Para's beliefs."

"Av has no title, but he is Aren's mate. The only reason I have title is because I'm steward."

"And didn't Lady Para spend the whole winter complaining loudly about the fact that her daughter is to be mated to some mutt?" the head cook snapped in response.

"Where's Balya?" Jer asked.

"Why?" demanded several voices at once.

"Because I said so. This estate must be open to me to investigate all things. Aren will want to know anything that may cause distress on the estate."

"Out by the well," the head cook said with an edge to her voice.

"I don't plan on hurting her," Jer said as the kitchen went dim.

He frowned up at the light orbs as the door behind him opened. He turned as Para slipped into the kitchen. Her eyes flickered over Jer, then to the cook.

Para opened her mouth, then closed it, and looked at Jer fearfully before she focused on the head cook again.

"Dinner will be done to the utmost perfection, Lady Para," the head cook said in response to the look. "I will send tea to your rooms right away. You could have rung the bell."

"I wanted to come down and see you about it," Para said weakly.

"If you'd like to make certain the tea is made properly, by all means, have a seat there." The head cook motioned to a chair. "Lord Jer was just leaving to speak with Balya."

"Why?" Para asked, turning to him. "Why do you wish to speak with Balya?"

"Are you afraid she will tell me something that she shouldn't?" Jer asked.

The woman trembled. "Balya was my personal servant for a time. She lies often."

Para didn't sound like herself. She sounded desperate. She even seemed to struggle to get the last sentence out. When she finished speaking, Para moved to the chair the head cook had motioned to. She sat, back straight and a distant look on her face.

Nothing about Para had ever sat right with Jer. From the first moment they had met, the woman had managed to drive a wedge between herself, Jer, and Av.

He was beginning to think that Para was just a little mad, but not enough that her blood recognized the signs. Was this a lucid moment then? Was Para fighting with something inside of herself?

Maybe the anger and hatred Para put into the world was the only way she could stay stable enough to function. Anger was used by commoners to keep queens out of their minds, but also because an angry person could act and react. If the option was between crying and throwing something, Jer had been told to choose anger.

Would the servants tell him what was going on?

Jer glanced at the head cook and found her glaring at him. The woman was bristling with anger.

"Well's out that door, I presume?" Jer asked, motioning to the outer door of the kitchen, the one where deliveries of food would be brought through.

"Yes, it is, straight across the gravel, there's a big tree hiding it from the house."

He left the kitchen by the door and looked around him. Picturesque again.

Bilgern Vineyard was a storm of fighting emotions, but the light was winning over. A queen's anger and hatred took a long time to fade when the emotion had constantly been felt for years. The land seemed to keep that feeling, and the buildings certainly did.

Yet Aren hadn't been capable of feeling properly, and so already the estate was returning to its natural state of being.

Or at least it should have.

Jer walked around the tree and was caught again in sanctuary.

Startled, he turned back to the kitchen door. It was like looking out on a haze. He frowned and looked down at the girl sitting against the tree, a book in her hands and a light summer dress over her curvy, but not yet adult, form. Balya twitched as if she wanted to run, drawing Jer's eyes to her bare feet, then up the legs. This was a girl, fourteen perhaps.

He met her eyes and had to control himself.

This was a queen, and not just any queen.

"Calm yourself, warrior," Balya said, motioning with her eyes and a shift of her head to the well. "And move out of sight of the estate."

Jer shifted to the side, struggling with what he should ask first.

"How old are you?" he decided to start with.

Her body was that of a fourteen-year-old, but her eyes held the spirit of someone a great deal older. She had wanted to run, it had been her instinct to do so, but she had resisted it. Probably because she had known that just as it was her instinct to run, it would have been Jer's instinct to chase after her. He would have caught her and terrified her, might have been able to hold back until he met those eyes.

That was not what he wanted, and he prayed that if that ever happened that he was stronger than whatever created instinct.

"That's a funny question to ask," Balya said with a laugh.

Which made the world brighter.

Jer sank to the ground. "What are you? I'm sorry, I know you're a queen, but I've never seen anything like you before."

"I suppose the best place to start is my age. Do you mean the age of my body, the age of my spirit, or the age I was when I died the first time?"

"What?"

Balya hesitated and scrunched up her face. "They have very strict rules for this sort of thing. But she's been gone six months past now, so I think I'm allowed to say what I'd like."

"Who's been gone?"

Had Anue been out of the estate six months? Or had it been longer than that now?

"This body belongs to an unranked one," Balya said. "I know who you are, I know who your parents are, I had a tentative connection the first couple of months, but it's slowly faded."

"What... what? What, what?" It was the only word Jer could get to come out of his mouth.

Balya smiled at him. "Unranked ones come in many kinds, but those that warriors snip and snarl at are the type that this body belonged to. You snip and snarl because you can't make sense of the changes in behaviour. The original owner of this body was Bal, my name was Noi, together we made Balya. Now, Noi's an old name that won't sound familiar to your ears because I was born on the other side of this world some ten hundred years ago. I think. Time is a blurry thing when you're a spirit."

"What's it like to die?"

"While she has passed, I still have a vow to those spirits who remained behind," Balya said sternly. "I can tell you I'm a spirit if I know that the unranked one will not be harmed, and she cannot be. I can also tell you who of your relatives are amongst the spirits if I can find them. But I can't tell you things about what it's like to die or if there is a great big light on the other side, or if we are all reborn century after century. Do we choose to be reborn?"

"I... I think..."

"You're overwhelmed," Balya said, her smile returning. "It can be overwhelming. Bal came here because of Aren. All the spirits are talking about it. The throne is capable of finding unranked ones and combs through them from time to time, uses them to accomplish what it needs. Making certain someone carries on a family line is usually the case these days. Depending on the couple involved, it's a bastard, and off you go to live your life free as could be."

"So you came here because of Aren?"

"She's going to inherit the estate, leaving her younger brother free. The throne wants the bloodlines to cross, and I must admit, that is a fine boy who could grow into a great man one day. Bal liked him better than I did, but she still had that fresh outlook on the world. It was her first time falling in love, and it would have been her only time. The precious child would have had a splendid life indeed."

"What happened to her?" Jer asked.

"Para got drunk and strangled her." Balya lifted her chin and motioned her neck. "I knew, because of when I was born, that the spirit doesn't have to leave the body right away. A healer could bring a body back as long as the spirit was stubborn enough to remain. I remember it all went black. I remember slipping backwards, and I grabbed for her, and I kept her firm, but when I awoke, it was just me. I couldn't even bury her."

"Who healed you?"

"I don't know. There's no healer that I can find, but my senses have been muddled. Everything is muddy here. Most of it, I thought, was Aren. Part of how she hid so well was that she muddied the air, and by doing so she caused her parents to suffer, which was really just a marvellous side effect. Did you know her father made her do things for him? Or that Para has beat her so badly that several of her fingers were broken?"

"I didn't, but that's why I've come here."

"Is she mated to Av finally?"

"She is, yes, and they headed north."

"North, that's such a strange thing for me, to come back and palace lands have broken up. Good reason for the North to leave though. Took the palace, they keep saying, but not much of it has moved. Just the important bits they say... the whole thing was important."

"The whole thing was important?"

"That's what I said," Balya murmured. "I look at it this way. Each rank has a place in our world. Commoner is a rank, but those of other ranks have used the term to separate the two, makes it faster to explain. It's become like those with title and those without title. Those with rank think they can't mate commoners because nothing will come of it, just as warriors seem to think that mating anyone but a queen will produce fewer ranks."

"I think Lerd is a good example of how that is wrong," Jer said.

"He is a good example of how wrong that is."

"How do you know about him?"

"Hold on there, boyo, let me get there in my time. I'm very old and haven't had anyone's ear to talk off in a very long time. Naturally, if you tell anyone, I will put you in a hell the likes of which you've never dreamed of."

"Hell?" Jer asked hesitantly.

The brightness disappeared. Everything around him darkened and seemed to char. Even Balya seemed to wither and age, bits falling off her face.

And then it was gone again. Balya smiled at him as Jer whimpered.

"As I was saying... The ranks all have a place in the world. Queens lead, lend magic. Warriors fight and protect. Healers heal, trainers train and keep the other ranks in line, they are also the only ones not to want to attack an unranked one. They want to pet us and nurture us the way a warrior wants to raise an orphaned queen."

"Then what's the point of the unranked ones?" Jer asked.

"Bal's rank cannot access magic unless they link a spirit to their body. They are then conduits to the spirits. They have access to the magic of the spirits—which does things differently than magic of the living—as well as the magic and rank of the spirit they take on."

Jer whimpered again, to which Balya nodded slowly. "The reason why warriors fear them is because they see the two different spirits. When we join in harmony, as myself and Bal did, the reaction isn't so much fear as confusion. You probably would have given me enough time to explain, but Bal would have run away from you, and I would have come to protect her, and she was chosen to be with Eln for a reason.

"I had hoped the world would move away from breeding and constantly wanting stronger blood. It did, but then it cycled back, and that makes me sad. I mean, yes, the desire for breeding is much like regular attraction, we're attracted to those who would breed better children, but the fact that it can overwhelm us to the point where we go along with something as strange as chasing down a woman who is barely an adult is... it's just so odd, once you've lived through an enlightened time.

"In that time, at least the one I lived during, warriors didn't go chasing queens. There was seduction and subtle claiming. Instead of mounting and tumbling and romping, all these things that were said to happen a generation before I was born, the warriors danced with the queens and simply looked at commoners. People now remember those times, like something passed through the blood, but none of you remembers that in order to have the light, you need to suffer through the darkness.

"But that little queen of yours? Aren? She's suffered through the darkness. Now she just needs to be shown the light."

"I have about a hundred questions I now want to ask you, but I need to focus on why I was sent here."

"It's not like I plan on going anywhere," Balya said, setting her book to the side. "Para may have been drunk, but she knows I was dead and now thinks I might be a healer in hiding. She's deathly afraid to come near me. And I may not know all that happened, as I've been back in the world of the living for six years and things escalated, but I do know how to bring her back to the light."

"And, besides because it's the right thing to do, why is that important?"

Balya smiled. "Let me tell you the story of my mother, the woman who began the last period of enlightenment the world saw."

"From... the other side of the world?" Jer asked.
"It was a very different world then."

Chapter Nineteen

Av gave Aren's temple a peck as the queen let out a small purr of delight and tried to burrow closer to him. He moved away and replaced his body with the pillow he had laid his head on as she drifted in and out of sleep.

People liked to assume he was stupid or unobservant, but normally he just left others to their own mistakes and problems.

In the bathing room, he had smelled something on Url. It was a smell that he was acquainted with from his adolescence.

He had romped with the guards more than a time or two and, as his instincts had awakened, he had ended up in awkward positions before. That smell should have been enough to put off another warrior from trying such a thing. Somehow Av doubted it, given the odd fear in Url's eyes.

Someone wanted to dominate Url, who had found himself in an unfortunate position. Av didn't understand how it had happened, because Url was dominant for a reason, not weak by any definition of the term. Url should have bent the one who tried to bend him and broken him in many places.

That hadn't happened for a reason, and Av had a nagging feeling that he knew what that reason had been. It was shorter than even Aren, grey-haired and should have kept her damned hands to herself.

Av picked up each piece of his clothing and pulled it on carefully. He looked down and straightened his shirt, then bent and gave Aren another kiss on the temple.

After the bathing room situation, he couldn't very well leave her there in the rooms by herself. Something about conquering a rival had put a fire into Aren. Watching her fend off the other queen had put a desire into Av, but it wasn't one that he couldn't have handled on his own.

Once back in the rooms, however, Aren had launched herself on Av. She had got in a few blows before Av had pinned her to the floor, and that was when things went outside of Av's experiences.

In the past, he had been beaten by a woman and then had her jump his bones; he had taken down more than one woman and then had her weep and cry.

He had never bested a woman and had her grind against him with need. For a moment he had resisted, but then she had said please, and all thought of saying no went out of his mind.

Av wanted to stay in the room, stay in bed, but this had to be nipped in the bud before it got out of hand, if it hadn't already. He wondered, as he searched for his boots, if the residents of Castle Grey had been affected by Aren's desire. It might be too late, but if it was...

Av grinned, baring his teeth at nothing in particular.

If it was too late to prevent it from happening, that only gave Av a reason to make an example that the others wouldn't soon forget.

"Where are you going?" Aren asked from the bed as Av's hand touched the doorknob.

"There's something I need to do. I'll come back as soon as I can," Av said, struggling to calm his expression before he turned back to the bed, where she sat up and watched him warily. "When I get back, we need to have a talk about what happened before."

"If someone—"

"Not about that," Av said a little louder. "Your whole technique was sloppy. What I want to discuss is teaching you to protect yourself without a weapon."

"Suddenly you want me to train?" Aren asked.

"I've wanted you to train since you came back for the winter, but it was suggested that I keep my opinions to myself and let you do what you wanted. That's what we're going to discuss once I get back."

"Maybe I should nap while you're gone, and when you get back..."

Av smiled. "Maybe you should."

He turned and left the rooms before he changed his mind and decided to stay with Aren.

Just because he could be more violent if something had happened first didn't mean that he should risk it.

Moving through the hallways, he realized his problem was an unfamiliar building with unfamiliar people. Normally when he had to find someone, he found Jer first, and his brother did the hunting for him. Even if Av had experience searching a building alone, there were too many new things in Castle Grey. When things were new, they were easier to pick out of the background. When everything was new, it was overwhelming.

He found his way into a common area of some sort. Large windows overlooking the cliff and down. A little lower, he could see the ballroom, which looked out over the valley behind Castle Grey, into the North. The other side of Castle Grey also stood over a cliff, though not so steep. It overlooked palace lands, but that side of the castle had few windows.

That was the side from which they expected to be attacked.

In the common area, warriors were gathered in clusters, some playing games, some simply sitting and talking.

Finding warriors in Castle Grey wasn't difficult. Even the men on the serving staff were warriors. The servants weren't afraid of the lords, and the lords couldn't take advantage of the women serving the castle because most were already claimed by warriors. The few children Av had seen, even the commoners amongst them, had stared openly at him, not afraid, but curious about the newcomer.

They were happy children, clean and healthy. The babies—he had seen plenty of babies but few children—were fat and bubbly. They were alert, and giggled at a smile from an adult.

Av liked Castle Grey, but there was a danger to that balance.

"Lord Av, how surprising and—"

Av grabbed the warrior who spoke to him by the throat, lifted the man off the floor and then slammed him into the table where he had just been sitting. Straightening, Av huffed out a breath and tugged his shirt back to where it belonged.

He sniffed the air on purpose and detected just a hint of the smell that was around Url. Av looked down at the man he had put through the table and bared his teeth.

"I don't know how you were raised, but my father taught me that's rape," Av said, smiling all the while. "Try it again. I dare you."

"Don't you think that's between him and me?" the warrior demanded.

Av reached down and dragged the warrior out of the remains of the table by his foot. As he did so, the others came close. The warrior struggled, trying to stand as Av gave the foot a yank. The force would have been enough to cause some damage, but two warriors getting riled just meant that they'd beat on one another until they were tired unless one of them could cross that line and hurt the other.

When the other tried to get to his feet, Av struck him down. Each time the other tried to get to his feet, Av batted at him. The warriors who had gathered around watched silently. They didn't try to interfere or call out support for one or the other.

The anger of the other warrior turned to frustration, which caused him to attempt to tackle Av. Anger could be a powerful weapon, but in a fight, it was a danger to the one who felt the emotion. Av stepped to the side, and the warrior stumbled back to the ground.

"Stop playing with him," an older warrior finally called out.

Av turned to the warrior. "Excuse me?"

"I was talking to him."

Av ducked and turned at the same time, slamming his hand upward as the other tried to sneak up on him. The blow sent the other one back, giving Av the leverage he needed to slam his hand into his rival's chest, which thrust the other into the floor. There was a whoosh of air and the distinct sound of bones snapping under his hand.

He dug his hand into the other's shirt and dragged him off the floor by several inches. "Queens backing you? Doesn't stop me. If you want to take down a rival, do it on your own two feet. Don't take down a good man just because you want to wet your dick."

"He likes his own," someone muttered with disgust.

"What in the name of the spirits is going on here?" Url bellowed, parting the crowd as he came forward.

Av looked up as Url came to a sudden stop and paled. Standing, Av stepped casually away from the warrior on the floor. There was no need to tell Url why Av had chosen that specific warrior to pick a fight with.

"What are you doing?" Url demanded of Av.

"He touched something which is mine," Av said.

Url went bright red, which made Av frown and consider his words.

"I don't know how else to put it," Av said carefully. "I only had Jer to contend with at the palace; the other warriors simply stayed out of my way. When I say that to Jer, he knows what I mean. I guess I didn't say what I thought I meant."

"You should only ever say that about Aren," Er said, coming up behind Url. "I think you meant to say that he touched your family."

"If you say so," Av said through gritted teeth.

"What exactly do you think he did?" Er asked Av.

"If I need to, I will beat him into the floor, but what he did? That's between him, me, and whom he did it to."

"And you saw what he did?" Url demanded.

"No," Av said, approaching Url. He grabbed his cousin by the shoulder and dragged him close. "I smelled it on the one he touched."

Url trembled.

"Let him go, Av," Er said with a growl.

Av looked at Er but didn't release Url. "I hold the two of you responsible for this, especially since you're so casual about it. That is not how things are done here, and that's certainly not the way things are done on palace lands."

"Mounting happens at gatherings all the time," Er said calmly.

"I'm talking about having a queen back a weaker warrior to take out another because the queen has a problem with holding true to honour," Av snapped back, shoving Url away from him. "You two came to my land and lectured me on bowing to the commoners and giving in to the court and how to be a warrior, but I come up here, and you're doing the same thing, except it's a queen so old that you could look at her and her hip would break.

"She is messing with my toys, and I don't like it. Do something about it."

"She's an elder," Url said steadily.

"Next time I kill the puppet," Av bellowed at Url, causing everyone in the room to take a step away from him. "And if you don't try to stop it from happening, after I kill the puppet I will kill her and anyone who tries to stop me."

Er looked at Url pointedly. Url dragged a breath through his nose and got a distinctly annoyed look on his face. It seemed that whatever was going on between the two didn't necessarily have to do with what had just happened. There was an edge to Url's look that strongly implied that his father had told him to do something and Url hadn't done it.

"Take him to the healers," Er said, motioning to the warrior wheezing on the floor. "Av, why don't you take a walk, cool your head. Stick it out a window or something."

Av growled at Er. The baron met his look with an expressionless face. Av struggled with himself but brushed past Url and left the common area.

It hadn't been enough. He still wanted to break something, destroy something, shout at someone. Av rounded a corner and came face to face with a queen.

She watched him calmly with her strange eyes. Her hair was black as black could be. Her presence was not all over the hallway, as most queens at Castle Grey spread out. Av knew she was a queen, but not obviously so. She reminded him of Aren in that manner, and that reminder calmed Av's nerves.

"Av, finally we meet," she said with a smile.

"I've not met you, no," Av said, reaching for that black hair.

She batted away his hand. The hair looked silken like his mother's had been. Her features, however, looked nothing like those of the Hue bloodline.

"Shouldn't you be hiding with the others?" Av asked.

"You can't hurt me," the queen said pointedly. "I came to see why you weren't calming her down."

"Calming who down?" Av asked.

"Aren."

"Aren is fine," Av said, moving around the queen.

"No, she's not. She's the same as she's always been, hiding behind a mask."

"I beg your pardon?" Av asked, turning back to the woman.

"You haven't noticed an odd fragility to Url? That he's not inserting himself over you as he should?"

"I think you mean asserting," Av said sternly. "And I'm above him, he bows to the throne, I am mate to the throne."

"No wonder the palace lands have stalled," the queen muttered, then met Av's eyes. "He bows to her, not to you. Url is reacting this way because he is connected to her. When a queen is mad, so too are her people. Have you never heard that?"

"I have, but I fail to see what you mean. Aren is stable. She's a great deal calmer."

The woman frowned at the floor for a moment, her head moving slightly as if reading a book. Finally, she took in a sharp breath and looked up, surprised.

"I'm going to try to explain," the woman said, then sighed. "This would work better if you knew of daily pain."

"My father has explained daily pain, as warriors, we could be crippled and that will end up hurting the rest of our lives."

"So you are familiar with the sadness that can come over a cripple? What is it that the trainer taught you about if you find one who is crippled?"

"You have to get them out of bed and moving. Staying in one place will make it worse, make the pain worse."

"Think of what has been done to her like inner damage you cannot see," the queen said. "She looks stable only because she decided a long time ago that not feeling at all was better than crying all the time. Crying doesn't change anything. Typically it makes things worse."

"We're working on that. It doesn't solve itself overnight."

"B-but no. No, you don't get to say that. I tell you to do something and you do it!"

"Then tell me what to do specifically! Don't tell me to fix the world and then hand me a damned bandage. I don't know what to do, I can't fix it!"

The silence over the hallway was brittle. Both realized at the same time that they had just lost their temper over two different problems. The queen looked embarrassed. Av looked up and down the hallway to see if anyone had heard them.

"Do you know how to fix her?" Av asked.

"Each mind is different. It makes it difficult to put the pieces back together. Only one who can see the pieces can put them back together."

"Well, Danya's not here right now."

"Who is Danya?" the queen asked.

"If I'm right, she can see the pieces, because she certainly seems to be fitting them back together."

"Of course, the cracked foundation, that's not breaking down, that's building up."

"What are you talking about?" Av asked.

"You have to solidify the foundation before it breaks back away to nothing. Otherwise, it could be years before the pieces could be put back together again."

"Again, how do I do that?" Av asked.

"I don't know if you'll recognize this term, but I want you to give her a nice sociable time," the woman said quietly.

Av chuckled. "Yes, that at least I know. I'll give that a try. I just don't know how in Castle Grey to do that."

"See the warrior she almost hit with the food," the queen said quickly. "His rooms look out over the North, and come night time it is quite beautiful. Tell him it will help settle what he accidentally moved. He'll understand."

"Thank you?" Av said. "Why are you...?"

"We have a common goal."

"And Aren being more stable is part of that goal?" Av asked.

"Aren being more stable means she will begin to trust the world enough to feel." The queen watched Av for a moment and then smiled slowly. "If this is what she's capable of when she doesn't feel, what do you think she'll do once she does?"

Chapter Twenty

Jer sat through a very awkward breakfast, during which time he had to watch Para make a fool of herself, already drunk and complaining about the dinner from the night before, the dinner that Jer had missed. After talking to Balya, he had gone directly to his room and churned the information over in his mind.

She had told him all about her mother's and then her own life.

Times of enlightenment came after periods of great darkness. Those darkest times caused the people to desire a change. During the grey in-between times, the people had simply existed. They knew things could be better, but also knew things could—and had been—worse. No one tried to fix anything, no one tried to improve on anything, and most people looked the other way.

When things seemed darkest, enlightenment happened. There wasn't supposed to be a grey period between the darkness and the light. First came dark, then someone stood up, and the light happened.

Periods of enlightenment could last for between fifty and five hundred years.

Balya's mother had been raped, beaten, and sold into slavery. She had been brought to palace lands by the slavers, and a warrior spotted her in the markets. He had purchased her, used her as he saw fit and then gifted her to a lord at the palace. That lord had gifted her to his son, a young warrior who seemed incapable of claiming anything, one of the first lessons a warrior had to learn.

The young warrior claimed the queen, tried to free her and was denied. So he killed the one who sat the throne and half the court. His queen had taken the throne, but because of her time as a slave, she hadn't bent once she had a taste of freedom.

She abolished slavery, waged war across the seas to retrieve her daughter, reunified the lands across the ocean with palace lands, and launched an enlightenment period that lasted two hundred years. Noi had taken the throne after her mother, then her son's mate after her.

They hadn't had a dark period. Em had only counted as grey, and a light grey at that, from what Balya had said.

Had lacking the darkness needed to give rise to strong queens given the throne's ability to convince others to breed to create stronger bloodlines? Jer didn't doubt for a moment that there had been more than one opportunity to save Aren, that the throne could have put an end to it and hadn't.

What did he do with this information, now that he had it? Tell Aren that her life was bad because of the throne? That she should suck it up because it would make her stronger in the long run?

Balya had watched her parents struggle in private for years. She had, in the end, done her mother a mercy because the madness had taken too much hold over her. The wavering emotions, the fits of rage, and the weak moments helped fuel the queen for years, but eventually, it broke down.

Unless the warriors around the queen created a better cage than they normally did.

Balya knew about the careful controls, knew why they were there and had even taken advantage of it at times to get what she had wanted. Just as the warriors around her had done the same.

He had instructions on how to set it up, but Av had to be the anchor for the whole thing. It only worked if the queen's mate took—and kept—control. The foundation was slowly setting up. Balya had been surprised by what Jer had told her, but the problem was that Aren was also showing instability.

"Lord Jer?" Cerlot asked.

"Just Jer, I don't hold title," Jer said in response. "Steward, but that's it. A steward doesn't get the title of lord, that's only for landed bloodlines."

He glanced to Eln, but the boy was focused on his food and had an unhappy look on his face.

"Jer then, I had just asked how long you planned on being here," Cerlot responded sternly.

Jer wiped his mouth and stood from the table. "I need to see your records today, speak with the masters, and then I could probably be on my way as of tomorrow morning. I'm eager to get back to the palace."

"Of course, I can take you to my study right away," Cerlot said.

"First I'd like to have a private conversation with young Eln here, considering he will be coming to the palace next spring."

"Fine," Eln said sullenly, standing.

Jer wondered how he had stepped on the boy's toes. The only person he had spoken to the day before had been Balya, and once the sun had begun to go down, they had ended the conversation. Jer had gone back to his rooms, and that was that.

Except Balya had come to his room and slipped the list under his door sometime in the night.

Stalking a crush could happen, but Jer had to nip that before it became a problem. Together Balya had agreed to mate Eln, and the original spirit of the body had been taken by his looks. The queen who remained in the flesh had loved and lost; she had been mated and had known the love of a warrior whom she still believed had been made for her.

The Balya who remained would not put up with a pup sniffing after her and acting creepily.

Jer left the dining room and led Eln out of the estate. No one was in the yard, leaving them space to speak in relative privacy.

Aren learning to see things she wasn't a part of was one of the items on Jer's list. At some point she would stumble upon the ability, as most queens did. The point of teaching Aren how to do it on purpose was to keep her from thinking she had been seeing things. Seeing things meant madness, and madness meant instability.

Balya could see anything that happened on the estate. Saying her name would draw her attention, but learning that tidbit had been a warning to Jer.

"Are you being sullen with me?" Jer asked.

"No," Eln said to the ground.

"Eln, as a lord, you basically have to act like a warrior. This land is yours to protect, and no one else will do it for you. If you don't stand for what you believe in, people will suffer. So I'm going to ask you again, are you being sullen with me?"

"She's too young for you!" Eln shouted and then burst into tears.

The boy looked surprised. He turned away from Jer and wiped at his eyes as Jer waited. Once Eln turned back to him, Jer decided to pretend Eln hadn't been crying at all. Standing up to someone could be difficult, and sometimes the only response was to sob because one simply didn't know how to react.

"We were talking, Eln," Jer said quietly. "It's come to my attention, and to most of the servants, that you are taken with Balya. You like her. And as the son of a vineyard, that was fine, but as the heir..."

Eln frowned at Jer.

"Your parents dictate who you can mate. You need their permission. Your mother will never give her permission, and you are not a warrior."

"What's that mean?" Eln demanded.

"Which part?" Jer asked.

"That I'm not a warrior, that's obvious to everyone," Eln said. "Mother wishes I was a warrior. Everyone here looks at me like I'm broken or something, just because I'm the only one without rank."

"I more of meant how Aren ended up mated," Jer said quickly, holding up a hand to stop Eln from protesting. "A warrior can claim a person beyond any doubt. By doing so, Aren broke off her arranged mating with the Southern baron's son."

"I thought that was broken off because you slept with her intended."

Jer blinked at Eln as the boy blinked back at him.

"In fact," Eln continued. "I thought I could trust you around Balya because you had slept with my sister's intended. I thought you wouldn't want mine."

"Yours?" Jer asked.

"Balya's been acting funny since last fall. She promised to mate me, she was even going to tell Mother. And then she got distant."

Because Para had killed the girl rather than let her mate Eln.

Jer clenched his teeth. He drew in a long breath. "I think you should speak to Balya about what happened when she spoke to your mother—what happened that she no longer works with your mother, that your mother will no longer go near her. Eln, I don't think Balya is avoiding you. I think she's been hurt and threatened, and is now afraid of what might happen."

"But if my parents need to agree, then I'm never going to mate her!"

Jer sucked in another breath. "Yes and no. The law specifically states that your guardian has to agree to it."

Eln frowned at the ground, then turned that frown to Jer. "When one becomes a ward to the throne, the throne becomes that one's guardian."

"I know, and I figured you'd know that," Jer said quietly. "I can't get Balya to agree. She would have to leave the vineyard and come to the palace and mate there. The problem being, unless your parents up and die, you'd have the same trouble a year from now or ten years from now."

"I'll mate her for life."

"You barely know her—"

"Aren barely knows Av, yet they're mated for life," Eln countered.

"Actually…" Jer said, then winced. "None of us knows how long they're mated for and, at this point, we're too afraid to ask."

"No, if Aren ever mated it was going to be for life, it's the only way to secure a position and result in a contract that allows her to achieve the freedom that she wants. Tell me that you didn't mate my sister without drawing up a contract!"

And there was the man that they needed Eln to be.

"Matings at the palace rarely have a contract."

"The arranged one between her and the South did," Eln said as if Jer were stupid.

"Av didn't mate her to gain anything besides her."

"Who looks out for her interest if he dies?"

"I do. If she dies and has children, my daughter will look after Aren's children. If, at any point, Av fails in his duties to protect Aren, the entirety of his bloodline will come down from the North and murder him, then me, for not protecting her. Is that good enough for you?"

"I want them to cripple him and bring him to me," Eln countered.

"No," Jer said with a shake of his head. "They are already mated, it's too late to negotiate. They are also all warriors. There's not a chance of you standing against them."

"She's my sister!" Eln shouted

"She has claimed no brother!" Jer shouted back.

"Just because she hasn't claimed me doesn't mean that I'm not her brother. It means that she needs me to carry this damned line and take care of the vineyard. It doesn't mean that she doesn't trust me!"

Eln spoke with all the conviction of someone who needed something to be true.

Aren had forgotten Danya even though she spent the whole winter with the woman. How much of Eln did she recall? A sibling, certainly, but what else might she remember? That one time that her mother had made Eln punish her, in an attempt control both her children?

Yes, Jer and Balya had had some time to talk about what Balya knew for certain had happened on the estate. It had expanded Jer's image of Aren and ended up explaining so many things.

"Would it be better if she didn't remember you?" Jer asked.

"What do you mean?"

"It seems that when life gets tough, we lock away what we can't handle at the moment." And thanks to Balya, Jer now had a way to explain it to everyone else. "But when a child is confronted by time after time of tough moments, they start locking everything away. By the time they're an adult, they don't know how to handle things in any other way."

And once she was introduced to another way, she had a screaming fit, threw things, then broke down into tears. Eventually she would adjust, but when it first happened, it would seem as if she had lost her mind.

Spirits were good for some things, if only one could find a spirit and pin them down long enough to get an answer.

"Oh," Eln said.

"Don't feel bad, she's probably forgotten I exist as well," Jer said. "Then, when we meet again, hopefully, she'll recall more than my name. She didn't quite recall Anue either. She knew Anue existed and was concerned about her, but it was like 'out of sight, out of mind'. That really should have been our first warning."

"What was the second?" Eln asked.

"When she was angry, the walls didn't explode," Jer muttered. "Or when she and Av had sex the first time, the commoners didn't end up clobbering one another."

"That happens?" Eln squeaked out.

"It does, and it didn't. Or when your parents came, and she bubbled a table instead of making the room explode. Or the fact that we saw very little actual magic use until she came back from the winter. There have been a hundred things that should have tipped us off and didn't."

"I've seen her angry," Eln said. The boy looked down and scuffed his foot on the ground.

"When?"

"Something, uh, happened, at our old home. I don't think they think that I remember."

"You mean when your mother burned a queen at the stake?" Jer asked.

Eln nodded. "I guess that's what it was. I just remember her lecturing us on ranks being beneath us and the girl being dragged out there. And then the pyre was lit, and she started screaming. And then she stopped. Everything went still, it got real dark, and the ground moved. Mother said it was a sign of the girl dying, and she *was* dead, but not by the fire. It went out, and she was barely touched, was the heat she was screaming about."

"Then how did she die?" Jer asked.

"Father made me help build the second pyre to burn her body. He said that her heart exploded, said it wasn't the fire, that she died because someone else, someone without skill, had taken pity on her. That day he asked me if Aren had rank and I looked at him and told him the first lie I ever told."

"Why?" Jer asked. "You were too young to understand, surely."

"I was old enough to understand that queens died and Aren was a queen. Therefore Aren would die. She told me funny stories and always told me when I should hide from Mother and Father. She protected me. I knew, as the brother, I was supposed to protect her, so that day I did. And every time afterward when Mother would come and ask if I noticed anything odd, I'd say no. She trusted me and I know she's my mother... but I knew what would happen if they were queens."

"And what about him?" Jer asked, motioning with his head toward the barn.

Eln had mentioned that he was the only one without rank, but no one else in the vineyard talked about the other brother.

"I don't know what happened to him."

"No. Wait. What do you mean, what happened to him?"

Chapter Twenty-One

Aren walked awkwardly into the rooms. She was dressed in a black gown provided by Olea. Black in the North was not a colour of grief but instead was reserved for queens who held title. It took them a great deal to make a true black.

Grey was the colour of grieving, and also the colour that healers wore.

Her skirts rustled as she stopped in front of the lord whom she had almost struck with the tomato. She looked down, and he dared to touch her to draw her chin back up.

"Lady Aren, I hardly blame you for the tomato. Whenever those things are served whole, someone ends up catching one in the eye." The lord pulled away. "My name is Ord. This is my mate, Coranna."

A queen stepped up beside Ord and smiled at Aren, her eyes a distinct shade of grey. Aren blinked at the other queen, then looked to Ord.

"You're a warrior. She's a queen and... Marilton?" Aren winced and looked at Coranna.

"I am born to that line, yes," Coranna said with a smile. "Er's my eldest brother, I his youngest sister. I met Mirmae. I think she'd approve of you."

"I've heard stories?" Aren asked. "Av said he'd be here, has he arrived?"

"He has, he's on the balcony."

"The... balcony?" Aren asked.

"We were waiting for the food," Ord said quietly. "I apologize if he didn't explain that we will be dining together. I wanted to apologize for my inappropriate reaction, and he wanted to do something for you. We both had a desire that I could fill."

"Right this way, Aren," Coranna motioned. "I will take you there while Ord waits for the food."

Concerned because she didn't like surprises, Aren followed Coranna through the rooms. At the glass doors, Coranna stopped and turned to Aren with a smile.

"The men have put a lot of effort into tonight. Normally I don't allow visitors to my rooms. These were gifted to me by my father, and not even Er dared to question the assignment. This is my room. I can't stress that enough."

"Are you afraid I'll make it explode or melt it or something?"

"No." Coranna sighed. "You're the first visitors we've had because I deny every other request. I don't want you to think I'm laying down my territory, though it is mine. I want you to understand that what Av's managed to do, just getting dinner in my rooms, is very special."

"Why for me, then?" Aren asked.

"Because I want to speak to my nephew and his mate without ears or eyes prying," Coranna responded. "I don't want to talk about politics tonight, or how I can help you, or you can help me. I just want some time with my nephew. Except the only way to get it is this dinner. And I don't have a problem with that. But at some point during dinner, no matter how well he's pulled this off, I'm going to start prying. Ask about his life. I'm not doing it to be awkward."

"None of his other aunts or uncles are trying this," Aren said quietly.

"They have families of their own and children of their own," Coranna said just as quietly. "One of us may be infertile, or almost unable, and we can't figure out which."

"Oh..." Aren said quietly. "Well, there goes the possibility of asking for help talking to Av about waiting on children."

"You aren't pregnant yet?" Coranna asked.

"I was in the fall," Aren said.

"But you've been back for some time, and you aren't pregnant yet?" Coranna asked.

"No, of course not!"

Coranna nodded slowly. "Then I have to say that he knows. You'd be surprised how there are no children when both set their minds to it, but the moment one of you wants one, it just happens."

"So do I bring it up?" Aren asked.

"No, you don't bring it up. If you want to set a timeline, then you bring it up. Tell him that you'd like to enjoy him for four years, and then have children. Even a man like Av can understand that."

"And that means..."

"He..." Coranna hesitated. "Av likes children, and everyone in Castle Grey knows that except for you. Which must say what he thinks of the matter between the two of you, that he keeps himself under control when you are around because he doesn't want to pressure you into something you don't want to do."

"I suppose I shouldn't keep him waiting."

"Sometimes it's good to keep a man waiting, to remind him that you do have a mind of your own," Coranna said before she walked towards the front of the rooms.

Aren watched the other queen leave and then turned to the glass-panelled doors. She suspected that Av could see her, so she tried not to hesitate as she opened the door and walked onto the balcony.

It was huge and stone, looking out over a lower bit of land lit here and there with different little clusters of houses. She stared at the dark view, at the specks of light that were almost like stars fallen to earth. And then she turned to Av.

He was dressed formally in a vest and a tie, even though Aren knew that he didn't like wearing either of those things because he found them restricting. He stood by a table set for four, lit with candles. No light orbs around or on the balcony.

Aren turned to the rooms and realized that they, too, had been lit by candles. It had been an entirely different sort of light than what an orb gave off, but she had been distracted by her own concerns. She turned back to Av and then noticed the flower in his hand.

"What's that?" she asked, approaching him.

"A red rose," Av said, raising it to smell. "I haven't seen a rose in any other colour but white. I thought all roses came in that colour. Olea has a love of roses. I got to thinking it might be a queen thing. She calls this a long-stemmed rose, and if she ever finds out that I bartered with her grandchildren to take the blame, she will throw me out the nearest window."

"A long-stemmed rose?" Aren asked, reaching to take it.

Her fingers touched something sharp. She yanked her hand away from the flower and immediately stuck the hurt finger into her mouth as she glared at Av.

"Uh, I think of roses when I think of queens," Av said carefully. "Beautiful to look at, silken to the touch, if you know where to touch them and when. But touch them the wrong way, or in the dark without caution, and your fingers will be caught by the thorns.

"Most of the time you remind me of the flower."

"Only most?" Aren asked.

Av set the flower on the table. "Sometimes your thorns bite into my flesh, but I like the way it stings."

"Are you making reference to yesterday?" Aren asked, feeling her face flush at the thought.

"A little, yes," Av murmured, closing the remaining distance between them. He lifted Aren's chin and frowned, eyes roving over her face. "Did he touch you?"

"He just lifted my face when I looked down, why?" Aren asked, confused why there was suddenly an edge to Av's voice.

The warrior struggled to relax. "Just worried me for a moment."

"Worried you, why?" Aren asked as she tried to pull away.

Av wrapped an arm around her and pulled her closer, his hand still on her chin. With his hand on her chin, she looked up and met his eyes, trembling at the hunger they contained. Av leaned in and captured Aren's lips, kissing her deeply for less than a moment before it softened and he pulled away. Aren whimpered and tried to follow those lips.

When had he learned to kiss like that?

"Not tonight, darling," he said quietly.

"Why not?" Aren asked breathlessly.

"Because tonight isn't about that, it's about pretty well everything else."

"I can't make any promises," Aren said, moving to the table to sit before her legs gave out on her.

"If I need to, I will sleep in another bed," Av said quietly, taking a seat beside Aren slowly. "Call it an experiment, but I'd like to not do what started our relationship, for tonight only. Tomorrow morning when we wake up? Certainly. But I didn't do all this to have sex with you."

"You don't have to do all this to have sex with me," Aren said pointedly.

Av smiled slightly. "No, all I have to do is point you to the nearest rival."

"Or look at me," Aren said.

"I'd still like to chase you down one day," Av said, going red as he played with his empty wine glass. "But I want you trained first, trained to take down a warrior. I want there to be no question, when I take you to ground, that you gave in and weren't just tired, that you chose to be caught and under me."

"Who says I'd be *under* you?" Aren asked, watching the red deepen as Av took in a sharp breath and stared at her.

"Dinner," Ord called as Coranna opened the door to their rooms.

"Can I pour the wine, then?" Av asked, sounding strangled.

"Go ahead, dear," Coranna said, taking a seat across from Aren.

Av stood and pulled a bottle of wine from a bucket. He poured wine for each of them, but less for Aren. The look Av gave her seemed to imply that he was worried she might try something if she drank too much. After a long consideration of his own glass, Av poured less into his glass than he had Aren's.

As Av moved around the table to help Ord serve dinner, Coranna looked across at Aren and smiled. Then she looked down, and the smile faded.

"That's not—" Coranna looked up at Av. "What did you do?"

"Nothing, they had already ripped it up," Av said. "I figured if I had it, she couldn't blame any one of them."

"Av, that's not Olea's rose, that's Vivlia's. Olea has red, that's burgundy."

"Apparently queens do like roses," Aren said to Av with a smile.

"Vivlia is Er's mother," Coranna said sternly to Aren, then looked at Av, who shrugged as he placed a plate in front of Aren. "Well, I'm glad you are so bold as to shrug at the idea."

"Not my fault that I can't tell the difference between bright red and burgundy. It's all red to me. And your mate might have been more helpful. He wouldn't even look at them for fear someone might know."

"They grow side by side," Ord protested. "And... frankly they're both the same colour to my eyes."

"Men and colours," Coranna muttered. "I wonder how many wars began because you people can't tell the difference between burgundy and red."

"It's why bloodlines have emblems, not colours," Ord said calmly to Coranna. "Wouldn't want to stab the wrong man."

"They have emblems in the North?" Av asked. "Palace lands still have colours. Take Bilgern, wonderful blue that no one else can make, you definitely recongize that when you see it."

"Surely you recognize the red of the palace, then," Coranna said. "Olea's roses are that colour."

Av took his seat and picked up the flower. He turned it this way and that in the light and frowned at it, then looked to Coranna.

"Looks the same to me," he said.

"The palace is the colour of fresh blood," Aren said calmly to Av.

The warrior looked at Aren, then the rose. Very quickly he set it down on the table.

"It's the thought that counts, isn't it?" he asked.

Ord laughed, but Coranna glared at her mate. "She swore death to the next lover who stole one of her flowers to prove his prowess. Aren't you the least bit concerned?"

"By what?" Ord asked. "They didn't know, and we certainly didn't go in meaning to take that one. Surely she's not going to kill the one who sits the throne and her mate because of a threat uttered twenty years ago? By the spirits, Aren wasn't even conceived yet, how would she know about it? Or Av? I thought their beds were separated."

"They had to combine the two because Vivlia's kept dying," Coranna said.

"It's the conflicting rage and disrespect mingling with excess magic to drag down the land of a rival," Aren said, picking up her wine glass as three sets of eyes turned to her. "What?"

"It's what?" Av asked quietly. "No, I don't care about the what. How did you know that?"

Aren thought back and frowned. "I don't know. Someone must have told me at some point. I've been learning an awful lot about magic recently."

"We don't teach that," Coranna said with a shake of her head. "We eventually come to suspect, but once you know, it's far too easy to spoil the land of a rival or cause her estate to fall because her crops fail."

Av looked at Aren pointedly. She paused with the wine glass to her lips.

"Possibly I know from my time at the vineyard?" she asked. "Though Anue and I didn't exactly fight, let alone show one another disrespect."

Coranna used the mention of Anue to redirect the conversation. While they ate, they talked about many things, with Coranna or Ord changing the topic of conversation as it pleased them. After dinner, they retreated to the hearth in the central room for tea and more talk.

At the end of the night, they said goodbye and Av took Aren's hand as they walked back to the rooms. Outside of the rooms, Av hesitated. He drew Aren close and kissed her on the forehead, then hesitated again as if considering whether or not he dared kiss her again.

Her heart skipped a beat as he thought, then did a pitter-patter in her chest when he bent down to capture her lips once more.

When he pulled away, she wavered on her feet.

Aren swallowed, recalling what Av had said at the beginning of the night.

"I think we should do this more often," she said quietly.

"As do I."

"With one small change to the rules," she said, and watched him pull away from her. "I think that sometimes, not every time and not a majority of the time, but sometimes, we should toss the rule you made at the beginning of the night."

Av considered Aren thoughtfully, then he smiled. "I think I can agree to that."

"Good," Aren said, opening the door to their rooms. "Will you be sleeping here tonight?"

"Does that mean we have to break the rule?" Av asked.

"No, I'm just asking. I sleep better with you in the bed."

Av closed the door and immediately tugged at his tie, tossing it onto the nearest chair. Aren waited patiently as the vest, then the shirt followed.

"Wouldn't want you losing sleep," Av said, coming to Aren to hug her.

Not what she was expecting, nor what she wanted. Aren watched silently as Av went to the bathing room and then she sighed to herself. She stripped off the dress, pulled on a nightgown and climbed under the covers in the time it took Av to relieve himself and wash his hands.

The warrior came out looking rather pleased with himself. He climbed into bed beside Aren and pulled her close, tucking himself around her, draping an arm over her possessively.

"Goodnight, Aren."

"Goodnight."

Chapter Twenty-Two

Av and Aren awoke early the next morning to enjoy one another's company, and then he sent her to training even though she made a comment about being tired. After training, he met with her and walked her to the informal breakfast that happened every morning in one of the side dining halls.

Breakfast was held in various places of Castle Grey, with some families gathering in specific halls to spend some time together before splitting off into their days. The Marilton bloodline came together once every four days for just such a breakfast, where the various families and branches of the line could talk and exchange news.

Walking into the dining hall, Av felt delighted. He was looking forward to the day and another night with Aren. He had arranged, during his training, to take Aren for a horseback ride so that she could see a bit of the land. Olea and Cara would be going with them, along with Url.

Av had a feeling that his aunt was trying to push Cara on them. The more he heard about his cousin, the more he understood why. She didn't fit in with the Northerners and was exactly the sort of queen that palace lands were known for. The lords and ladies would be able to tolerate her a great deal better than those of the North.

And if it meant that Aren might get in another tussle with the other queen, well… Av wasn't exactly going to complain.

When they walked into the hall, everyone went silent. Av glanced around and caught Coranna's eyes. The queen paled and looked away quickly.

He had just enough time to utter a silent curse when there was a crack. A light orb shattered overhead and sprinkled those in the hall with glass. Aren moved backward, yanking Av with her and turned as if facing an opponent.

"That's not how magic works," Av muttered to her.

"It is if I say it is," she responded with a resolve Av hadn't heard in a very long time.

There was another crack and the floor around them blackened, but not near enough to do them any harm. Av watched it happen and knew they should have been dead, but he didn't know why they weren't. He frowned at the floor, and looked up as the elder, Vivlia, stepped out of the crowd and raised her hands.

Aren sighed. *Sighed.* Like Vivlia was inconveniencing her.

"I just want breakfast, is that too much to ask? That I get to eat before someone tries to kill me for something *you* did?"

Av gave Aren a look, and the queen responded by shaking her head as if he were the biggest idiot in the world. She lifted her hand, and the space between them and Vivlia seemed to explode. Av threw his arms up to protect his face, but nothing struck him.

He looked over his arms cautiously, then dropped them entirely. Smoke danced at the edge of the blackness on the floor but came no closer. He could smell the smoke, but it and whatever had caused it, stayed on the other side of the invisible line.

"What did you do?" Av asked, turning to Aren.

She turned slowly to him, wavering just slightly. "I didn't do it, Raven did."

Aren fell, but he saw the way she went limp just before she did. Av caught her and eased her to the floor, his anger bursting from him in a growl as he lunged into the smoke.

Only to hit that damned wall as if it were made of solid rock and bounce back off of it, startled, confused, and frustrated.

The smoke settled and then swirled, coming together to form a woman.

"My name is Raven," the smoke said, then it vanished and reappeared, flicking several times as it said, "Raven, Ra-Raven. Raven. My name is Raven."

The form solidified and the woman turned to Av. It was the woman from the hallway, the one with the oddly coloured eyes. Av bared his teeth at her, and she arched an eyebrow at him.

"You're staying in there until I know you won't hurt yourself," Raven said, then smiled. "No worries, Av. I've not hurt her any, just tapped into her magic and the chaos that ensued. Vivlia probably didn't fare so well, but I don't take kindly to her type of woman."

"Raven?" Olea asked, moving through the crowd quickly. The queen came to a stop at the edge of the crowd and stared at the woman standing in the middle of the blackened floor. "Aren told us about a Raven. Who are you? How did you do that?"

Raven flickered, then solidified. "My name is Raven. I am what you would call landscape magic. I have been a part of Castle Grey since it was built. I have watched you all for centuries, though I have faded to almost nothing in the past. With Aren here, I was able to reunify my pieces. Her magic reactivated the latent processes that would have kept me alive indefinitely if only we had known before the move. Olea, if you would please come here."

Olea moved forward without fear and took Raven's outstretched hand. The queen gasped.

"You feel real."

"For all anyone or anything can tell, I am," Raven said. "Vivlia is coming to. I don't want to deal with her."

"She's an elder," Olea said.

"I know what she is, I've watched her grow from a child into an ugly old woman," Raven countered.

"Then you know about our elders," Olea said insistently.

"They are like the priests of old. Miring the people in a swamp of tradition and rules. Like the priests of old, they are made up of people, and people can be stupid, ignorant, and plain evil. Power corrupts. I killed off the priests to cut away the cancer, and your people agreed to never do it again. I can hardly blame you for not recalling the promises you made ten hundred centuries ago, but I do have the magic to enforce it myself."

"We will have a hundred questions for you," Olea said.

"And I can answer almost none of them," Raven responded. "I can only give secrets to the one who sits the throne. What I can do is teach you how to maintain my processes. If I could reach the palace, there would be no need. But you are linked to Aren and will be able to. I'll be damned if I remain invisible for another six hundred years, listening to you people whine about your lives."

"How dare—" Vivlia's voice stopped suddenly.

Av bent and tried to look around Raven. Vivlia was clearly speaking, he could see her lips moving, but he couldn't hear the words. Suddenly that invisible wall was keeping sound out.

"Av, if you will behave, I will let you out," Raven said, appearing beside him. "Will you behave?"

"Can I stab someone?" he asked idly, glancing down at Aren's still form. "But that's not going to help her, is it?"

"She will be fine, she will wake shortly with a headache and be a bit blurry, but otherwise no lasting side effects," Raven said gently. "I needed a chaotic moment to open everyone else's eyes to see me. This wasn't the moment I was planning on appearing, but I'm sick of queens trying to kill one another over petty arguments. It's a damned flower, who cares? It'll grow back. You know what wouldn't grow back? Aren's head! I keep saying that we need her head attached to her damned body but does anyone listen to me? No!"

"Raven, they're listening now," Av said, motioning to the Mariltons, who were all staring at Raven in various states of defense.

The queens had been pushed behind the warriors, for the most part. Olea and one of her daughters stood near Vivlia. The elder was quieted finally, but she was pale and shaking.

"What did you do to her?" Av asked.

"Nothing on purpose. In order for me to be seen, I had to absorb a great deal of magic. Vivlia likes to throw magic about to make a show, and it was attached directly back to her because the woman doesn't know how to send magic across any distances. Aren does know, but I needed it attached to her so that I could… basically give her a library."

"On what?"

"Magic."

"How much magic?"

"How to use magic in every way it can be used."

"Won't that…"

"She won't have access to it all at once, that would make her head explode," Raven said idly as she waved dismissively at him. "I thought this would happen in a few more days, that I would continue to absorb and be able to do this in such a way that I could walk into a room instead of appearing in the middle of breakfast."

"What did you do to me?" Vivlia wailed.

Raven frowned at Av. "Everyone else in this room is terrified, why aren't you?"

"She attacked Aren and is now suffering every moment I distract you from getting on with whatever it is that you want to say," Av said with a smile that grew slowly.

"Some queen messed you up in a special sort of way," Raven muttered.

Av could only shrug in response. Life on palace lands rarely allowed a warrior to stomp his feet and kill the person he wanted to kill. Sometimes he had to find other ways to cause damage, ways that couldn't necessarily be traced back to him and didn't result in blood.

"Good morning, everyone," Raven said, raising her voice as she walked back into the blackened area. "My name is Raven."

Why did she keep repeating that? Like the few Av had seen who were troubled, they would repeat the same sentence over and over again. He recalled when the healers had shown him a young woman with a troubled past who kept repeating her name. She had been trying to remind herself of who she was.

Or was it like the older folk, who repeated themselves because they kept losing track of what they had been saying?

Could landscape magic go mad?

"I was once a part of the palace, and when the people demanded the palace be destroyed in the hopes of wiping the slate clean, your ancestors took me from them. You have told palace lands for centuries that you took the palace north, but you've muttered amongst yourselves, 'only the important bits' while never understanding what those bits meant.

"The tale of what I was wasn't meant to be told, for fear that those on palace lands would realize that the stones they destroyed were just that, stones from the outer walls. Only the baron and his heir were ever to be told the tale. They were to tell their mates what to do, to keep me alive.

"But something went wrong over time. A baron didn't trust his son, the mates didn't understand what the barons wanted of them. There was a rift between mother and daughter. No one was weaving magic the way they should have been, none of you were linking. Even now, the only links being created between queens are the ones being created by the young one who sits the throne.

"None of you trust one another, all of you harbour secrets, and I know them all. I may not have started as a part of Castle Grey, but there is no longer any part of it that can be hidden from me. Not if you put up your magics, not if you can block the sight of another who has magic.

"All people have secrets. All people hide things from their loved ones. They let someone steal something for the sense of adventure, they let their siblings take the fall for something they did. But a man shouldn't have to hide his preferences or his desires simply because the elders say that a baron must mate a queen."

"I love Olea," Er protested loudly and very quickly.

"Not you," Raven grumbled. "The two of you make me sick with how devoted you are to one another. All lovey dovey, as if you just met.

"There was a time when the elders held purpose. They replaced trainers to keep the baron from grasping at power, from abusing his people. Ever since you were gifted with a trainer, you've blackened your lives by believing the elders over him. You sent him away because of your elders."

"To be fair, the throne wanted me in the south," Av said.

Raven turned to Av and glared at him. Her eyes had changed from the odd colour to that of blood. There was a raging fury to her face that was difficult to hear in her voice.

"It's true," he insisted.

"The throne has no influence here, it wanted Aren," Raven said carefully. "If you really are such a good pair for her, the distance between here and there would not have stopped you from finding one another."

"All right," Av said, moving towards Raven slowly. "I understand you're angry, but why?"

"Jer was supposed to be here!"

"Is he..." Av glanced at Aren, then back to Raven.

"He is my Aren," Raven snarled.

"He's the product of rape," Av responded. "You can't just rape people to get the lines right. You can't do that to someone's life!"

"I can, and I will if it means saving the land."

"No, because how does that save the land?" Av demanded.

"Jer would have your grandfather's blood and power, his title. He'd also have your mother's bloodline to back him and the knowledge of queen's stone. With the power of his title, he would have either taken palace lands by force or traded into it. He would have gone to the palace and found the books and then read them. From there he's got the intelligence necessary to put it all together."

Av shook his head. "The books from the palace were moved south after the palace was rebuilt. And what does he need to know? Because I can tell him. We already know the stone grows, we know it comes close to the surface. That only a queen on the throne can stop the growth, and only the strongest could make it retreat. What else could he possibly need to know? About the infection? About the madness that follows? What is so important?"

"He would have bred to create the queen to sit the throne, to save the world."

"He has a daughter, she's a very good queen, but she will never sit the throne," Av said. "And I hate to be the bearer of bad news, but Jer prefers males over females."

Raven almost smiled. "And? He only needed to have one, and he did. He's now probably found himself some slip of a thing who blushes and trembles, is shy and needs protecting."

Av thought of Laeder, wondering what the young man would think of being spoken of in such a manner. He also wondered what Jer would say to that.

"My brother is not being brought to you. You'll have to make do with Url."

"Jer was my first, Url my second. I also have a fourth, fifth, and *thought* I had a sixth, but it turns out he can easily be turned."

Behind Raven, Er made a motion at Av. He caught the motion and knew it because his father had taught it to him, but he didn't dare look away from Raven. If Raven were an actual queen, with a living, breathing body, this would be the point in which Av had to take her down. Maybe not kill her, but at least lay her out.

"Where are you going with this, Raven?"

The woman looked startled. Her hands clenched and she growled through gritted teeth. The sound was inhuman. It couldn't possibly have come from anything that walked on two legs.

Av watched her struggle and approached her slowly. "Tell you what. We'll get ourselves settled and fed, and you take the time to sort things out, how about that? We'll get Vivlia to the healer and put Aren to bed, and it'll be less of a standoff and no one's going to distract you with all these questions. How does that sound?"

"The elders need to go," Raven said, sounding desperate.

"I can't just kill them, but if any of them interferes while I'm here, I'll kill them then. You're still technically a part of the palace, so that means you are technically mine to protect. Right? So no one's going to question my right to kill a person who does something stupid around you."

The features cracked. Raven struggled and almost became solid once more, but she shattered and fell to the floor. Av stared as the pieces seemed to melt into the floor and disappeared.

He looked up at Er, who stared back at him.

"That was madness," Av said to the baron.

Er nodded slowly. "Uh, what's that healer say? Uh, alone too long can fracture the mind? Does she still work, or is she retired?"

Olea jumped when she realized Er was talking to her. "How would I know? What is even going on? Vivlia is a blank space, Aren's all fuzzy like she's made of fog. A woman was just arguing with Av about her right to have people raped for the betterment of the world, and you two are just standing there as if this is a normal day?"

Av and Er motioned to Aren at the same time.

"Infected," Av said. "Best to just not act surprised all the time, because it's going to slow things down rather than solve them faster. Now, if I'm right, what you've got on your hands is a piece of landscape magic that was once a part of the throne. It's been broken because it was almost destroyed several times. The best thing for you to do is work with her to repair her... What did she call them?"

"Processes?" Er asked.

"Right. Magic made her go from invisible to nearly everyone to visible to us, but getting that time put a strain on her. When I talked to her, she was very stable and collected. Rational, very rational. Likely the same when she spoke to Aren."

"If Jer were here he'd say we needed to check the library."

"I have a private one," Er said suddenly. "I'll take Url and Olea, and we'll start searching."

"What about your mother?" Olea asked quickly.

"I think Raven made it clear that anyone who is aligned with her is not aligned with Raven, and as we may or may not be living inside of Raven..." Er grimaced and looked at Olea. "Send her to the healer hall until we sort this out. Av, take Aren back to your rooms. Trust me when I say it's best for a queen to wake up in familiar surroundings when something involves her and magic."

Chapter Twenty-Three

"Aren?"

She groaned and rolled over into the warm comfort of fabric and pillow.

"Aren, wake up."

Something jabbed her in the side, and Aren groaned, burrowing deeper into the blankets.

"No, seriously, *wake up*."

Unhappy with being forced awake, Aren sat up but pouted. She should have been able to sleep, not just be woken up at someone else's pleasure. It wasn't like she fell asleep in the middle of the dining hall on purpose.

"No, it's not like that, but while I could smash my way in and drop what I pleased, I thought it high time you and I have an honest talk," Raven said, crossing her arms and looking down at Aren.

Aren assessed her situation. She had just pouted; she never did that. She wasn't tired physically. Then again, she wasn't entirely certain she could feel her actual body. Everything around her was dark, and Raven looked like Raven, but also different at the same time.

"Where are we?" Aren asked. "And how are we?"

"The answer to the first is complicated and linked to the second. The good news is that I'm now giving you the knowledge you'll need. Basically, no, you cannot give someone information in this matter. I can because it's written into me. This is technically your mind. Though most people have a happy place that they retreat to when angry or upset."

Grass appeared on the edge of a lake. Aren ended up sitting on a bench, blinking at Raven in surprise. She wasn't certain where to begin with her questions.

"As I said,"—Raven moved to sit beside Aren— "the knowledge I'm imparting on you will tell you how I did this, but you won't be able to achieve it yourself. I've been slowly loading the fundamentals since you touched the stone, but you won't be visiting long enough for that to work. You know almost nothing, and yet things which queens who have been through training find difficult to manage. That won't work, not with what the throne has planned for you."

"And what is that?"

"Save the world, which sounds ridiculous, but you'd be surprised how often it happens. That information, the magic, is being given to you in the background. I have some time to talk, but I'm also splitting myself between here and the outside world. The mind moves a great deal faster inside one's own head."

"Then what do you need me to talk about?" Aren asked.

"For starters, I need to keep you talking so that I know if you hit a point where it's too much," Raven said, then smiled and almost grimaced at the same time.

"Why do I get the feeling that will result in my head popping open like one of those stink bomb mushrooms?" Aren muttered.

"More like an egg thrown against a wall."

"Why does this keep happening to me!"

Raven studied Aren, her eyes roving up and down her. "Fascinating. Now that I see it, I know they're wrong. You do feel, but you are just very good at hiding those emotions. Where did the magic go, then?"

"It's not in what you'll be giving me?" Aren asked.

"No, but that's not surprising. The knowledge I carry comes from hundreds of queens, all of whom sat the throne before you. I've picked and chosen what to give to you, just as I've chosen what to keep. No one needs to be taught how to castrate a man with magic, or how to take the innards and bring them to the outside of a body without damaging anything."

"Basic teleportation with a sadistic mind," Aren countered quickly.

Raven hesitated. "You are more intelligent than I expected you to be."

"When reading is considered rebellion but isn't something you can exactly be *caught* doing, you read."

"Fair enough," Raven muttered. "You seemed surprised when I told you that the world had to be saved. You are aware that our world cycles. The archivist told you."

"How do you know that?" Aren asked.

"The archivist needs magic to access the long-time storage." Raven motioned to herself. "I am the long-time storage."

"Oh? Oh..."

"So I know what information he has accessed for you. You know the world cycles, but were surprised when I told you that it was in need of saving. The world being on that balancing point is a part of the cycle. Now, no—no one has ended up destroying the world before. They have, however, ended up tortured, beaten, raped, murdered, and burned to death, which I think is just plain worse than the others. They have ended up losing all of their loved ones by inaction, or the wrong action. They had also started some of the longest dark periods the world has ever seen."

"I can't fail, but I can regret ever being born."

"Yes. The reason for the cycles is a rather large and accidental landscape magic. When queen's stone was first discovered, the nobility of the world all infected themselves. Many were lost, but they were considered weak blood. In a way that was true, there was a weakness of the heart among many of the people, and queen's stone certainly reduced the occurrence of it.

"The nobility at the time were mainly commoners and twisted just as often as they were good. On the throne sat a strong queen, one strong enough to revive the river of magic."

"A source of magic that spreads from the palace and ever outward, which anyone who knows how can tap in to and use to their own pleasure depending on the strength of the queen and her skills," Aren said. "When it's restricted to palace grounds, it's referred to as tapping in to the throne and can only be done by those who are a close friend or family of the one who sits the throne."

"Or blood, which causes problems," Raven said. "Each of the nobility tapped in to the river nearly constantly to light their houses and then, once the infection started taking hold, to do things like teleport, change the composition of things. A few were even able to create something out of nothing. They called it enlightenment because even commoners had magic and the villages grew, and the ranks multiplied. And one day a farmer found a vein of queen's stone in his field, where the year before there was none. And then another, and another. I still don't know how it happened, but as a living stone, queen's stone likely changed itself. If landscape magic can change itself without the direction of a queen, then surely the stone could as well."

"What happened?" Aren asked.

"What caused it to grow seems to have been the death of the queen who was infected the first time. She died by her own hand and in terror and sadness. Her mate left her, called their children monsters because he had just discovered that his son, her heir, wasn't a queen at all—the boy was a nihally."

"What's a nihally?" Aren demanded. "What does it do? What's its function?"

"It is an unranked one, and if you take that name to the archivist, he will tell you everything. He has to."

Aren tried to relax. "Fine, I will do that. But, ranks are things like warrior and healer."

"Which were once all referred to by some other title. The language is no longer in use, and the rank nihally doesn't translate into the common tongue."

"Oh, I see."

"The throne sat empty for six years because it was made known that the heir wasn't a queen. Back then they could do that. The throne was new and had no understanding of its function, but the longer it sat empty, the more the stone grew. People came from all over, scholars, queens, ranks I'm not even allowed to mention because they were killed once discovered."

"Does that happen often?" Aren asked.

"Rank is not usually a slippery thing, but if you take a child and it dies, and you bring it back to life, it's not quite the rank it was supposed to be. And just like sometimes babies are born blind or different, so there can be oddities in rank. They rarely turn out well."

"And all these people, what did they decide?" Aren asked. "And before or after the strangers were killed?"

"Before the strangers died, and what we discovered was that queen's stone could not live on palace grounds. We began to theorize, because at that point it was all we could do. The river of magic had already gone dormant, the throne was running out of magic and, as it did, queen's stone crept ever closer. So the heir came and sat the throne. Slowly the stone retreated. His rank can sit the throne, you know that, yes?"

"Someone might have told me, or it's in what you gave me," Aren said with a shake of her head. "I don't know."

"His daughter, his heir, went to war and died. His mate wasn't capable of carrying a second rank, despite being a queen, and he was unwilling to bed anyone besides her. When he died, the throne had more magic, because he pushed as much magic into it as he could, and his mate did the same. They were worried the world would be taken over by queen's stone in the time it took another queen to be found.

"Upon his death, the throne latched onto a lesser queen within the palace walls. She was the first taken by the throne. This happened every time, and each time the stone got to be smaller. One day it seemed there was none at all, but keeping it at bay had put stress on the throne's processes. What it was supposed to do was fracturing and it was all over the place. Madness I suppose is what it would be called in a real person. The throne was mad, and it retreated into itself, picking any queen at all. The strong ranks of the infected days were long dead, as were their children. During enlightenment nothing was about breeding, it was all love and sparkles and yet wasn't at the same time. Men mated women with the title they wanted or the fortune, or because their parents said to. For a trade agreement. I gently suggested to a couple that when their parents tried to make them marry different people—because that's what it was called then, that they elope and call it mating. They were doing it for the breeding."

"Mating is what it's called nearly everywhere. It seems it was a fashion for arranged matings and carried on from there."

"Many of those arranged matings are done by the throne, but it still infuriates me that they changed the meaning," Raven grumbled. "One day consumption struck. I recalled it happening the first time, but had thought nothing of it because it was an illness, and they pop up constantly. Fearful of what might happen, I started strongly encouraging couples whom I thought would breed ranks. I wasn't right all of the time. I was new to it even then. Ranks came back just as the stone was reaching the surface and in two generations I had a queen on the throne who was the same strength as the one who had started the entire thing, but only her strength before her infection. It took sixteen cycles for the throne to awaken, to gain any thought. The last time I saw the throne, it still could rarely manage to speak, and when it did, it did so to me and usually to wake me from my sleep. 'Wake up, wake up, sleepy butt.'"

"I've never watched another magic wake up before, but I suppose we were all children once."

"So am I the queen who makes the stone retreat?" Aren asked.

"That's when things get complicated. Oh, you may be able to take something on besides magic, what would you like?"

Aren thought for a moment. "Teach me to rule."

"I can do that, but how about I teach you to lead, instead of rule?" Raven asked, then watched as Aren shook her head, not understanding the difference. "Em ruled, Mirmae led."

"Lead, then, definitely lead."

"Good, now, where was I?" Raven asked herself. "Oh yes. You, Aren, are infected. Now you tell me how you were infected."

"I ran into a cave and then straight into the back wall, smacked my face on it and sat in there for a little bit," Aren said.

"No, while slightly amusing, I meant: Did you have consumption beforehand? Did you break your skin, or bleed at all while in the cave?"

"I had consumption first, yes. I bruised in the cave, but I didn't cut myself if that's what you mean."

"Good, directly afterward was there any bodily damage done besides the bruise?"

"Av hit me once we got back to the palace."

"He what? Why would he do that that?"

"I ran and hit him with a book through magic use, to get away."

"That doesn't give a person the right to hit you, Aren."

"He's a warrior and thought a blow for a blow was fair," Aren countered, then shook her head. "Everyone is all shocked that he hit me. Em attacked me. Women kept dying on palace lands, but everyone is scandalized when a man hits a woman. No one even cared when Jer literally ripped Em's head off."

"I think you mean—"

"*Literally.*"

"Oh dear," Raven murmured.

"Why does all that matter anyhow?"

Raven took in a slow, deep breath. "How you are infected will change how it affects you. Those nobles I told you about? They did the healer's hall, stick your hand in a box filled with living stone thing. Throughout time it is the ones who stumble onto—or into, in your case—queen's stone, who bond with it more thoroughly. If you sustain damage while it works its way into your body, it will assume that damage is a normal thing for you. If you had broken a bone or had cut the skin, it would have been an almost instantaneous infection because once the stone has found a host which can keep it alive, it keeps them alive. Sometimes that means you heal right away, sometimes that means that every bump and scratch turns your body, ever so slowly, into the stone. There are a couple of statues I could direct you towards which did not start as stone."

"Does being infected also have something to do with all the trouble that keeps happening?" Aren asked.

"Things will happen that are out of the ordinary, but they happen like that around those with a great deal of magic. Think of magic as a light and everything else in the world is a moth. It will be drawn to you. The reason why the draw is stronger now is because your magic is getting stronger."

"That's not possible," Aren said. And then the thoughts began flitting through her mind about what was possible for those who were infected. "The stone is literally inside me, and I can change it like I can any other object, once I know it's there and what it is. It's what your anchors are based on, self-replicating. All they need is the slightest drop of magic, and they will continue to build upon it. Will it ever stop?"

"Eventually, I think it will," Raven said quietly. "Most don't live long enough to see it slow down. The next part I'm going to tell you, but only if you promise not to tell Av what we talked about."

"I think I can do that."

"As far as anyone who isn't infected is concerned, a side effect of queen's stone in the body is madness."

"As far as anyone is concerned?" Aren asked. "What does that mean? And why do I have nothing on that?"

"Because you won't be going mad. Remember, you are a light for the moths. Eventually, things will begin happening to you that others simply cannot comprehend, or cannot see, or cannot keep up with. The leaps and bounds that those who are infected make are too complicated for anyone else to explain. Eventually, they say that the one in question has begun to go mad."

"Are you telling me this to reassure me that I'm not going mad?"

"I'm telling you this because it's what they believe and with this event, they will probably start planning, preparing to keep you sane as long as possible. I find that those who know this last longer, and some even died of old age rather than any other cause."

"But there will be times where those I love look at me as if I've lost my mind."

"Yes, there will. Av and Jer have likely been raised on Mirmae's words, those same words which Url believes whole-heartedly and they were taught those words in case this very thing happened."

"To those without faith, it would seem madness."

"Exactly. I don't think they fully understand because they think you will go mad, but they do, on some level, know that you aren't crazy at all."

"None of this says anything about reliving the same day—" Aren stopped and stared at Raven. "I did what, now?"

"I'll explain it to Av. That is a bit extreme for someone newly infected." Raven sighed. "This would be so much easier to talk about if I knew what the throne knew, but I can't find it. Like it's blurry, or in a different room and shouting through the walls."

An idea occurred to Aren. After the discussion they had just had it, seemed like a better idea by the moment. She smiled at Raven.

"You want to talk to the throne? Because I have a way you can talk to the throne, or at the very least it can talk to you through me."

Chapter Twenty-Four

When Jer saw the palace come into view, he was relieved to say the least. Dropping the horses at the stable, he shot the stable master a look when the man tried to babble. Jer then took his two wards to the healer hall, where the healers asked about the younger boy.

Jer had given his word. He couldn't very well break it.

After leaving the healer hall, he ran into Laeder but told the scribe that he needed to speak to his father first. Something about his tone must have scared Laeder, which cut Jer like a knife, but he hadn't the control to make amends.

Walking into the master's house, he found it empty. Furious, Jer left the house and opened his senses enough to find the trainer. Through the palace and to the war room he went, slamming the door as he entered for good measure.

Ervam stood at the table with several messengers and papers scattered about in front of him. The trainer looked at the messengers, who left quickly and closed the door behind them.

"You look like you carry a burden, Jer."

Jer tried to speak but couldn't. Furious, he kicked a chair, turned back to his father and ran into another, which he picked up and threw to the other side of the room. Ervam stood motionless as this happened.

"He's a rank," Jer snarled. He waited for a response from Ervam but realized that he had too much snarl and not enough words. "He's a rank, the dimwit is a rank."

"It can happen, there are several historical instances of a male queen getting into a fog, mainly because he doesn't understand that what's going on is real, so he just sort of quietly goes mad."

"There's nothing wrong with his body. He's not a queen. Physically he looks like a normal person. He… he looks like he's Aren's brother. A year younger, maybe, but Eln wasn't certain."

"Who is Eln, again?" Ervam asked.

"The heir. You'll like him."

"Funny, that's not what Aren implied," Ervam muttered.

"She didn't mind him, but wouldn't want to be ruled by him. You know why? Because whenever a man tells her to do something, it disgusts her. You know why? Do you know how many…" Jer stopped to take another breath. "You know the lord we can't find?"

"The one who is leasing Em's land?" Ervam asked, sounding surprised.

"We can't find him because an unranked one went on a little trip and put a blade between his ribs, and then threw him to his dogs. Who, thankfully, he never got to use on Aren, like he had bought the contract from her father."

"Is Cerlot still breathing?" Ervam asked, going perfectly still.

"The man made to purchase Aren's virginity. He wasn't specific on the details. It would be prostitution, plain and simple. We can fine him and remove her by the laws, but Cerlot had no knowledge of what the lord planned, which was encouraged by Em. Do you know why it was encouraged by Em?"

Ervam swore. "She knew more than she told us."

"Yes, or so an unranked one tells me. Did you also know that unranked ones are linked to spirits and have pretty much all the knowledge of the spirits, should they dare to ask, as long as the original spirit of the body is alive, did you know that?"

"Your trip was educational in more than one way."

"And for the love of the spirits, never tell her to smile. Not in any context."

"But the lord in question's land…" Ervam said slowly.

"It's in the borderland," Jer said. "She even gave me the keys."

Jer fished the keys out of his pocket and tossed them to Ervam. The trainer stared at the keys for a long moment and then looked up at Jer.

"And all of this was *before* she was infected?" Ervam asked, his voice barely above a whisper.

"Yes, but there's a reason for that. See, the unranked are known to the throne, which has said that if some of them don't help it, it will out them to us—the warriors, who will kill them and they will then be replaced by those who will obey."

"Except it only needs some of them. There are those who are fighting against it," Ervam said with a nod. "So the ones who knew the throne's plot were fighting over Aren. To either save or destroy her so utterly that she couldn't be put to whatever tasks it was that the throne had for her."

"And some of them made her life a living hell because the throne told them to."

Ervam swore loudly. "We can't take that to Av. He already wants to bash the seat to bits!"

"Can we drink yet?" Jer demanded.

"No," Ervam said sternly, moving away from the table. "No, damn it. But I want them both dead, I want their house purged, and I want that boy back here on palace lands. I want the names of everyone who has had anything to do with her and I want them executed."

"She won't come forward, the unranked one."

"Why not?"

"Because the original spirit died and all that's left is a queen from a very long time ago who sat the throne and has said, without a doubt, that if you go down there to drag her out, or Av does, she'll make our lives a living hell."

"You keep using that word as if I know what it is," Ervam said. "Hell?"

"Take your happiest memory and turn it on its head. That for all eternity, or until you die, and it's been made to sound as if she can make a moment in your life seem like an eternity."

"So we won't have a trial. It wouldn't be the first time."

As his father became angrier, Jer felt calmer. While he had been at the estate, it had seemed as if he were the only sane one in a mad world. That wasn't true, however. There were a great many people who thought the same way he did.

"We can't kill her parents," Jer said calmly.

Balya had given him the solution, but Jer had been too angry to see it. She had even suggested keeping Aren's parents alive for the same reason Jer had originally wanted to. If they ever needed Aren to produce more magic than normal, all they had to do was bring her parents to the palace.

"Why not?" Ervam demanded.

"Because if Av ever found out and they were already dead? Or worse yet, he found out and discovered that we had hidden this information from him?" Jer watched the trainer go perfectly still, as if the life had drained out of him. He gave the other man a moment before he dared continue. "We have little experience on the fields, and Av, near as I can tell, has never dealt with that emotion. We want him to bleed a man, not fall to the fields or rise to them, or whatever it's called, because we killed the object of his hatred before he even knew that he should hate the man."

"What about that other lord, then?" Ervam asked. "Surely we'd have to include that in the number."

"She killed him and fed him to his own dogs. I don't think Av is going to do more than chuckle at it. Hopefully, he never asks about other victims, whom I will be talking to the captain of the guard about shortly. See if we can't find them and undo some of the damage."

"We tell Av, then what?" Ervam looked frustrated. "He passes judgement? Certainly, he is the mate to the throne, and it is his right, but what about our right as her family? Do we get no say in this?"

"Did Mother's family have a say in your judgement?" Jer countered.

"What happened to your anger?"

"You taught us never to make judgements while angry. We need to get over this and calm down so that when Av returns, we can sit him down and tell him what I've learned. If he wants them dead, then we will go down there and do it, but not unless he says so. There's no denying that Aren wants them alive. Otherwise there are a hundred ways we could have ended them before she banished them from court. In a way she's right, we can't leave Eln down there by himself, and we can't put someone in charge of the estate while he's warded out. They maintain the status quo, and they aren't going to do any harm to Eln. Are they a danger to everyone around them? Yes, but so was Em, and we kept her alive for years without seeing the end of the road. We just need to keep them alive until Eln turns eighteen, and then he can take over the estate, and we can put an end to them quietly in a field somewhere. Where no one is going to be asking questions, or making demands, or whispering things about what the warriors did to bad parents. Because that's all the court sees them as, bad parents."

"You're a very good steward," Ervam grumbled. "I still want to break something."

"Break a chair, break a table, break a stone for all I care, but you cannot ride down there and do what you want to do, because it's not your thing to do," Jer said, frowning when he realized he had suddenly stopped being specific.

He turned towards the door, where Danya blinked several times in surprise. The woman came deeper into the room, turning her face slightly away from Jer.

"You've changed, Lord Jer."

"Just Jer—we need to nip this title thing before it gets out of hand," Jer said quickly.

"The both of you are worked up enough that the servants are beginning to feel it and several of the lords have already begun to cry for drink," Danya said.

"It's very complicated, Danya."

"Quite, from what I overheard," Danya murmured in response, then smiled when Jer growled at her. "I was recently taught by a boy how to see without seeing. Marvellous thing, with magic one does not need eyes, simply needs to know how one is supposed to see. It works quite a bit better if I'm not in the same room as what I am viewing, however. It also seems to dim the other senses I use to find my way around the palace."

"Mie," Ervam grumbled. "Is he teaching everyone to do that?"

"Just anyone having trouble seeing with their eyes. He believes, with the war coming, that we should have every advantage against possible attackers. It even seems that he believes it in his right to command us to training."

"Are you trying to lodge a complaint, or distract us?" Jer asked the woman.

Danya turned her body towards him. "Both. I waited until you returned because the boy was certain that if I went to your father, he would tell me that it was a matter for the throne to decide, not the master, and as you are steward, you represent the throne."

"You'll train," Jer said sternly. "Maybe not with the rest of them just yet, but you will train."

"Jer, I can't see!"

"You can see well enough to walk around, and that's just from a desire to learn. I'm sure you'll be able to see just fine when someone swings at you, but I want you to know how to stop them in such a way that I can come and gut the moron who tries to attack the crippled."

"I am not a cripple!"

"First you can't see, now you're not a cripple," Ervam rumbled with a laugh. "You're digging yourself a hole, Danya."

"Ah, a laugh, we are getting somewhere," Danya said quickly. "Good, that is good, because we have actual problems to talk about."

"What has happened—" Jer attempted to correct Danya, but the room filled with a queen's fury so quickly that he stopped speaking.

Fury was supposed to be a step above anger, not below it. A queen was angry for quite some time and then became furious when things still did not go her way. There was throwing things and kicking things and her stewing in her thoughts for some time before it escalated to that point.

"…Is in the past, Lord Jer. That is where we leave it, in the past. Aren doesn't speak about that because she doesn't wish to bring it up. She doesn't wish to speak of it. She wants to move on with her life, not dwell in the past."

"Not facing it is obviously not helping."

"She is not *running* from her past. She is simply not chasing it down. Aren doesn't recall a great deal of what you are talking about, some of which she didn't even know was going to happen. You two morons want to, what? Add to her pile? Tell her that her father was going to sell her? That her mother killed more than one rank? What does it matter?"

"I just want to kill them all," Ervam said. "I don't want to tell her about it, just bathe the estate in blood."

"To which Aren will demand an investigation," Danya said. "Until Aren has satisfied whatever curiosity has taken her, her parents are to be protected as her parents would be protected. Jer, you have come back with more tales than what you've shared, surely. Would you say that she likely has trouble with trusting others?"

"I would, absolutely, and I don't blame her."

"Would you not also think that she has put her trust in you to care for her parents?" Danya asked, turning her full attention to Jer. "If you kill them without her say so, you will not help her. If anything, you will hurt her."

"Can we ask her to kill her parents?" Ervam asked.

"Can we ask if *we* can kill her parents?" Jer corrected.

Danya's head turned towards Ervam, then back to Jer. "Now you're thinking in line of trust. I wouldn't suggest being insistent on that point."

"Write the report," Ervam said to Jer. "Gross abuse of wardship, we can start there. It'll give us legal grounds for the boy coming here next spring. We might even be able to counter the laws and bring him immediately."

"Now we're all thinking with our heads," Danya said happily. "If details are asked, do you know how to work around it?"

Jer studied the floor, trying to sort out the various aspects that he knew. It wasn't the first time he had been asked to alter the details without outright lying. Living mated to a queen made it a necessity to know how to tell the truth while lying.

"Are we talking about Aren, or lords?" Ervam asked in a low rumble.

"The lords are simple, Aren will want to know who, what, and why. Most especially involving her parents."

"Gross abuse of wardship," Jer said in a tone of voice that he had used on Mie a time or two when the boy wasn't taking 'no' for an answer.

"I like that," Ervam said, pointing to Jer. "She knows what they did, so us summing it up in a few words is as far as we'll go. Covers us, keeps her thinking we don't know anything extra."

"Abuse of power, killing ranks," Jer offered up. "That results in a fine for each time. We can't prove murder without bodies and witnesses willing to come forward, but we can charge abuse of power, allowing us to fine her which is us telling her that we know what she did, even if we can't hang her."

"Fine her?" Danya asked. "Fine a woman with no income, who is on a warded estate?"

Jer looked to Ervam. The man seemed to consider carefully.

"We can place a burden fine—debtors fine is what the lords call it now. If she ever has money, we take it. We can also contact her bloodline, the Argnerns on the coast, to collect the coin. We can also take that coin and give it to those who suffered under her. So let's come up with some more fines."

"Aren wants a cottage," Jer said.

"And we might have just found a way to pay for it."

Chapter Twenty-Five

There was some confusion over the next four days, and Av seemed to be the only one able to keep his head on straight.

Aren woke up on the second day early in the morning, ate a meal and then demanded Av bring her something to drink. Confused, he had brought her tea, only to have her give him a look that he hadn't realized she had known.

It was the look that questioned whether the male on the receiving end was actually that stupid, or was just pretending to avoid doing what she had asked.

Av had quickly corrected his mistake, but only after he realized that she wasn't drinking to drown something out, but to speak with the throne. He had then sat to the side, because she hadn't told him to go away, and watched patiently as she seemed to talk to herself and then switched to another language entirely. It was a language that Aren was unfamiliar with, and for the moment the alcohol began to fade as she stumbled over words.

When she demanded more drink from Av, he had denied the request and she, or the throne, had thrown the bottle at him. Considering the spot-on aim, Av assumed the throne had thrown the bottle.

He put Aren to bed, and she slept late the next day but rose without a complaint.

Castle Grey was in an uproar. Er was limping badly because his mother had attacked him once she came to her senses somewhat, but that didn't seem to slow the baron down. He was swatting warriors and elders out of his way as one. The only ones who didn't get snarled at were the scribes, who were poring over the library records that Er had opened to them.

The Marilton bloodline had many secrets, was all that Av could take away from the visits. Each time the scribes thought they had found the one that would link to Raven, Er grumbled and told them no.

Stealing artifacts, sabotaging boats headed across the ocean because the Eastern Baron owed a debt, and Jer wouldn't have been the first product of rape to become baron. Though on the last item, it wasn't always the woman who was raped, a fact that Av found interesting but hadn't the courage to ask anyone about.

There were mentions of a queen's library, which no one had any knowledge of. The baron's library referenced it so often that Er and Olea had gotten into an argument and come to blows over whether or not Olea was trying to safeguard knowledge for Url's mate. Olea won… Av thought. After the first strike and a brief struggle, the warriors not involved turned on their heels and left the room, dragging any commoners with them.

They saw no sign of Raven, heard nothing from the— they hadn't even decided on what to refer to her as. She wasn't a woman, wasn't quite a queen, though every Marilton attested to the fact that Raven held the rank of queen. Did they call her the castle, then? The palace, as was her origin? Or did they simply refer to her as landscape magic?

On the fourth morning, Av walked Aren to training and then went to pick her up afterwards. She was standing to the side as the boys stared openly at her, apparently arguing with someone who wasn't there.

Raven.

"Of course," he said with a sigh, coming to a stop just short of Aren and hoping, praying, he hadn't just stepped into Raven's image. "Aren, no one else can see Raven."

"Oh?" Aren asked, then turned to the boys she had been training with. "Oh… Does everyone in the castle know?"

"Yes, and no," Av said with a grimace. "We thought she had gone to sleep again. She was a bit fractured."

"Too many suppliers of magic without clear direction shuffled bits around. She's trying to get it back into place, but it'll take time, and Olea needs to know how to direct the magic. I should probably talk to Olea to make certain she knows what to do."

"You should. Why don't we go do that now?" Av asked, taking the training sword from Aren gently.

He took the sword to the training master, who took the sword as if it might bite him. The man gave Av a questioning look.

To those without faith, it would seem madness.

His mother's words didn't just apply to those who had been infected. It also applied to magic and, it seemed, strong queens.

"Long story, but if you're concerned for public safety, speak with Er. He'll explain it all."

The training master nodded and glanced around Av, to Aren. "She didn't train much today, argued most of it away. You tell her that if her friend wants to visit, that's fine, but she needs to keep training."

"Will do," Av said.

He returned to Aren and pulled her from the hall as she continued to argue with Raven, only this time in a broken language he didn't quite understand. It seemed like a garbled form of real words.

"Training master said if Raven wants to visit, fine, but you have to keep training at the same time," Av said sternly, pulling to a stop when he knew it was safe. "Yes, there are some odd things going on, yes, it is a big deal, but your training is also a big deal and you wanted this, so now that you have it you can't just decide to drop everything."

"She was trying to tell me that Olea and Er are fighting," Aren protested.

"Then you argue with her while you keep training," Av countered.

"I tried that. The boy kept smacking me," Aren grumbled to the floor.

"It'll teach you to do two things at once," Av said quietly. "And they are fighting, Olea and Er. The scribes have been going through things and keep finding references to a queen's library. Not the one at the palace, but one here at Castel Grey and Olea says she's never heard of such a thing or found it. Er can't help but feel she's hiding something, perhaps because of something she's said before."

"Where are they now?" Aren asked the air.

"Could you make her visible so that I can see her too?" Av asked.

"No, she's not strong enough for that. She told me what happened when she tried to talk to you all and, between you, me, and her, she's a little embarrassed because she miscalculated how much magic it would take to do that and what she did for me."

Av stood rooted in the spot as Aren walked off on him. Finally, he gave himself a shake.

"What did she do for you?" he asked Aren as he tried to catch up.

"Not right now," Aren growled.

She walked as if she knew where she was going. Av supposed that was true, in a way. Raven was likely giving Aren directions, or simply leading her through the palace.

He thought back to the palace and wondered just how useful a magic like Raven would be. There'd be no need for guards when she was awake because she could alert anyone to anything that was happening within her walls. The one who sat the throne wouldn't need a guardian because Raven would be the guardian.

"Raven is very useful," Av said.

The palace's landscape magic flickered into view for a moment and then vanished. Aren pulled to a stop, looking to where Raven had been, then back at Av. They both frowned at one another and looked back to the spot where Raven had been.

"Try that again," Aren said quietly.

"Raven is very useful. I wish we could take her back with us, just think of how much trouble we'd be able to avoid and how many people would love to talk to her. The archivist, Telm. Laeder would lose his mind."

Raven flickered back into view and looked down at herself. Ever so slowly she looked up at Av, surprise playing over her features.

"What did I just do?" Av asked.

"You strengthened Aren's magic," Raven said, sounding as surprised as Av felt. "Say that about her."

"About?" Av motioned to Aren. "She wouldn't believe me if I did say it."

Raven gave Av a frustrated look as Aren turned to him, surprised. "I wouldn't believe that you find me useful? Of course, I'm useful, I make the lights shine, and the water run. Only a moron would assume I think otherwise."

"I think Raven more of meant that I should say something like… you're beautiful."

Aren flushed red. "Don't be ridiculous."

"There, it happened again," Raven said. "You must be reacting emotionally to hearing him say nice things about people in your life."

"While it's not what I'd think of when I think emotions, feeling good about yourself is an emotion," Av said to Aren. "Feeling good about yourself leads to happiness, which is usually a strong emotion for a queen."

"Anger and rage tend to be stronger," Aren said idly, then turned to Raven. "Save your strength to shift things back to where they belong. We need you fully functioning so that I can access the records when I get back to the palace."

"That might burn the poor man out," Raven said as she faded away.

"His apprentice is almost trained, might even be able to take over for him," Aren said in response.

They set off down the hallway again with Aren in the lead. There was no longer an explanation or any talking, but Av at least felt as if he had a firmer grip on the situation.

He also now knew that Raven would follow Aren's commands.

"Is part of the plan to get Raven back to the palace?" Av asked as Aren pulled to a sudden stop.

Aren looked at the door before her. "Yes, it is. We have to find where I put the fountain first. Moving her to a new location when she's so fragile could be disastrous. If she can shift from here, to where the fountain is, it should place her back to where her other pieces are, the ones the commoners didn't know existed. There's enough magic stored in those rocks to keep her alive indefinitely, but if I'm also there, she can consume whatever is necessary to repair herself."

"Good, because I'd love to introduce her to a few lords," Av said with a grin.

"Once she repairs, she'll be able to lift physical objects just like a person," Aren said, frowning at Av.

"Which means she'll kill people," Av said with a shrug. "Maybe if she starts killing lords, you won't frown on me killing them."

"I don't, but we need to end the war first. Raven's pointed out that we need the lords to pay for the war, and then we need to pay back the lords before we kill them. Otherwise, it'll appear as if we are killing off those we owe coin to and that's not a good way to bring loyalty."

"Can we do that for a couple of the worst ones first, then kill them?" Av asked. "Then, to warn the ones who are sort of on the line, we'll repay our debt not to them, but to their heirs as warning!"

"Sure?" Aren asked with a shrug. "I don't know, let's get through the war first. Do me a favour and knock on the door."

Av reached around Aren and knocked with all the authority he could muster. Loud and hard, as if he were in charge of Castle Grey, because he assumed that's what Aren wanted. Er snapped open the door a moment later and glared first at Av, then at Aren as she pushed past him and into the room.

"Raven's invisible and talking to Aren," Av said to his uncle.

"Oh." Er moved to the side and motioned for Av to come into the room.

"Where's the baron's library?" Aren asked.

Er motioned vaguely. "Northern side of the castle, in a watch tower."

Aren chuckled to herself. "And you never thought it odd that the queen's symbol is carved above the door?"

"Queens have symbols now?" Olea asked, coming out of the bathing room wrapped in a robe. "Come to think of it, that did look familiar to me. Maybe that's what's carved under the rug in the heir rooms. They used to be the rooms for the queen who was mated to the baron. You know, for those times it was just about breeding."

"That's why you looked like you knew it?" Er asked with a frown. "Could have saved us some trouble if you hadn't hidden the damned thing."

"It bothered me," Olea muttered, moving towards Aren. "But if that's the queen's library, where's the baron's library?"

"It's supposed to be in these rooms," Aren said. "It must have been moved to the queen's library at some point, and the books were just mashed together. You'll have to read them all."

"There are over five hundred books," Er protested. "And I've only got three scribes."

"You won't need to look for the information if we can get Raven working properly," Aren countered, reaching out to take Olea's hand. "You and I need to have a chat about linking on purpose and directing magic. The problem the mates of the barons have had is that they are linked to their daughters, but their daughters aren't linked to them. Raven thinks this has something to do with how you're raised to protect your daughters over your own life. She also thinks that you have the best chance of breaking this idea because you weren't born in the North."

"What's that mean?" Olea asked in response.

"Instead of having five or six flows of magic, there would be one into Raven, yours. Because you're linked to me, we think we can speed up the process. We want her as solid as possible when we transfer her back to the palace."

"You can't take her. She's ours!" Er shouted.

"Calm down," Av said to Er.

"You can't keep her," Aren said calmly. "Raven *is* the palace. Her absence has caused the foundations to no longer link to the one who sits the throne, which is likely the cause of the short-lived queens. She's a buffer, a direction for our magic. Raven is the one who multiplies the magic in the stones. Unless a queen knows how to do it with her magic, only the palace can do it."

"That would give her control over who sat the throne," Av said quietly.

"And how powerful the queen became," Aren added. "She calls herself a kill switch. Her processes act as archives, well for the magic, direction for the river of magic, and as a balancing point. Queens didn't go mad while sitting her because of everything she did. The reason why she does so many things—whereas normal landscape magic does one thing like, teleportation—is because each part of the palace is a part of her. Separating the two of them is like separating the spirit from the body. The body has continued to live on, but it has barely survived, and it is slowly dying.

Er moved to Av's side and bent in close. "Has she been doing that since she woke?"

"Archives," Av muttered. "Raven had said she was going to teach Aren about magic, but I thought she meant how to use magic. Not the entire history of it."

"I can hear you just fine," Aren said from Olea's side.

"I thought you couldn't access that all at once?" Er said.

"I can't, if I did, it would make my head explode," Aren responded. "Like an egg against a wall. The more times I access the knowledge, the more likely it is to stick. Like learning in a round-about way. Plus, Raven's still here explaining it all to me."

"Raven is ours," Er said sternly.

"No, she's not. Raven is a thinking landscape magic, and while she appreciates all you've done for her, she wants to go home. You swore you'd bow to the throne."

Er was bristling, and Av didn't blame him. Sharing something was a lesson warriors had to learn hard and fast; no doubt Er had learned that lesson. But there were some things that a man never thought he'd have to give up and when it came time, it could be difficult.

"Do you appreciate what you are asking me?"

"She's already begun work on Grey," Aren said.

"Grey?" Olea asked.

"You can name it whatever you please, but it would insist on the name of the building it resides in. The palace was named after Raven when other such landscape magics were created and placed in other locations. Those magics have likely passed, or fractured to the point of utter madness.

Castle Grey, on the other hand, was built on Raven's instructions, it can be made into what the palace once was."

"I beg your pardon?" Er asked. "What's that mean?"

"Raven will help Olea create a magic like herself, with all the benefits of having Raven remain here at Castle Grey. But only if you do as she asks. And as I ask. If at any time you or yours become disloyal to the throne, Grey will end you all. Or Raven will, if she's still here."

"The high lord is here to bring us the throne's wishes," Olea said.

"With Grey, I have no need of a high lord in the North. The title would be removed, leaving only baron in its place. However, to retain the ability to call yourselves baron, and to collect taxes before paying forward to the palace, I will require a change, or forty, to your laws. I don't quite know how many yet."

"Let me guess," Er growled. "You want us to be figureheads?"

"Under Mirmae's treaty, you would have been figureheads," Aren said calmly. "Under my offer, you would have the right to rule the North as a land attached, or under palace laws. A... province, I believe the South wanted to be called? A nod to your independence and what you have done for us by keeping Raven alive, safeguarding our history."

"What do you know you want to change?" Olea asked.

"The baron will no longer be bound to mate a queen, we already discussed that. If you wish to keep the strongest warrior inheriting, by all means. But the North has few queens, and you know the other reason why, Er."

"It was a fling," Er protested.

"The lines of magic between the pair are no longer faint," Aren said. "Their blood has mingled, and your son is not one to walk away from a child, or half-guard it. He has to mate palace blood anyhow. What's wrong with her?"

"She's not a queen!" Olea protested.

"She's stronger blood than you," Aren countered. "She may be a healer, but she is stronger than any healer on palace lands, and I'm willing to bet she's stronger than those here in the North. Yes, she's a healer. But I can't name a rank who I would say is stronger than her. Besides. Raven says they could have fourteen healthy, living children, all of whom could be ranks."

Av managed to get his mind to work. "I don't recall Aren giving you a choice. You said you'd obey. She's given you the terms of your obedience."

Er growled at Av, who smiled slowly in response. He made a motion to his uncle, certain that he could win a challenge.

Chapter Twenty-Six

Url walked into his father's rooms, a pup under each arm. He moved around Av and Er, and went straight for his mother, who was seated before the fire with Aren.

"Here," he said, dumping the puppies into Aren's lap and watching the woman's eyes go large. He had meant to hold them, not to keep, but seeing the look of childish delight on Aren's face, he couldn't very well take back his word.

Url glanced at his mother, whose eyebrows were almost to her hairline.

"You like dogs, Aren?" Olea asked.

"Yes," Aren said, lifting her head as the dogs tried to lick her face. "I've wanted one for a very long time."

"Well, you are in luck. Those two are mutts. One of Er's prized dogs got out while in heat and found herself a wolf. They won't be any good to us, and if you don't take them, we'll have to cull them to keep our lines pure."

"Er won't mind?" Aren asked. "I know how breeders get with their dogs. Don't want the line spreading any which way, and mutts need to be culled, not just given away."

"He won't mind at all," Url said quickly.

Er would mind, he'd mind a great deal. But he also wasn't heartless. If Er had seen the look on Aren's face at the implication that she could keep the dogs, he wouldn't have made a fuss at all.

The reason the baron would have cared wasn't even because he wanted to keep the lines pure. It was because mutts amongst the line were gifted, or sold when no one was found deserving of a gift. Er liked to gift one to his children upon their expecting their first child, to protect them no matter where they went.

A Marl and a wolf made for a large, intelligent dog. They were the types of mutts that Er liked gifting to his daughters, and there wasn't a doubt in Url's mind that the prized dog had been let out on purpose.

There were still two others, but these were smaller than the rest. He had been bringing them to his father for special care, not to give to Aren.

The queen giggled, then laughed.

The whole room went still. Url swallowed the lump in his throat and looked to his father and Av, still on the floor, their challenge forgotten. Av helped Er to his feet and approached Aren cautiously.

"What have you got there?" Av asked, his voice low as if he were speaking to the puppies and not to Aren.

Aren gathered the two of them up and showed Av as the pups struggled and wiggled in her arms, trying to lick her face.

"Url, those were supposed to be a surprise," Er growled.

One of the pups, the male, growled at Er from Aren's arms. There was something about the deep voice of the baron that brought the dogs to heel, but only after they learned who was pack leader.

"Oops?" Url said, looking to his father for forgiveness.

There was a sort of pity on Er's face when he turned to Aren. "Go get them some rope at least, son."

Url nodded and went to the chest where his father kept items for the dogs. As he returned to Aren and motioned to the floor, he tried to listen in on the conversation his father was having with Av. What he did manage to hear were instructions on how to train the dogs.

Marls were fiercely loyal to their master. Er kept only a few very close to him because the creatures tended to lose their minds when their master died. Just as Er mourned the death of each he held close.

Aren laughed again as one of the puppies tumbled over.

Url wondered why there wasn't magic flooding the room. Her giggle had been broadcast across most of the palace. A laugh surely should have done something besides startle the people in the room.

He showed her how to play with the puppies and explained how to play with them to train them. Once he was certain she had the basics, and he knew that Aren had played with dogs before, he moved to his father's side.

Av motioned out of the rooms with his head and the three men left, closing the door behind them.

"I'm sorry," Url said to his father. "I didn't mean to, but you should have seen the look on her face."

"I had intended to give them one, but one of the larger ones," Er grumbled. "I wanted the runts for myself. To keep me busy while you all went off to war."

"I'm sorry," Url said again.

"How difficult are they to train?" Av asked.

"Not difficult in the least. If you have a kennel master, he could show you how to train them to hunt, but they aren't meant to be kennel dogs. At least not with your dogs, they'll eat your dogs. Or terrify them to death."

"There's no kennel on palace grounds, we don't use dogs to hunt," Av said, then shrugged. "We hardly hunt. Most of our food is purchased or donated by locals depending on how much they owe in taxes."

"You mean to tell me that the North isn't the only land to use items to pay taxes?" Er asked.

Av winced. "Aren doesn't know that part, only the coin master and kitchen master. It's cheaper because donating an animal is half of what it would cost if we purchased it. Works out for the most part, and if a hunter is behind on taxes, we don't put pressure on him, which has in the past resulted in donations after taxes have been paid."

"If you raise them with you, they'll never leave your side," Url said.

"Is there a way for me to train them, but have them never leave Aren's side?" Av asked.

"No, she'd have to be the one to train them," Er murmured. "Once they impress on her, once they decide she's their leader, you can train them but only if you are fully submitted to Aren. If you try to do it otherwise they'll... uh... they'll try to rip you to shreds."

"They'd have to be trained to attack a person to do that."

"They'll come to about here," Er said, motioning towards his leg. "You might not have seen our wolves, and you haven't seen a Marl yet, but I'll be sure to show you a pelt, and their mother before you go. They aren't small dogs, not by far."

"They were bred, to start, for the size of the animal, to scare off palace lords," Url said. "We just have to release them, and the dogs think it's a bit of good fun and the lords piss themselves in fear. Once we had the size, we started breeding intelligence and other factors. They've crossed with wolves before, but we tend to keep that thread small. Easier to control them."

"And to maintain the wire coats, which help in nearly all weather," Er murmured. "I'll provide you with the necessities for their diet and care as they age, as well as a few toys and maintenance items. You may wish to trim their coat from time to time, depending on how mangy you want them to look. Brushing helps, but lords are all about these sleek dogs this generation. The wire coat isn't as loved as it once was."

"Unless it's to keep the dog cool in the summer, there's no way Aren will trim a dog's coat for its looks," Av said sternly. "Especially for the sake of a lord's precious belief of proper dog grooming."

"Did you only come for the dogs?" Er asked.

"I feel that some of the younger warriors are getting riled up, I was wondering if you felt the same way," Url said quietly. "I've never really felt it like this before, so I'm a little confused."

"They are riled," Av said.

Er nodded slowly. "First Aren arrives and fights a warrior. Then the elders getting uppity over the fountain disappearing, and this one,"—with a motion to Av—"putting Reld in his spot over an as yet unknown warrior. That's a great deal of new for such a short time. They could be wondering if the hierarchy is going to change, which means if we have a gathering they may attempt to challenge your rule."

"I can take the ones who are getting riled," Url growled.

Av made a sound at the back of his throat, drawing Url's attention.

"Why don't you redirect that energy instead?" Av asked. "We've got a war to plan, a war that needs voluntary bodies and the young among our rank are most likely to submit to an army to bloody their hands and come back victorious and with a built reputation."

"You can't just redirect a warrior's murderous rage," Url said with a shake of his head.

"No, no." Er held up a hand to stop Url. "Ervam mentioned something about the master title. There aren't enough warriors so the master is to keep them from killing each other."

"Sometimes it meant asking the lords for a criminal that was about to be executed," Av said with a shrug. "Sometimes it was sending them out to fight a skirmish on palace lands to justify the rule of a lord. Or to slaughter a man and his bloodline for some crime against the throne. You just need to dangle something in front of them which is worth more than tearing your throat out."

"That would require a great deal of respect, a reputation that can't be beat… and…" Url struggled.

"Maybe up here it would, which means I'll need your help," Av said, then smiled. "You may end up needing to crack a few skulls, but only because they'll be clamouring over one another to be on the front line."

"I don't have that kind of a reputation," Url growled.

Av looked to Er for help. The baron stared back at Av, then turned his attention to Url and jabbed a finger at Av with a frown and a head shake.

"What, he doesn't have that sort of a reputation either," Url said.

"The hunt," Er said. "Rewel. Reld. If Av attacks one more warrior with an 'r' in his name, I'm going to start thinking he has something against specific sounds. He is also mate to the throne, as in leading the army that he wants to recruit for. He hasn't revealed, to anyone, who he was protecting from Reld's advances, he stabbed your grandmother—"

"Gently, I stabbed her gently."

"—when that was exactly what he said he was going to do. And let's not forget that he had the balls to call us out on hypocrisy in front of your cousins, several of whom will be at the gathering. If that isn't enough to sway them, I don't know what is."

"How do you two not have this reputation?" Av asked.

"We were called out on hypocrisy," Url said.

"We didn't put Reld in his place for putting another warrior at risk," Er added quickly.

"Shouldn't you have done those things?" Av demanded.

"Elders," Url and Er said at the same time.

"If anyone else had been involved, if anyone else had tried to tell us what to do, we would have stepped up," Er said. "But we couldn't because of the elders, and in the case of Reld, he was pulled in to punish a warrior for stepping out of line. So how well do you think it would have gone if I had disobeyed? My mother tried to stab me in my bad leg!"

Av pointed at the leg and then set his weight. "Now's a good time to talk about that, since you brought it into the conversation."

"It works," Er growled through gritted teeth.

"Most of the time," Av countered. "Let's forget the fact that you need to set an example for aging warriors for a moment, and instead talk about what I'd actually like to know. How did it happen?"

"There's not much to the tale," Er said shortly.

"When we were out hunting, and I almost turned on you, that other one to the side said 'like father, like son' and asked if you were prepared to lose a chunk of your other leg."

"You were aware of that?" Er asked.

"Sort of, it was a bit like I was drunk," Av said with a shake of his head. "But that's not the point."

"And he can remember what he's done in a rage and still get out of bed in the morning," Url grumbled to himself jealously.

"It's a blessing not to remember," Av snarled at Url, then turned on Er. "What happened?"

"Have you met my bodyguard?" Er asked, motioning to Url.

He smiled slowly at Av, showing off his teeth. The only time Url was introduced as such was when he was allowed to cause bodily harm.

Av looked at Url, frowned, and then looked at Er. "But he had guards. My father killed them all."

"No one but the heir and the baron are supposed to know," Er said quietly. "It's in the heir's best interest to keep the baron alive, but also places him in such a position that he learns everything that is going on, all the dirty secrets."

"You knew?" Av demanded.

"I knew that your mother went walking and my father went out after her. I didn't know what took place in the woods because if I had gone sniffing after her, I might be the one who was dead. Did I suspect? Yes. But I didn't tell your father, I didn't ask her, and when I heard what the mate had planned on doing, I tried to stop her. The boy had Marilton blood in him and if Mirmae didn't want to out the baron, then so be it.

"By the spirits, how was I to know that he *made* her run? That he went after her, fully knowing that she wouldn't be able to say no to *any* available body? That he could control the rage? Which is something I should probably start teaching you how to do because being aware is the first step."

"Don't change the subject, what do you mean, made her run?"

"Your father has no doubt taught you about holly and pine."

Av nodded. "Are you telling me there's something like that for queens?"

"It drives them almost mad. They aren't aware. They don't remember the next morning. She might not have remembered, except he stayed with her and made certain she knew. When a queen walks with the spirits, she rises with child. There's never been any other way to it."

"There are surely options here, just as there are at the palace," Av said.

"No one who walks with the spirits has been able to shake the child," Url said quietly. "The healers won't even try any longer. The only option is to carry to term and then do what you will with the babe."

"When Mirmae was to announce paternity, she was going to say Jer was your father's. The mate accused her of adultery, of Jer being a bastard. Mirmae called the queens, including my mother and my mate, and they listened to her story and agreed unanimously that while the child was my father's, it was not the product of adultery. These tribunals, when they come together, draw a great deal of rumour. To squash any stories from being told, everyone is told what happened. The day your father found out what had been done, he taught us a fear of ranks we had long forgotten. He took your mother and you and Jer back to the room. Said he needed to walk to clear his head. By that time my father and I were in the map room, we were arguing about it. I remember that. I remember hearing the sounds outside the door. There wasn't a doubt in my mind what was going on, and I'd heard the old tales just as my father did, just as those on the other side of the door had. If a trainer or warrior starts hunting in the castle, or at the palace, those who are not a part of the hunt are to kneel with their heads down. A warrior will not attack a person who is submitting in such a manner, as long as their eyes remain on their lap. I went down, but was a fool and looked back up."

"Story around the castle is he pulled Ervam out of the rage," Url said quietly.

"What did he do?" Av asked.

"Stabbed into the meat of my leg and ripped the item out, tearing muscle and other bits," Er said, rubbing the leg absently. "Healers stopped up the bleeding to keep me from dying and when Ervam woke, he demanded they finish the job, but bits were missing. It looks whole, but doesn't feel it some days."

"How many did he kill?" Av asked.

"One," Er responded. "My father. The others were still alive. A few have passed from age, but he didn't kill any of them. He crippled them to uselessness but didn't take it that extra step to kill them. We... we told him that he had killed them. That rests better on a man's conscience, rather than knowing that he had not only destroyed twenty lives but forced them to continue living as an example of his rage when his family is hurt."

"I don't feel so bad about killing Rewel," Av said with a desperate sort of laugh.

Chapter Twenty-Seven

As Av readied for the gathering, Aren put on her training clothing and braided her hair. It wasn't until he turned to say goodbye that he realized what she was doing.

"You can't come with me," he said in a strangled voice.

"Raven says queens used to go to gatherings all the time," Aren said shortly. "I'll be perfectly safe."

"If anyone touches you, I'll break their legs!"

"That's why I'll be safe," Aren countered.

Av gritted his teeth and glared at her, well aware of the fact that she wouldn't back down, not from this. Whatever her reasons for wanting to go to the gathering, Aren was not about to share them. If Raven was about, she wasn't yet strong enough to appear and tell Av what was going on.

"I have an issue with you going to a gathering," Av said, shaking a finger at her. "But I also know that I have no way to convince you otherwise."

"Why do you have an issue?" Aren asked, blinking at him.

"It's dangerous," Av said.

"You're not afraid that, while at the gathering, I might spot another warrior whose blood is better than your own and I might decide to have a one-night stand to strengthen my bloodline, thus denying you your right to be the only one to breed with me?"

Av opened his mouth, staring at Aren.

That was *exactly* what he was afraid of.

"Perhaps now is a good time to talk about the fact that I have no intention of sleeping with other men while mated to you," Aren said quietly. "And these creatures at Castle Grey, while they are near to warriors, are not so close to the full rank as yourself, who I know for a fact will breed true with me every time. So why risk a maybe when I have an absolute?"

"No comment on liking my bed manners?" Av asked.

"Raven's teaching me a few things about that too, by nattering on when I want her to remain silent," Aren grumbled irritably with a glance to the other side of the room.

"Wait, mating means you don't mate with others."

"It's called breeding, and if I did, especially at Castle Grey, how would you ever know?" Aren asked.

Again, Av was stunned into silence. Because Aren was right and yet at the same time, he was afraid that just such a thing might happen to him. He hadn't realized that that had been why he was upset about Aren going to the gathering, but now that he knew, he was thinking back, wondering how many other times his irritability could have been explained by something so simple.

He was afraid. As a warrior he couldn't be afraid, others would see it as a weakness.

"I've just scared you more, haven't I?" Aren asked.

"I'd say that's an accurate statement," Av grumbled in response.

"Then I suppose it's a good thing I don't care about breeding," Aren muttered, walking around Av to the door. "Try to act like you knew I was going to do whatever I do, would you?"

"Out there? Of course. Except in your defense, I will never say that your behaviour was unexpected. But in here? In the privacy of my rooms? You're damned right I'm going to question you."

"These aren't your rooms."

"I could pee on everything, then it'd be mine," Av growled back with a grin.

"Olea would blame me for that, I'd never hear the end of it," Aren said as she opened the door. "However, these rooms are not private, not by far."

Av grudgingly agreed and followed Aren out of the room. She looked around, wondering where to go.

It was his turn to lead the way.

No warrior was ever told where a gathering was, he simply found his way to it. A few might pass on word to their friends that there was a gathering happening, or the women might be informed of when and where, but normally one had to follow their instincts.

It didn't take long for Av to find the large hall where warriors were gathering. Some were half his age, not even old enough to shave yet. Many ranged from Aren's age up past Av's age. These were not the young riled warriors that Av thought he would be meeting with, these were…

Everyone at Castle Grey who felt out of place. They would never cause trouble for those above them, but these warriors didn't feel comfortable around Olea and her daughters.

Any queen born in the North made her way to Castle Grey when she was ready to find a mate. If a warrior wanted a chance at a queen, he had to get into the castle early and young, before he was old enough to be thinking about mating. That meant that the men in the hall had come looking for a mate and hadn't found one, but couldn't leave if they wanted to still have a chance at capturing the attention of a queen.

The warriors looked to Av, then turned to Aren as one. A quiet came over them as Aren drifted around Av and approached the group. She poked a youth between the eyes, and then laughed at his startled response.

Her laugh made the air around her waver, sending a warm tingle through Av and then the crowd.

Suddenly warriors were claiming dances and jostling one another for a chance to present themselves to Aren. Av noted that none of them did the jostling near enough to Aren for the queen to accidentally be struck, they left a circle around her while they tried to sort out the pecking order.

"Enough!" Av called, his voice echoing off the walls.

The warriors stopped in various degrees of motion.

He watched them for a very long moment, making certain that they were going to obey him.

"Url will have the first dance with Lady Aren, then you." Av pointed out a warrior in the crowd who looked to be about his age. The man had green eyes instead of the

Marilton grey. "After that, no one will dance with her unless she approaches them. Do I make myself clear?"

"But—" one of the youths tried to say.

"I choose my dance partner, not you," Aren said.

Av looked to her and found that she was watching him.

"I suggested Url because he knows you've never danced these dances before. I suggested him"—Av motioned again to the other warrior—"because I'm sure he knows that if he steps on your toes, I will gut him with his belt."

"Not because of his eyes?" Aren asked.

The chit knew that he had chosen someone who was not his blood to dance with her. He wasn't even entirely certain why he had chosen that warrior, but it seemed the right thing to do.

"He does have pretty eyes," Av offered her in response. "That'll give you something to look at as he bores you with war stories."

"I suppose," Aren sighed out. "When's Url arriving?"

"Shortly. Eat something before you start dancing," Av said, motioning to the tables off to one side that were overflowing with food.

There was no one tending the table of food. There were no women in the hall at all. Av knew that the North encouraged women to attend gatherings, but if none of them wanted to be there, there was no way to force them to go.

He knew the other warriors were wary of him. He was a rival for whatever blood was available, even if he had brought his mate with him. Av didn't doubt that there were a few warriors in the group wondering if they could best Av and take his place at Aren's side. He even caught a few of them watching the queen as she walked to the food tables wondering what to eat.

This was why he had wanted Aren to stay in the rooms. He couldn't fight them all off, if they decided to turn on him. He couldn't—

There was a yelp behind him, followed by a solid thump.

Av turned to the food tables where Aren stood with a dented serving tray in her hands and a cowering youth at her feet.

"Try that again," she snapped down at him, throwing the tray at him as he skittered back and limped away from her.

Av tried to wipe his smile away as he turned back to the group of warriors.

They were now keenly interested in the queen in a different sort of way. A few eyes were going a little wider, and Av could almost see them making the leaps and bounds, at what they were thinking about.

Having a queen willing, and able, to fight back physically… No more fear of the queens because a queen might light them on fire or make them explode. They would be on an even ground, that they knew how to handle and how to confront, perhaps even best.

And then he saw a few of the older ones shudder as old instincts kicked in.

They were wondering what it would be like to capture a queen who beat off all the other warriors.

"She's mine," he said to the group.

The group moved away from him, and thus farther away from Aren, as one. He smiled at them.

"A queen who is taught to fight will bite, scratch, and claw at anyone stupid enough to try her," he said calmly to them. "Instead of wasting her magic, which she may not have much of at the time of an attack, she will stab her foes, and she will beat them with whatever object she has at hand. She doesn't fear a warrior, even if she's not fully trained because she believes she can defend herself, and so she can."

"What about chasing?" one of the older warriors asked.

"No one chases queens on palace lands," Av said.

"But what if we organized a chase and…" The warrior motioned behind Av, towards Aren.

"I would beat you all into the ground and still claim her as mine," Av growled in warning.

"Wh-what about having women just speckled along?" offered a youth. "We, uh, we could. And then…"

It seemed the group was thinking as one because there were several whimpers and some uncomfortable shifting. Av understood, slightly, what they wanted.

They wanted Aren to lead a run and for Av to chase her, bringing the other warriors along just for the run. There would be women, volunteers looking to breed, along the way for those who fell out of the chase.

What he didn't understand was why they wanted to do that, why they would settle for commoners over the queen they were chasing. Why would a warrior chase a queen he knew he couldn't have?

"What did you say to them to make them go that colour?" Aren asked.

Av leaped a foot into the air and skittered away from Aren as the queen's innocent look darkened. Only for a moment, and then she gave the warriors gathered that doe-eyed look.

"What were you talking about?" she asked them.

To which the group of warriors looked embarrassed, then surprised before they all found everything else in the hall interesting.

"They want me to chase you while they chase after," Av said. "Their idea is to do it, and I still take you to ground, but they get to take others to ground who volunteer for that sort of thing."

Aren's eyes seemed to fog over. She turned her head slightly as if listening to someone. Av assumed Raven was saying something, but whatever it was made Aren frown and look back at Av.

"But what if one of them jumps me?" Aren asked.

"They wouldn't."

Aren pointed to one of the youths, not the one she had smacked with the tray, but another one. "He would. He especially enjoys his women resisting him. So far he's found willing volunteers, but in a chase, who's to say he could keep his head?"

"I didn't say they could do the chase," Av said quickly.

"Not right now, no," Aren said sternly. "Maybe near palace grounds, with palace women. Maybe not the ladies. Maybe a couple of the wards, if they want. And are over eighteen. So, women who were once wards and don't yet have a mate but are interested in breeding. I'll check around. And not right away. Once I'm trained, so that if they do catch me, or try to cheat, I can take them out."

Av stared at Aren. Desperately, he jabbed a finger over Aren's shoulder, to where he assumed Raven was still standing.

"All she said was that she understood why they'd want to chase after a queen, even if they knew they weren't going to catch her. It's the chase they're after, and their instincts drive them to do it... They seem drawn to it like you were drawn to me."

"What does that mean?" Av asked as Aren turned to the spot where Raven stood.

"Oh," Aren said with a nod. "You have a point, that's a really good reason for a queen to take that risk."

"Still standing here, can't hear the invisible person," Av said sternly.

Aren turned back to Av, then to the group of gathered warriors. "It will be done on palace grounds before you go to war, but as you're about to. If you don't go to war, you don't get to chase me. I cannot promise the number of willing women, but I do promise to try to match one for each of you, perhaps more if I can manage it. I also will not promise not to kill one or more of you, if you are overcome and attempt to take me against my will."

"You'll let us chase you?" one of the older warriors squeaked out.

"Only those who go to war for me."

"Why?" Av asked.

"Your instincts lead you to good blood. It's entirely possible that chasing me will be the same as them taking a queen to ground, even if they take a commoner. When a warrior takes a queen to ground, there's almost always a rank born of it."

"By letting them chase you and take palace ladies to ground..." Av trailed off as the idea occurred to him.

"And those who were wards but can't find mates are more likely to find mates after producing a rank. But if they don't, the rank will grow up around the palace."

"I'm training you, not the palace guard," Av said sternly to Aren. "And if you need to use magic to make someone explode, you do it."

"For starters, there would have to be volunteers for the army first," Aren said. "No volunteers, no chasing."

Av bared his teeth at Aren and growled. The queen shifted her weight and gave him a look that stated he had best bite her and stop growling about everything.

Instead, Av snarled at the warriors gathered. "Some of you are going to volunteer, or I'm going to start slaughtering idiots."

Chapter Twenty-Eight

Url walked into the hall and found an odd thing.

Aren drifting among kneeling warriors.

Av bristling with a frustrated anger that was slowly tapering off.

He walked up to his cousin and looked him over, then looked at Aren. Av's look was that of a frustrated man who had been denied his right to a woman. The kneeling warriors accepted Aren's hand as she moved amongst them, touching it for a moment and then lowering their heads.

In his gut, Url knew what was going on, but his rational mind couldn't put it together.

Warriors didn't kneel for queens, except his father for his mother, and Url hoped to never walk in on that again. But when a queen arrived at Castle Grey the warriors did not kneel for her. So how did these ones know to kneel? By following instinct alone?

His rank had come before Aren's surely—

Aren glanced over her shoulder, at Url, and his knees buckled. She drifted away from the group, hardly seeming to move as she came towards him and set a hand on his head. Not allowing him to take her hand, but accepting him nonetheless.

He couldn't put words to the frightened warmth he felt. The acceptance and yet the fear of that feeling, because he had no idea what was going on and Castle Grey knew almost everything there was about being a warrior. Aren's hand travelled down the side of his face, to his jaw. The shudder that rolled through him was near to sexual pleasure.

Av reached out and set a hand on Url's shoulder, causing a different sort of warmth. In that strong grip was the comfort of home, the promise of protection, and so many things that Url shouldn't have been able to feel from touch alone.

When Av offered a hand, Url took it and was pulled to his feet, then slapped on the back.

"Looks like we have the start of an army," Av said with a large smile.

"How?" Url asked. "I mean, I know plenty of warriors who are starving for blood, but few here are on that list."

"Men starve for different sorts of blood," Aren said distantly, drifting back towards the food tables.

"She's volunteered to be chased," Av whispered quickly to Url. "Those here that volunteered will be able to participate with women from palace lands volunteering to be taken by those that fall behind."

Url's breath hitched for a moment. His heart seemed to skip a beat at the idea.

And then he thought of Nae and relaxed.

"Oh, by the spirits, Nae is pregnant," Url gasped out before he realized what he was saying.

"From what Aren says, yes," Av said. "Why do you think that?"

"Because I felt upset by not being invited until I recalled Nae," Url whimpered out. "My mother has told us often enough. I can't mate her. I have to mate a queen."

"As of our mating, you can mate whomever you please, by Aren's command," Av said quietly. "It's one of the few demands the throne would make on the North. The baron mating a queen implies that up here is a throne. It's not. You should be encouraged to find a queen, but if you can't find yourself a queen and find yourself a healer instead, everyone's to keep their complaining to themselves."

"Oh?" Url asked, feeling a bit faint.

"No, that's not true. You have to mate a woman from palace lands, don't you?" Av asked.

The idea of introducing Nae to his grandmother ran through Url's head. It made his stomach twist in a funny sort of way.

"I'm going to be a father," Url protested. "I'm younger than you are!"

"So was Jer, so are a lot of warriors," Av grumbled, then frowned. "Actually, I'm the only warrior I know who hasn't had a child by my age. That's odd. I should ask Raven about that."

"Raven?" Url asked.

Something flickered beside him. He swore it was a woman in a gold and red dress. Recalling Raven from breakfast, what the magic had looked like, Url looked to the spot, then Av.

"I'm going to be a father, and you just want to talk about you?" Url demanded.

"We could talk about how she's going to gut you when she finds out," Av muttered. "Or what her reaction will be once it clues in that you, the father of her unborn child, is marching into war. I hear healers are especially stabby about warriors they find themselves linked to."

And a slow, knowing smile.

"What did she do to you?" Url asked.

"My father's been training her for the past decade," Av said, lifting a finger. "And she liked to bite all through child and teen years. She is not a woman to be taken lightly."

"Does that mean Nae is mine?" Url asked.

"No, it means you bred her."

Url considered the information. "What if I wanted to make her mine?"

This time Av was silent, considering. "You bed a queen to claim her, but that's acceptable. You bed a healer to breed her. The difference between the two is that queens can be caged because we've been taught how to keep them close. Healers look for reasons to prove that their rank is dangerous. Queens don't have to because we protect them."

"What are you talking about now?" Aren asked, approaching them with a plate of food.

"Url just realized Nae was pregnant."

"Nae?" Aren asked.

"You've made mention to her!" Av said rather loudly.

Aren chewed on a carrot stick and looked innocently at Url. The queen chewed for far too long as she studied Url.

"Oh," she said, drawing out the word. "That's what that is."

"She doesn't have access to all the information at once, does she?" Url asked Av.

"No, only parts at a time," Av muttered. "I'm guessing accessing it on purpose takes time."

"No, I see the connection, I just didn't remember what that meant," Aren said, motioning up and down with the remains of the carrot stick. "By the way, Url, I'd strongly suggest you keep her on. Mate that woman. It's good, the... Raven says I'm not supposed to actually tell people that."

"She and I would make good breeding?" Url squeaked out.

Aren nodded and bit into the carrot again. "But Raven says people like this idea of having control of their choice in mate. And... has just now used *me* as an example. Then again, I see her point with that."

"The fact that you two were basically humping one another, and then you mate and start fighting?" Url asked, then smiled slowly as Av attempted to murder him with a look alone.

"It's very normal for a queen and warrior to fight once they're mated," Aren said, nodding as she did. "Em and Jer, Er and Olea. They liked each other before they mated. Telm would probably say that we're being stubborn and trying to protect ourselves, and in the past these instincts have saved many warriors and many queens, but we're just being stupid."

"Then why didn't Jer's save him from Em?" Url asked.

Aren shrugged. "His instincts told him that Mar was his. Em was good blood, but she obviously had some way to stop it. Or maybe Mar was just so good that Em wasn't actually capable of having more."

"You talk funny now," Av said sternly to Aren.

"It's a lot of information, and it changes the way I look at the world," Aren said. "There are so many magics to change instincts, or initiate them. When it comes time, I'll have to tell you how to bring it out in me, to drive me to that point, but even that is magic. I mean, even instinct in general. Url knows he's going to be a father on instinct alone, but he never realizes that he and Nae are forever connected and even if they don't mate, he will always know if she's happy or sad or angry because they pair so well that they've meshed together.

"It's not just queens who can make others feel things, anyone can. Anyone can make anyone else aware of their presence and demand to be seen and... and no one ever uses that to their advantage because we tell everyone that they can't be that person, they can't do those things. Do you know why we tell them no? Because we want to hobble our queens and make certain that they can't see this giant world around them. I could leave tomorrow, I could cross the waters and none of you would ever be able to find me again, but I could find any of you, anywhere in the world. I could even contact you, if I had enough magic. And now I know how to get that magic.

"Seeing that makes the world so much smaller and yet so much larger all at the same time."

"Could you maybe get to the point when you talk to me?" Url asked, wincing when Aren frowned at him.

"You and Nae make sparkly babies, and I want you to make as many as possible," Aren said, frown deepening. "But only if she wants to."

"And why don't I want to chase you?" Url asked.

"Because you'd be chasing the wrong sort of rank."

"What if Nae joined you on this run to help keep others off of you?" Av asked.

Url whimpered as a heat came over him the likes of which he had never felt before. He blinked his watery eyes and rubbed at his face.

"Av, go play with the warriors, do what a master does," Aren said sternly.

"As you command," Av said quietly, moving away immediately.

Aren's full focus was on Url. "You are the culmination of warriors and queens breeding together for two hundred years. Your bloodline is well known for creating ranks, most especially warriors and queens. But a healthy world needs more than that."

"I'm guessing you'd use Ervam and Mirmae as an example," Url responded gravely.

"Two hundred years of warriors and queens produced one trainer," Aren said, holding up a finger. "A trainer and a queen produced two warriors, one of which is a true warrior, we both know what that means. Any child he has will be ranked. Raven's spent half her time telling me about sex and the other half telling me that if I find myself unable to have more children, I should ask him if he'd be willing to breed on another of her choosing because she can find one who could breed him."

"And what does she think Nae and I will make?" Url asked.

"She hasn't met Nae," Aren said with a shake of her head. "Telm would be the one to ask. Personally, I think a rank is still a child, something Ervam told me. No matter what is born to you or Av, they're still just children. They deserve to be able to be children until they turn ten at the very least. Let them laugh, let them play. This training from a young age, what does that do for you, exactly?"

"Warriors have a great deal of energy," Url said quickly, aware of how commoners viewed young boys training.

They looked down on it because children had to be children.

Having grown up training from the time he could walk, Url felt commoners were misinformed. Those training times were the only times that he had felt normal, that his energy was put to good use. Growing up without that training? Url pitied Mie for not starting training until recently.

Mie must have felt so out of place, so ready for anything and yet never understanding what he was ready for.

"I see," Aren said.

"You see?" Url asked.

"You think loudly, I see," Aren said with a nod, then patted Url on the arm. "I can't read your thoughts, but the thing is, we grew up in a world where no one is aware that one with magic, anyone with magic, is capable of hearing what we broadcast outward and we just shout out everything into the world."

"How do I *not* do that?" Url asked. "How do I hear others?"

"I can't shut it out at the moment," Aren said, then shook her head. "So I'm not teaching you until I know how to shut it out."

"Do you know how not to shout?" Url asked.

Aren chewed her bottom lip and looked over to the group of warriors. Url turned to where she was looking.

Av was laughing at something as he patted a warrior on the shoulder.

"You're... you're joking, right?" Url asked her desperately.

"I can't hear anything from him. Neither can Raven, so it's not just me being blinded. He honestly keeps it to himself. He doesn't demand the world see him for anything because he just doesn't care. I suppose. Raven says that those who don't shout out to the world hear it more clearly. It sort of makes sense. Av, shortly after he took me to see his father, stopped while we were speaking, looked at a man passing us and told the man not to do it. How? How did he know what the man was planning?"

"And he doesn't know what he's doing?" Url asked.

"Think loudly about doing anything to me."

Url hesitated, then considered how, when he had first met her, he had considered taking on Av to claim Aren. How capturing her attention and having her would have been his one and only thought at all.

Av stepped up to Aren, wrapped an arm around her and drew her close as he frowned at Url. Swallowing, Url blinked back at Av innocently.

"If you were about to do what I think you were about to do, I will bend you over that table and finish what Reld started, except I won't need a queen backing me to keep you down," Av purred out before he turned and kissed Aren's temple possessively.

"Point made," Url said to Aren, aware that no matter what he said, there was a good chance that he and Av would end up on the floor.

"You weren't just—" Av motioned up and down Aren with a finger and looked at Url pointedly.

"I have no interest in anything of that sort with Lady Aren," Url said quietly.

"Lie," Aren said with a small gasp, her mouth falling open.

"He could join us," Av purred to Aren.

Which made the queen go bright red and say, "I think I heard someone call me, who was that?" and walk off as Av grinned toothily at Url.

"No," Url said when Aren had left.

"Why? First cousins are a no because of breeding, not sex in general."

"Oh no," he responded with a head nod. "I grew up here, of all places. I know that line. But no. Are you mad? Why are you talking about sharing her already?"

"Aren's exploring her sexuality, I have no idea what she's actually into, and neither does she. A threesome could be extremely arousing for her, and you're the only one I know who wouldn't be stupid enough to try something, besides Jer or Laeder. And Jer is my brother, so no. And Laeder is Jer's, so... that's actually the more dangerous option."

"Why not Reld, then?" Url asked. "At least he'd enjoy it. And you could kill him afterwards."

"Aren finds him revolting, can't be near him. If he walks in front of her again, it's entirely possible she will show her violent side, and the thing is... she was like that before the incident. Because the more I think about it, the more I realize there are small communications in the hallways, and Aren has never liked that man, not even in passing."

"I can't," Url said sternly, wanting Av to understand what he was saying.

"That was more for Aren," Av said quietly, eyeing Url. "If I were to have you, I must admit it wouldn't be how Reld did it. I'd seduce you first and then as you begged for it, I'd leave you in that state."

Url's mouth fell open. "What did I do to deserve that?"

"You haven't submitted to me," Av said, then smiled. "Know your place, warrior. Or I'll put you in it and mash your face into it for good measure."

Chapter Twenty-Nine

It took a few days after the gathering to get back to normal. Not because there had been drinking, but because the entire world felt fuzzy and warm. Even attending training felt wrong and when he had shown up, fully expecting to be put to work, the training master had set him to the side and made him sit and watch.

While watching, he had learned so much. Weaknesses of other warriors mainly, but also how to stop certain moves.

Sometimes sitting back and watching was the best way to come up with a solution.

A number of other warriors seemed to be drifting the hallways, all ones who had attended the gathering. Av came across them from time to time, but they didn't seem to see him. A few times he saw others speaking with these warriors, asking quiet questions as to what was going on.

For the most part, the people of Castle Grey left the warriors to their own. They weren't disturbed, they were calm in an odd sort of way. The other ranks were disturbed by the sight of them only because they didn't know what had caused it, or if it would ever wear off.

He couldn't be certain, but Av thought he was the first one to shake off the comfortable fog. When he walked into training on the third morning, the others moved out of his way. It was good to stretch his muscles again and he used what he had learned during training, putting several opponents, and then the training master, into the sand.

Sand was much softer to hit than the packed dirt of the palace grounds. Av didn't even understand how Castle Grey had brought in sand for training, but he wasn't about to start complaining.

Aren spent her days with Olea and the queen's daughters, trying to explain how to link together to give magic to Raven. Av spent a majority of his time with Er, learning about military history while watching Er bite back questions as to what happened during the gathering.

Url was absent for the first five days after the gathering. When he reappeared, he had a goofy grin on his face and gave Av a playful shove. They ended up wrestling while waiting for Er to come, and when the baron finally showed up he had separated them, thinking they had challenged one another.

Av could see how it might be confusing to an outsider, but having been at the gathering, it just felt natural to let everything slide off of him. He felt playful and halfway through his lesson he had pounced on Url as Er sighed loudly.

They were dismissed for lunch and immediately went their separate ways. Url went off for food. Av went to the anchor room.

As he stepped into the room, Raven appeared and smiled at him.

"There you are," she said quietly, motioning to a bench in the centre of the room.

The bench was made of stone and had taken the place of the fountain. Av was afraid to ask where the bench had come from, given the fact that it looked as if it were made of a solid piece of stone. He sat on the bench nonetheless, facing the doorway as Raven sat beside him.

"No doubt you'll have questions once you come back to the world a little more," Raven said quietly. "Such as what's that wonderful fog that's come over you?"

"I don't care," Av said with a shake of his head. "It's probably something to do with Aren being at the gathering."

"And claiming the warriors," Raven responded, setting a hand on Av's arm. He could almost feel the weight of it against his flesh. "Not the way she's claimed you, of course. But a warrior who is claimed by a queen feels like he suddenly has a direction to his life. There's no more struggle because he knows what he has to do. Some of them may never come out of the fog, but they're muddied ranks anyhow."

"Muddied ranks?" Av asked.

"Not fully rank. They are more likely to birth rank than commoners, but they aren't quite either. Once, they were referred to as muddied ones because it was believed their blood was like mud. And they tended to be bad, and cause problems, but that's because they didn't understand what was going on around them or to them. Like looking at the world through a drugged haze."

"Are you trying to tell me something, and if so, please get to the point."

Raven drew in a slow breath. "The throne's actions have kept a real dark time from happening but has created many muddied ranks. The true ranks, full ranks, are now being born once more. That's why there was never a decline in ranks, but at the same time, due to the slaughter of the queens, none of you ever realized that the world is mainly populated by muddied ranks. The Marilton bloodline is mainly full ranks. Your father and your mother both were true and proper ranks. The other two barons are true ranks, a mark of breeding warriors and queens for so long. Yes, there is something to breeding warriors and queens, but it's not always a guarantee and certainly isn't the right of the matter."

"So they're all like me?" Av asked.

"A long time ago ones like you were called fathers," Raven said. "Because in times of darkness, if one of you appeared, you would be the father to an entire generation of ranks. The families would be large, not just from you and your mate, but you would draw other ranks to you and shelter them and protect them. You'd help them raise their children, even if those children were the spawn of, say, a queen and a commoner."

"Mar is my blood," Av said sternly.

"Danya technically is, as well as Nae. But what about Wena?"

"How do you know about Wena?" Av asked.

"I spoke to the throne when Aren drank all those days ago, do you recall that?" Raven asked.

Av nodded. He did recall that, he also recalled that he had assumed the throne had been speaking to Raven because otherwise there had been no point to that whatsoever. Aren certainly didn't seem to recall anything the next morning.

"Is Wena your family?" Raven asked.

"Yes," Av said quietly.

"Over time you may find yourself in the predicament of somehow acquiring wards," Raven said calmly. "The reason the throne has wards is because the mate to the throne sometimes needs more children than the one who sits the throne can provide. It's a nurturing instinct. I think you'll find that the more people a warrior protects, the stronger he is. The throne has settled for a strong warrior over a strong queen more than once."

"To protect the people."

"Exactly," Raven said with a smile.

"What did you do to her?" Av asked before he realized what he was saying. "She's… different."

"With me at her side explaining things, she is," Raven said. "But she's the same Aren. Queens who have set aside their pride and asked for my help are more confident. And why wouldn't they be? I have all the knowledge from thousands of queens. I know what did and did not work for them, and thanks to centuries of reflection I know why those things that worked for some didn't work for others. Aren's main problem is that she is young and everyone is used to a certain way of things."

"She's inexperienced. An untried chit, I believe is what the barons call her."

"Aren has plenty of experience. She's been the servant, she's been the downtrodden, she's been the rank afraid for her life. She's made difficult choices to keep her siblings safe, and she's witnessed what can happen when she makes a choice that someone else doesn't like."

"So have I," Av protested.

"You've never been a servant. You could have walked away at any time. You were never afraid for your life and the few moments of fear were that which anyone has when they stand up for themselves. Get your head out of the sand. Aren listens to those who would counsel her on how to rule, but ignores those who demand she obey their wishes."

"You mean, if I want to change her mind, I need to talk to her?" Av asked. "I do talk to her."

"You're a warrior!" Raven said sternly. "You don't talk to a queen, you place demands on her, and that is not how a healthy world works. It is a give and take. She cages you as much as you cage her. Otherwise one is more dominant than the other, and someone gets hurt."

"She knows a great deal more than I do," Av said quietly.

"Only because I am there silently telling her what she needs to know," Raven said. "Once Aren goes back to the palace—at least until I can be moved from here to there—she will have the knowledge, yes, but access to it will come and go. When she really needs it, or when she's finally ready to accept more. But I've linked it to her childhood memories."

"What's—" Av stopped and stared at Raven, recalling when Danya had told him to ask Aren what she recalled of her childhood. "She can't knowingly access the magic unless she remembers what happened to her."

"Exactly, it's a balance," Raven sighed out. "I don't believe Aren will use this knowledge for evil, but I cannot risk unleashing such a creature on the world again."

"What do you mean again?" Av bellowed.

"It's dead now. I killed it six times, and it will remain dead if it knows what's best for it."

"What do you mean *again*?" Av repeated sternly.

"Aren knows that story, she also knows that's why there is a balance, but she doesn't know what the balance is." Raven paused to stare at Av for a long moment. "You need to drive her to the point of remembering. Not everything, not by far. But she needs to remember the birthdays. The games in the fields she used to play with her brother. The nights she snuck out to see the village boy, not to kiss, but to be friends with."

"She has a friend?" Av asked, sounding strangled. "Tell me his name. I'll send for him."

Raven shook her head. "Confronting her with that could send her into the memories I'd rather her not recall. Those sorts of things tend to either drive a queen to madness or make her want to destroy the world and everyone in it.”

“She’s already going to go mad because of the throne and because of being infected.”

“The throne won’t drive Aren mad once I’m there and I reactivate the spells in the palace,” Raven said. “And the infection doesn’t make a person go mad.”

“But in all the stories—”

“All the stories say that she lived out her days as one with the stone,” Raven said pointedly. “Those queens who went mad were unstable to start with, or their families and court convinced them that they were mad. If you’re constantly told you are one thing, why keep fighting it? You just accept and become that thing people are accusing you of being because what’s the point in defending yourself?”

“So if we never call Aren mad for what she sees, or treat her like it…” Av trailed off as the idea took full form.

“She’ll not go mad from the stone. She could still go mad for all the other reasons, however.”

“How do I do that?” Av asked.

“I can teach you, but it would require you to build a cage, an actual cage.”

“Of metal?”

“No, the cage that just comes naturally to other queens to fall into, you need to make one of those for Aren. *You* do, no one else. You have to be the door and the lock and the key. Because at some point, no matter what you tell her, she’s going to think she’s losing her mind. Which is why, when you get back to the palace, you need to find someone who can see other things and get them to teach her how to do it.”

“Doesn’t she already know?” Av asked.

“She does, and one in her position tends to catch on, but unless she knows what she’s seeing, and what she’s doing, she’ll think she’s imagining things.”

“I see,” Av said quietly.

“If you do it properly, you and Aren could spend the rest of your very long lives together,” Raven said quietly. “But before we get into that, do you have any questions?”

“Is there anything she can’t do?” Av asked.

Raven smiled. "There's a great deal she cannot do. She cannot activate the Stone Circle, though that magic may be all but dead."

"What's the Stone Circle?" Av asked.

"Trust me, you'll have enough to deal with without poking that," Raven said quickly. "Aren also cannot fly, cannot heal others, but she may be able to heal herself. That's only because of the stone and the fact that you struck her shortly after she took in the stone."

"I didn't know," Av protested.

"You should have known better than to strike a woman who was barely on her feet. Your mother taught you better than that!"

"She did need to be brought out of her daze."

"Dump her into a body of water, splash her face with water, give her a little slap. What you did was not a little slap, and you had best pray she never finds out that she can heal herself because if she does, it will activate that portion, which means she will stop feeling everything. Do you know what happens when a queen stops feeling?"

Av felt a cold roll through him. "My father may have mentioned something of the sort."

"Idiot," Raven muttered. The woman paused to sigh out. "She cannot tell the future, but some queens can learn to read ones like themselves or their family and friends well enough that they can guess what a reaction would be and that might seem as if she is telling the future."

"What would that matter, when she can change time?" Av asked.

Raven frowned at Av, pulling away from him slightly. "No one has ever been able to change time. It's impossible."

"She lived through the same day twice and on the third day made demands on me," Av said quietly. "What would you call that?"

"Did you ever ask anyone at the palace how long you had been visiting your father?" Raven asked with a small smile.

"No... why would I?"

"A queen cannot change time," Raven said pointedly. "She can, however, alter your perception of the world around you. That doesn't change the world. It just changes what you see. If Aren tells you that the water is purple, then so the water is purple."

"That actually happened," Av said.

"Which is why I used it as an example," Raven muttered. "In those infected and who have a great supply of magic— say, a lifetime worth of magic that they have been storing up—there comes a unique ability to command people to forget, order them to do it again, only this time differently."

The cold came back and was followed by a sickening feeling in his stomach. "She didn't live through the same day twice."

"She lived through the day once, didn't like the outcome and, like puppets, rearranged you all until you behaved in a manner that suited her. Or in that case, when you put her out during the events. She has no control over that when it happens. It takes a great deal of emotion driving her to that point."

"How?" Av asked.

"When a queen is mad, so too are her people," Raven said. "It's an extension of the connection that you all feel with queens. If you upset a queen, you begin stubbing your toes and hitting your head on walls, become clumsy and have a foggy mind when making a decision. Why? Because she told you that you were no longer good at what you were once good at."

"That's hard to take in."

"Our world is great and large. But our people have forgotten how to see the world and what it means to be alive on it. I think it's time to remind them of the duties they promised to uphold. The throne thinks the same thing, which is why it was so driven to creating Aren, even if it meant destroying the innocence of a child to do so."

Chapter Thirty

Jer looked up as Telm entered the war room with the coin master. He elbowed Ervam, wanting to make certain the trainer put away the tally sheet they had drawn up.

While they were looking for any legal reason to fine Para, they had yet to draw anyone but Danya into the conversation. No need to get hopes up when they hadn't the first clue how much they could charge the Argnern bloodline with.

They did know that whatever the fines levied against the bloodline, Para would suffer dire consequences, if her parents didn't demand custody of everything that was Para's, to hold it for her heir.

"Did you need something?" Jer asked Telm innocently.

The queen looked at the papers scattered across the table and frowned at Jer. "A bench is missing from the artifact rooms."

"What sort of an object is a bench?" Ervam muttered.

"It was there to sit on and stare at the crown jewels," the coin master said sternly in response. "It was bolted to the floor, but bolts and all are gone. It was solid stone."

"We have crown jewels?" Jer asked. "No, no, the better question is: we have a crown? As in a ring of metal to put on Aren's head?"

"I doubt it would fit Lady Aren, as it was made for the last king."

Jer looked at his father, who shook his head, then to Telm. The head of house shrugged.

"What's a king?" Jer asked.

"As in a male queen?" Ervam asked.

Telm sighed loudly. "You are both trying to keep me distracted from those papers. I know that you both know exactly what a king is. Perhaps you should focus on the missing bench. The treasury was locked, there was no way in or out. That can only mean that someone teleported in, somehow unbolted the bench, and then teleported out *with the bench*."

"That's impossible," Ervam said with a shake of his head.

"Teleportation," Telm said slowly.

"It's not impossible," Jer corrected, "it's improbable. And if someone did teleport in, it was likely Aren. We'll ask when they get back. I bet she wanted to sit somewhere and there wasn't a bench, so one just appeared, and she sat, and everyone was stunned, but no one dared ask where it came from, for fear of her making them disappear."

Telm's frown returned, but the queen gave herself a shake and smoothed out her features. "You may be correct on that point. What are you two hiding?"

"Jer wants to fine the Argnern bloodline for Para's crimes," Ervam said absently, peering at a piece of paper as he pulled it farther from his face. "I may need reading glasses."

"Why not just kill Para?" Telm demanded of Jer.

Jer kicked his father sideways under the table, but the trainer seemed not to notice as he squinted at the paper.

"We can't kill Para. For starters, we don't have any hard evidence. Secondly, Aren wants her parents alive," Jer said quietly, trying to remain calm at the idea of not being able to do what he knew was right. "We can't fine Para because the estate has been warded by the throne, so we're going to fine her bloodline, because the Bilgern line can't afford it and because it seems Para was the main abuser."

"What have you got so far?" the coin master asked.

"I've got two counts of abuse of power. One at the maximum fine, one at half the fine."

"Abuse of power is for killing a rank without evidence of the death," the coin master said. "Why are you fining her twice?"

"I met an unranked one. It carried a second spirit in its body. Turns out all those stories about unranked ones coming back to life was the second spirit waking up and taking revenge."

"So Para killed someone, but the body is still alive?" Telm asked.

Jer nodded and pulled the list out that he had hidden under another paper. "I've got the endangerment of a victim, maximum fine. Dickery, maximum fine. Warmongering, minimum fine. Destruction of an heirloom, minimum fine."

"Dickery?" the coin master asked.

"Can I not fine someone for annoying me?" Jer asked in response.

"No," Telm said with a shake of her head. "The victim, I'm guessing, is the brother. Warmongering, yes the war is at least in part due to her interference, and she was likely plotting against the throne while here. Hence Anue's timely arrival. Destruction of an heirloom, though?"

"Bilgern Vineyard was once an heirloom in and of itself," Ervam offered up.

"Abandonment of heir, maximum fine," the coin master said suddenly. "It's a thousand coins unless the new heir is a different gender than the old one, then it's two thousand. The fine was brought about to protect the female heirs."

"What about the dress?" Telm asked.

"Which one, exactly?" the coin master muttered. "We can, however, charge her for the destruction of Lady Aren's wardrobe. It may have only been a few hundred coin worth, but for the blue one we will need to confer with the dye masters."

"She took apart an older item, the fine would never hold up under the throne," Telm said.

"And if any of this goes back to Aren, she'll dismiss it," Ervam added.

"I thought we had learned our lesson about not killing people?" the coin master said sternly. "You want to do something, you do it, or bad things happen."

"It's Aren's parents," Jer protested.

"No, what we decided was that killing them before Av has a chance to would mean putting ourselves into danger," Ervam said. "Whether he kills them or not, I'm still fining the Argnern line. As is my right as master. I only need one other head to back me, and that's Jer. If he pulls support, he

won't have to worry about his brother killing him because I
will."

Jer stood and moved around the table to stand beside
Telm.

"I'd support you if Jer had to withdraw," the coin master
muttered.

"Or I would," Telm added. "Para may have been blamed
for what happened before, but her bloodline needs to answer
for her misdeeds. If this were any other line, we'd be holding
them accountable and demanding reparations. The village is
under Gamen, isn't it?"

"It is now, it wasn't then," Jer said quietly. "The border
villages have a right to come or go. Para chose to be with the
palace, but her father supports the baron."

"Then send him a fine just the same," the coin master
said. "Happens all the time. He is responsible for all his
lords. You are fining one of his lords. That lord is being held
responsible for his daughter. Both should have had some
control over Para; after all, she's just a commoner."

"We want to stay on Gamen's good side," Ervam said,
sounding hesitant.

"When a lord or lady from another land does something
stupid, we fine the bloodline and the baron," the coin master
said sternly. "It has always been that way and will always be.
It may be decades before we collect from the baron, but the
message is clear enough."

"We can't afford to go to war with the Coast and the
South," Ervam protested.

"There would be no war with the Coast," Telm said. "The
queens have already come to their agreement. It doesn't work
unless they all participate. If the Coast tries to withdraw, the
North will lay waste to them."

"The North doesn't have that sort of manpower," Jer said,
looking to his father for help.

Ervam stared back at Jer. "It wouldn't be the first time."

"Fine. We'll give Gamen a list of the fines as well as a
stern letter commanding him to control his lords' behaviour
on palace lands."

"That needs to be signed by Aren or Av," Telm said.
"The command, not the fining."

"Av'll sign it," the coin master said quietly. "We simply need the opportunity to present it to him while Aren is not around."

"If we're sending the fines to Gamen, we need to be very careful," Telm said.

"What are you planning on doing with the coin?" the coin master asked.

"Buying a cottage," Jer said.

"I'm guessing for Aren," Telm said.

"Well, yes," Ervam said. "What else would we do?"

Telm looked at the coin master, who peered back at her. Both sighed at the same time.

"The warded estates won't work and those which have been abandoned or donated to the throne..." Telm shook her head. "She might be able to accept something of that sort, but I doubt she would be comfortable. Most have been abandoned because they don't have pipes and lighting. You can't add piping to these places, the pipe masters spend a majority of their time just replacing and repairing pipes."

"I have, however, found four plots of land where there are pipes, but the estates and homes which were on the plots are gone," the coin master said hesitantly.

"The nearest, let me guess," Jer said.

"We're still removing bodies," Telm muttered. "Worl died far too quickly. There's a mark on the land. There's no helping that."

"The other plots are farther away, a day and a half, two days."

"There's a plot right near mine for sale, if we're looking for one with pipes and no home on it," Ervam said suddenly.

"What?" Jer asked. "I thought that was all bought out?"

"Around the lake, yes, but there's one right behind the house," Ervam said. "Backs on to mine. The reason we chose that was because when you're on the lake, you control who can move in behind you."

"Yes, yes," the coin master said, nodding. "I remember your land now. There's an entire village plot behind you. Yours was the connection to the lake, the queen's home."

"Probably why it was maintained while the rest fell," Ervam said quietly. "How much does that go for now?"

"Sixty thousand," the coin master said.

"What?" Telm shouted.

"It's the key link to the village plot behind it," the coin master rushed to say. "I don't set the prices, they've been set like that for generations."

"Can you lose a zero?" Ervam asked.

The coin master motioned to Jer.

As steward, it was Jer's duty to make certain that all the masters did their tasks with honesty. While he completely understood what his father wanted, he also knew that he couldn't just allow it to happen. Were Aren to live a long, long life, then there would be no problem.

But Jer had to err on the side of caution.

"How much would it cost to build a home on the plot?" Jer asked.

"Once the pipes are laid, I could do it," Ervam said.

"You're master of palace grounds," Jer countered.

"I have a young boy and a young ward, they're going to need romping time in the woods," Ervam said sternly.

"You're over fifty," Jer snarled.

"Are you calling me old?"

"I'm calling you stupid!"

"Depending on the home, between nothing and fifty thousand," the coin master muttered. "Considering this is Lady Aren we are talking about... let me ask the master builder. Since she's taken the throne, he has had to do minor repairs, and that was all from other queens."

"What's that mean?" Jer asked.

"He has apprentices who need training somehow," the coin master said. "It wouldn't be the first time they built a home in their training time."

"The neighbour of the plot is a surly old man, though," Jer muttered. "What are the chances of selling the land otherwise? The palace takes how much of that cost?"

"The palace owns the land. Technically speaking, Aren could gift the land to anyone besides herself and as long as the masters agreed, it would be free."

Telm smiled slowly. "What if I were to donate my wages to pay for the—"

"No!" Ervam shouted, standing quickly. "You don't take your damned payment as it is, you don't get to just bandy it about like that."

"I think the reason we're fighting like this is because Aren wouldn't accept charity or any other way," Jer said to the table. "Fine Gamen, tell him where the money is going to, tell him why we are fining him, skip the command. Fine the Argnerns. Tell them that if they don't pay, I will be coming for them and I will bring the mate of the throne. Pin the notice in the square or to a house, hand it out to the villagers. I want them to know that if the Argnern bloodline does not pay up, I will be coming and I will hunt through the streets until payment is had in blood or in coin, and I don't care if it's villager or Argnern because there aren't enough Argnerns to slate my thirst."

"Slake, Jer," Ervam said sternly. "Slake your thirst."

"Keep quiet. You know what I meant."

Chapter Thirty-One

"Why didn't he question us sending Cara with him?" Er asked quietly.

Url stared at the greeting hall's doors for a long moment before he turned to his father. "He and I agreed it would be best if she were removed from a sympathetic environment."

"Her and Aren are going to end up killing one another," Olea grumbled.

"But Av will have a great deal of entertainment," Url said with a smile, a nagging thought coming over him. "We're certain she's not going to attack Ervam, though?"

"She doesn't know Ervam killed her father," Er responded. "All she knows is her parents went down for a visit and never came back."

"One of you should have gone with them," Olea said pointedly.

"We've a castle to settle back into place," Er said, holding up a finger as he hesitated.

"Er!" Vivlia shouted.

"There it is," Er said under his breath, then glared at Url. "I ever catch you talking about your mother like that, and I'll whoop you, even from the spirit world."

"My mother never tried to sell me to slavers," Url countered, stepping around his father to place himself between the baron and Vivlia.

While Vivlia was Er's mother, the history was long and complicated. She hadn't wanted children, but as a queen, she was presented with little choice. Her good friend had offered to breed her once and then give her the freedom she wanted.

Vivlia wasn't cut out to be a mother.

"Vivlia," Url said.

"Lady Vivlia Marilton," she snapped back at him.

But the words no longer had the bite to them.

Vivlia's magic was still recovering. There had been some debate as to whether or not the queen would ever be able to use magic again. Raven hadn't explained much and Vivlia was so dazed and afraid after the event that she hadn't been capable of reaching for magic.

It was possible to cut a queen off from her magic, but it involved twisting her instincts and redirecting her. She wouldn't have access to the magic, but someone else would.

"Vivlia," Url repeated in the same tone, causing the woman to flinch. "this is Castle Grey, the Mariltons run it. While in the past we have granted a council of elders to exist and guide us, Raven has made her demands very clear."

"Frankly I'm happy to be rid of the yoke of servitude," Olea spat out.

"In order to facilitate the changes, the elders have been stripped of their rights, those which they took on when they became elders. Many have been reassigned as teachers to the children, as was the original intention for elders."

"And I'm stuffed off into the shadows someplace?"

"My father's misplaced loyalty will no longer stand," Url said, lowering his voice and trying to put a softer edge to his tone. "You are his blood, not his family. It was by your actions that the elders lost their rights, because when you accused the one who sits the throne of treason, you endangered us all."

"She destroyed the anchor room!"

"She awakened Raven!" Url bellowed back, revelling in how the older queen flinched again and moved backwards.

He gripped his hands tight, reminding himself that Vivlia was now under their protection. She was elderly, had no family elsewhere, even if they were stupid enough to place her out of reach. Her magic might never return.

Vivlia was now a ward to Castle Grey. Url could shout to discipline, but he had to be careful at the same time not to cross a line.

"Aren awakened a magic older than the castle, a magic which has been nothing but useful and will continue to be useful in the future," Url said in a flat tone.

"She's creating a magic like herself for Castle Grey," Olea said. "Imagine us with our own palace. Our queens wouldn't need to do more than speak to Raven and give over a small portion of their magic for the stores. She would do the rest. We could venture far and wide, hunt with our men without fear. Go to war."

"This is not the way of things," Vivlia protested.

"Things are changing," Url responded. "That much was made clear to you when Mirmae sent us her letters. When we signed the treaty."

"I agreed to submit to Mirmae," Vivlia said.

Raven flickered into view beside Vivlia and moved to Url's side. The magic set a hand on Url's arm. He felt the weight of it against his flesh, the warmth of another body. She smiled at him and then turned to Vivlia.

"Vivlia, your years of service have done Castle Grey a favour in protecting it until it was time to shed the past," Raven said. "And I deeply regret what has happened to you in order for myself to be solid. But the time for change has come and passed. It has already happened. Nothing you say will change things now."

"I am an elder."

"The North is united once more with the palace," Raven said, giving her head a small shake. There was no hiding the giddiness she felt. It was infectious. "Soon I will rejoin the throne and then one by one the other lands will also join."

"The throne only did it to—"

"To link Marilton blood to it in order to solidify the treaty," Raven said. "Av was mated off as so many women have in the past. He's happy though, and she's happy. Your blood is happy with the arrangement. They will make many ranked children. Strong children. It mated off a strong warrior to a strong queen to keep her sane long enough to find me, so that I could tell it how to keep her sane indefinitely. Now it knows how to. Now it knows for certain how to unlink someone to it if it needs to, while I transfer down there. Giving it, and her, the time they might need. Is there anything else you would like to try to bring to light?"

"Raven has been open with us on every point," Url said placidly.

"You are no longer in control, and you are not the first queen to struggle with submission," Raven said. "I could quote a list of queens so long it would make your head reel. Why, when the warrior queen stepped off the throne, and her son took over, she had to leave palace grounds and go to a place nearly half-way across the world. She loved her son, she wanted nothing to do with ruling, but when it came time she fought him every step of the way until she removed herself. Of course, she could teleport, so if he did something stupid she'd just flicker over and cuff him upside the head."

"He?" Vivlia demanded, staring at Raven.

"With any luck, Aren will birth a male queen and put to bed this muttering about those of your rank but not your gender," Raven responded coldly. "Vivlia, why don't you go back to bed, you look faint."

Two healers approached cautiously.

"Apologies, Lord Er," one said, taking Vivlia by the arm gently. "She wanders and isn't quite herself yet. Come on, dear. I've got a nice tea for you."

"Tea?" Vivlia demanded, then wavered slightly on her feet.

"Yes, tea, you like tea, don't you?"

"I do like tea," Vivlia muttered, turning with the healer to leave.

Url waited until he was certain they were out of earshot before he turned to Raven and jabbed a finger to where they had disappeared.

"Did you just do that?"

"No, Vivlia has turned inward," Raven said quietly. "I may be able to access her magic if I needed to, but I suspect that would kill her."

"Turned inward?" Olea asked. "As in what she's done to others in the past?"

"Yes," Raven responded, turning round to Olea. "I was hoping I could reach her but either I haven't enough magic to break the inward turning or she's started to slide into madness."

"Reach into her mind?" Url asked.

"No!" Raven said, exasperated. "For the last time, I cannot enter anyone's mind. The few who can are killed on sight to prevent it from spreading. I was reaching for the magic she's using on herself, to break it. Those who could do what she can do, but used it wisely, were once called spiritual healers. There was some debate as to healers being a type of queen, or queens came from healers, because of that."

"But you can change someone's perception," Url said. "And command us about."

"I can only do that if you trust me or fear me," Raven said. "The perception is just... I can see how in the world as it is now, you think it's mind reading. Your language doesn't even have words for what it is that queens do."

"Compulsion," Olea offered. "That's what my mother once called it. The throne tells those what to do, but it's only a compulsion. They have every right and every ability to say no, but they follow the suggestion blindly because they want to submit to a greater power."

Raven considered for a moment and then nodded slowly. "That may be as close a translation as you have."

"Thank you for saving us from that," Url said, glancing at his father.

Er looked rather unstable. Url had wondered why his father hadn't stepped in, but it had probably been because of seeing his mother in a weakened state. It was difficult to see a parent hurt, or to think of a world where they were no longer there.

Even if there was a difficult relationship between parent and child.

"I didn't come for that," Raven said with a dismissive motion. "I've been wrapped up in Grey's activation."

A warrior appeared beside Raven, his dark grey eyes and grey hair a reflection of the stones of the castle. There was something about his presence that was commanding. Url couldn't even quite put words to what he felt from the new magic.

"Good morning to you all, my name is Grey," the warrior said without emotion. "I am responsible for the upkeep and maintenance of Castle Grey, where the ruling queen is currently Olea Uthernol."

"Marilton," Raven corrected gently.

"She should be sitting the throne," Grey said back to Raven.

"That plan changed."

"When her mother disobeyed a direct order," Grey grumbled.

"Olea is happy here."

"The world is not happy because of it."

"You are in charge of their well-being, you cannot point out every fault," Raven countered, looking at Grey.

He stared back at her with all the annoyance of a warrior who was being commanded to stand down by his queen. Grey took in a long breath and gave his head a little shake.

The same shake Url had seen his father do behind his mother's back as she spoke, which was dismissive and had an eye-roll to it as Grey looked away from Raven.

"What was that?" Url demanded.

"Creating another like myself takes generations," Raven said carefully. "To make him solid and able to speak, I had to write a few memories into him. As time goes on, he will become his own person. You may find he has small errors at first, you can write over the errors by correcting him. We're very complicated magics, just the processes to start the foundation of our magic usually takes five hundred years."

"He's not going to go mad and throw us off a cliff, is he?" Olea asked.

"There is that possibility if he receives too many conflicting messages," Raven said, then grimaced. "Which would have happened in about three hundred years."

Url's mind did a skittering halt. He closed his eyes and groaned.

"Please tell me we were not accidentally creating him and that you didn't use that foundation to create him!"

"I did, but I corrected most of the problems," Raven said. "Thankfully due to the barons coming and going and being a family, he seemed to understand that they weren't all right. When I first activated I tried to throw us off a cliff, but unfortunately the palace was very firmly attached to the ground. I just lit the dining hall and kitchens on fire and... might have blown out all the windows. But that didn't scare people off. So here I am."

"That is not comforting in the least," Grey said. "You need to lie sometimes. Everything will be fine, no one is going to die, and I won't trip you for being dishonourable. I'm looking at you, Url."

"Why?" Url demanded.

"There's a healer pregnant with your child," Grey said, motioning to the south. "And you're here?"

"I need to protect my father, unless you're solid," Url said sternly.

Grey folded his arms and made an annoyed face as Raven laughed. The queen covered her mouth and brought herself under control.

"No, Url. Grey can't be physical the way I can for some fifty years. He probably can't even make you stub a toe, but the day he can, you'll know if you're still alive."

Grey smiled all too knowingly at Url.

"Meaning what, exactly?" Olea asked Raven.

"Remember when you were trying to learn magic?" Raven asked.

Olea nodded. "My mother told me to do something, and I'd try and try and then when I got... oh... I was just supposed to light one thing, and it exploded. It all adds up over time. Oh dear."

"He's been instructed to try to hold back, but sometimes mortals are just stupid, and you want to peg them between the eyes," Raven said.

"Url, the others are looking for you," Grey said quietly.

"I need to go," Url said to his mother and father.

"Why?" Olea asked. "Who are the others?"

"The other warriors," Url said dismissively, walking away.

Those from the gathering; Url could feel them now. All of them could feel the loss of not only Av but of Aren as well. They were reeling from the change and needing direction. Url would have to step into Av's place and keep them at hand while they gathered others to them to go to war.

The faster they collected volunteers, the faster they could make their way south and rejoin Av and Aren. And take advantage of Aren's offer.

Url bared his teeth as the others responded eagerly to his call.

Something had changed in that gathering, and only they would ever understand it. But whatever had happened, they were stronger for it.

Chapter Thirty-Two

After travelling from Castle Grey to the palace with Cara and Aren, Av was pretty certain that bringing Cara along was not worth the effort. They were both about the same age, though Av was fairly certain that Cara was a few years older than Aren. Her parents had come to visit Av's family after Mar had been born.

Olerna and her mate, the one killed by the other and buried, likely, somewhere in the woods around his father's home. And the mate, who had answered to Ervam for killing his sister.

Aren stopped at the stables to show the boys there her new puppies.

Av pulled Cara inside to talk to everyone before Aren caught up with them. He pushed Cara in front of a startled Telm, who stared at Cara, and then looked at Av.

"She's not my blood, surely," Telm said desperately.

"What?" Av asked.

"The blue eyes," Telm said with a motion.

"Oh, no, those are from her father, along with the hair," Av said. "This is Cara, born of Olerna and her mate. She's ranked queen, and I want her to have absolutely no special treatment. She is a ward to the throne and nothing more, definitely, do not treat her like a queen."

"Lord Av, you're starting to sound like Em," Telm said quietly.

"You think the North would part with a queen willingly?" Av asked in response.

Telm considered Cara, then nodded once. "Very well, will she be doing training?"

"Yes, with Ervam," Av said, glancing over at his father as the trainer approached them.

"Where is Aren?" Ervam asked.

"Out in the stables, she recognized one of the boys and wanted to show him the two Marl pups Er parted with," Av said, turning his attention to Jer. He bared his teeth at his brother and watched the other warrior pale. "I trust Bilgern Vineyard, and the bloodline, is still standing?"

"They are, but I don't know for how long," Jer said. "That would be a discussion for another place. We've sent a list of fines to both Gamen Hue and the Argnern bloodline, holding them responsible for the actions of one of their people on our land."

"What exactly do you plan to do with those fines?" Av asked. "Fill the palace's coffers?"

"Coffers?" Jer asked. "You learned a new word, good for you."

"I learned a great deal more than just a word." Av jabbed Cara in the side, causing the queen to hiss at him. "Someone take her to a room to wash and eat and sleep, she gets haughty when she's hungry."

A servant stepped forward and offered to take Cara away. The queen glared at Av but went along with the servant. Av sighed out at those who remained.

"Fast and hard," Av said to Jer.

There was the sound of little thumps, and then a bundle of fur slammed into Av's legs as the other bundle stopped at Ervam's feet and began howling at the trainer. Not barking, but howling as it did to Aren when she left it alone for any period of time with Av.

"Tattletale," Av muttered.

The pup howled towards Av for a moment before hiding behind Ervam and continuing to yip.

"Here everyone is," Aren said, smiling at them all. "How's the war coming? Who have we heard from? How many men do we think we'll have and what have the scouts said about the South's army?"

Telm gaped at Aren. For a moment Jer did as well, but Jer knew what hard and fast meant.

"We have very little information at this point," Jer said. "The West sent word that they've begun recruiting. We haven't heard from Gamen yet or from Er, but I'm guessing you could bring us word from Er."

"And I have," Av said quietly. "But, Aren, war is something we can discuss later."

"You're right, what we need to discuss is the fountain that appeared without warning," Aren said. "No worries, I can put it back, it'll be fine. The fountain just marks the place of Raven's outer processes and the physical manifestation of the archives, though I know it's just in a room of stone. It'll all make sense very shortly."

"What…" Telm began.

"…Fountain?" Ervam asked.

"No fountain has appeared," Jer said, pressing a clenched hand into his stomach. "A bench disappeared from the treasury."

"That explains where that came from," Av muttered. "What do you mean there's no fountain? It teleported from there to here."

"The only room of stone is the one I showed Aren last fall," Telm said quietly. "The rest of the palace was completely dismantled and the remains of the stones were scattered across estates on palace land."

"Raven is still together on this side, she can feel that much of it," Aren said, sounding frustrated. "Of course the one person who could explain isn't here."

"What about the throne?" Av asked. "You could get drunk, and I could listen."

"If the throne knew, it would have told Raven before," Aren sighed out. "It's suffering the same effects as Raven, it doesn't know why something is wrong, it just knows there is something wrong."

"Raven?" Telm asked Av. "As in the palace?"

"Raven is a magic that is built into the palace," Aren said quickly. "She's as real as you or me when she's at full strength. Remember how Er said they took the palace?"

Telm nodded. "But when I pressed him on the matter he said he had only taken the important bits."

"They took Raven's anchoring stones. The restoration of the palace wasn't about fixing anything or getting rid of the bad emotions from queens over generations. It was about killing Raven so that the people could do what they wanted."

"What does Raven do?" Telm asked.

"She is the archives," Aren said.

"She also wrote the history of magic into Aren, but she can't remember it at all times, just sometimes if you catch her off guard or try to rob her on the road when she goes to take a piss and is out of sight of her warrior," Av growled out.

"They were still alive when you got there," Aren said pointedly.

"They had shit themselves in fear. I don't find enjoyment in taking on men like that. They stink, for starters."

"Why don't we know about this magic?" Telm asked suspiciously.

"Because when the palace was remodelled, the expansive library was all but emptied," Jer said. "The books were either burnt or sent south to the archives."

"Which Laeder worked in!" Aren exclaimed. "Raven worked closely with the queens who sat the throne, Laeder's studied queens, maybe he knows about Raven and where we can find her stones."

"He's in the library," Jer said, motioning as he moved out of the way.

"One question," Av said sternly to Aren, "and then you are to wash and eat before you ask more."

"I am hungry…" Aren muttered. She whistled to the pups and headed off in search of Laeder.

"By the time she eats, she'll be exhausted," Av said. "Because she'll ask, do we even have time to gather an army? Any word from the South?"

"Merkat sent word asking when and where we'd like to meet," Ervam said. "He seems to think this will be a war for the legends to speak of, and wants to make certain no side can claim the other was better prepared. I asked him for next late summer, he countered with late spring, so it's not so hot that his men have the advantage of weather."

"I want to call him an idiot, but I can't argue when his stupidity helps us," Av muttered. "And the where?"

"Someplace called the Plains of the Ancestors. Laeder was kind enough to point to it on a map. Neither side will have an advantage of territory."

"He's planned this well. That's not like the man I met, quick to anger."

"He may have a rank," Jer said. "The planning, this meticulous, is usually done by a queen. Laeder didn't meet one, but the land down there, flourishing suddenly as it is? A queen is the only explanation."

"I can at least take that to her, maybe settle her mind. Maybe she won't ask about skirmishes or raided villages over the next year."

"And in the meantime?" Ervam asked.

"Jer, gather the family that's in the palace to the family room. I need to talk to Nae, and then I'll bring her with me."

"When you say family…?" Jer asked.

"Em didn't have one," Ervam said quietly. "Is Wena a part of this? What about Anue and Mie?"

"Not Anue or Mie, let them be children a little longer," Av responded, "But yes, Wena. As of this moment, Nae is being removed from duties if she's not been removed already."

"Why?" Telm asked. "What's she done?"

"She's pregnant," Av said, turning the ring on his finger.

Url's ring, an oath that the warrior would keep, that Av knew his cousin had to keep, but not one that Nae would believe. He also had messages for Nae from both Url and Er. There was no telling how long it would take Url to gather the necessary men to contribute to the army, and he had to stay in the North until that was done. It could be months, or it could be years.

Until Url came down, or Nae went up, the healer was Av's responsibility. Even if that meant he'd have to toss her over his shoulder and cart her around like a sack of potatoes.

"Gather the family, meet me in the rooms," Av said, walking off.

"What about proper greetings?" Jer asked.

"Whether you get proper greetings will be determined by what happens in the family room," Av called over his shoulder.

He went straight for the healer hall. Walking in, he spotted Nae headed for the door. She came to a stop and folded her arms as she glared at him.

"That's what that command was?" she demanded. "I'm not yours to boss around."

"What kind of a healer are you, that you don't know the state of your own body?" Av asked quietly, aware that everyone in the hall was leaning in to hear.

"I beg your pardon?" Nae asked.

"When was the last time you bled?"

The woman went bright red. "That's none of your business!"

"It is when I'm told by two different people—in another land—that you are carrying my cousin's child," Av said, watching the red of embarrassment turn to a sickly white. "Now, he can't put you on bedrest or demand you only eat apples, but it is well within his rights to remove you from duty."

"But I can serve until my third month with minimal risk," Nae whispered.

Not quite protesting. Av felt as if Nae knew there had been a shift of control. She was speaking her mind to test the limits of the new rules, but she wasn't pushing.

"If you want to keep working, you can do so in the kitchens or any number of other jobs," Av responded. "I know you too well to let you keep working in the healer hall. You will give in to temptation, and he doesn't want to take that risk."

"And once the child is born?" Nae asked.

"That depends on how you're doing."

"I meant, what happens to my child, once it is born?" Nae said, finally meeting Av's eyes.

There was a fury there that Av should have counted on. He also should have explained from the start, considering he knew how hot Nae's anger burned.

"The next time Url is down, he will be visiting you," Av said, pulling off the ring to hold it out to Nae. "At that point, the pair of you will see where you are in life and whether or not you wish to pursue anything else. Url assured me that he has no intention to chase after other women.”

“Do you believe that?”

“Absolutely,” Av said quickly. “Url remained single for so long because no one in the North could draw his attention.”

“What if I need something?” Nae asked.

“Then you’ll come to me. Until he arrives at the palace, it is my sworn duty to care for you as he would.”

“My village—”

“Can have any other healer willing to move there,” Av said. “If you wanted to go back, you would have done so sometime over the past month. Instead, you remained here.”

“I suppose you’re right,” Nae said without any strength.

There hadn’t been anything in Nae’s village but for a few remaining blood. Most of her siblings had moved away. She had only stayed out of a feeling of duty towards the village. She had been the last remaining healer and hadn’t wanted to leave them with no aid.

“Where’s Danya these days?” Av asked.

“She’s been set up in a room in the palace,” Nae said. “Most days about this time she’s in the gardens teaching Anue and Mie about ranks. Others have started joining the lessons. She’s fitting in. Why?”

“I need her to attend a meeting with you, me, and the rest of the family.”

“I’m family?”

“Of course you are,” Av said.

“Am I only a part of the family because I’m the only healer you know?” Nae asked.

“I know lots of healers,” Av protested.

“Name one,” Nae said.

Av pointed to the healer at the desk, who blinked back at him in surprise. “That one.”

“What’s her name?” Nae demanded.

Av stared at Nae for a very long moment. “All right, I’ve lived at the palace almost thirty years, and I don’t know the names of any of the healers except for you. But I knew your name from outside of the palace.”

"I don't want to be a part of something just because you want a healer to add to your collection," Nae said.

"That's not why you're a part of the family," Av said sternly. "If it'll make you feel better, I'll forbid you from ever healing anyone ever again. Then you won't be a part of the family for your rank."

"That wouldn't make me feel better!"

"My father is the only trainer in the family. Laeder is the only scribe. Just because we all have a function that's useful to the others doesn't mean that we are only there because of our usefulness. Wena can't heal or use magic, she's not as well educated as the rest of us, she's still a part of the family. Danya's blind for crying out loud.

"Fine," Nae said suddenly, throwing her hands into the air. "I'll be a part of your stupid family."

"Good," Av said.

Nae muttered something very uncomplimentary about Av under her breath, but he chose to ignore the insult.

"Now that we're both in agreement with one another, do you have some information for me?" Av asked.

"Yes, but you aren't going to like it."

Av could only shrug in response. "If I were going to like it, I wouldn't have asked you to get it for me. Just tell me how slowly he's going to die."

"Jer says we aren't allowed to kill them," Nae said glumly.

"You didn't try to."

"Not try, I just made plans to go out, and Jer threatened to tie me up until you got back if I tried to leave palace grounds headed for the vineyard," Nae grumbled in response.

"Well, I can kill him. Though to my understanding, it's best to wait until his son is of age to take over the estate. So I have years to plan. How slowly, Nae?"

"Slow enough that I was going to offer my skills to you."

Av drew in a small breath. "And your parents are dead, correct?"

"My father died of natural causes, and my mother died in her sleep."

"What did she really die of?"

"I might have liquefied her internal organs starting with the ones she didn't necessarily need to live… and then as she died, put it all back together again."

Av nodded slowly. "And that…that is why I need you in the family. Because if you aren't with us, you might do that to me, and I like breathing."

Chapter Thirty-Three

Jer waited in the family room with the others, wondering if perhaps the war room would have been a better place to have the meeting. Something had changed about Av. He was different somehow. So was Aren, but that wasn't very surprising.

The longer she was at the palace, the more settled Aren became.

Yet it seemed the longer she was at the palace, the more unsettled Av became. He was no longer the same as he was before, he had changed, but Jer couldn't figure out how or why.

When the mate to the throne walked into the room, everything went still, and Jer realized just how Av had changed.

As master he was self-assured, but as mate he had Aren backing him as well as the throne.

Av was about to start a cull of those at court, and he was starting with the family.

Jer glanced over the people in the room. Ervam, Telm, Danya, Wena, Laeder, and Nae behind Av. If they had been on palace grounds, Url, Er, and Olea would also be in the room. Jer had to wonder if Van and Gamen would be among their number, or if the other barons were excluded because they didn't obey quickly enough.

Av closed the door and motioned for Nae to sit beside Jer. The healer complied and gave Jer a sidelong glance as if trying to warn him of something.

Jer hadn't warned anyone else because he hadn't quite been sure what to warn them against.

"I just want to have a chat with you all," Av said, standing as the others looked up at him. "While at Castle Grey, Raven explained a few things to me, including some startling facts about those who are infected. The main concern for us all has been and will continue to be Aren's sanity. We were told that those who are infected go mad; we were wrong."

"What do you mean wrong?" Ervam asked. "The tales clearly state that is what happens."

"The tales aren't wrong, they just have the cause wrong," Av said steadily. "Queens who are infected by the stone behave differently, and they are the only ones ever to be documented as going mad. Other ranks who are infected tend not to mesh cleanly, which is why the stone is named after the queens. Aren can pass it on to our children, protecting them from consumption. I might even become infected over time depending on our activities.

"My infection would be a good deal milder and would only really protect me from consumption, had I not had it in the past. Queens who are infected, as Aren is, mesh cleanly with it. This sort of infection is one in a hundred of those who survive the first few days. Not too impressive, Raven says, as there's another step above that, which requires infection from two of the living stones."

"Other stones can infect a person?" Danya squeaked out.

"She didn't tell me which ones, or the names of them, but yes," Av sighed out. "The reason those queens go mad isn't because the stone is meddling with them. It's because those around them believe them to be mad, treat them as if they have lost their minds. Eventually, they start believing it and begin sliding. There are times where you think there's a clean mesh but the stone is replacing bits slowly but surely inside the head. This can be viewed as madness, but often starts with forgetting words, places, faces. The problem with Aren is …"

"She doesn't remember half the time anyways," Danya said quietly. "Out of sight, out of mind, is the best way to describe it."

Av nodded.

"What's that to do with us?" Jer dared to ask, certain he would regret asking in a moment.

"If any of you ever tells her she's mad or treats her as if she is crazy, I will kill you on the spot."

Laeder raised his hand, drawing Av's eyes to him.

"What if in conversation she says something stupid and it slips out?" Laeder asked. "Or if she says she'll do something that we know is going to upset you, and we say it in exasperation."

"Good point," Av responded. "Obviously there will be exceptions to this rule."

Laeder raised his hand again. "I can't help but notice that everyone in this room is close to Aren, or at least as close as we could be. Does that mean I'm her family?"

"Yes, Laeder, that means you're her family."

Laeder raised his hand again.

"I've explained the difference between family and blood to you," Jer said quietly.

"It's still confusing for someone from a land where they're the same," Laeder said quickly. "But I also wondered if Lady Mar and Lord Perlon are only being left out because they returned to their estate, or because of another reason?"

Av stiffened. He shifted towards Jer and cocked his head ever so slightly to the side.

Jer might not have seen that look on Av's face before, but he had seen it on plenty of warriors in the past. Those warriors had been confronting stupid youths, sometimes even Jer, for doing something fundamentally wrong.

"You let them go back?" Av asked.

"We had no reason we could give her to stay," Telm said soothingly, trying to calm Av. "Lady Mar is aware a war is brewing, but we did not share with her how the lands will be attacked."

"Call her back, send a command," Av said to Jer. "From the mate, sealed by the steward. We cannot risk a queen of her strength that close to the border, not when she's carrying a child. Send an invitation with it to Perlon's blood—that's his immediate relations, Laeder—inviting them to join us or send their children to us."

"And if Mar declines the command?" Jer asked.

"I will go down there and get her myself!" Av shouted, causing everyone, even Jer, to flinch away. "They know who she is, they know what she is, and they know that she matters to you and me and to Aren. Send the command."

"Now, or would you like to finish?" Ervam asked, drawing the irate warrior's attention to himself. "Family meeting without everyone means a cage, boy. Don't think me too stupid to realize. Aren has made her thoughts on a cage very clear."

"I know that," Av said, finally taking a seat. "But Aren doesn't like the cage of lace and silk, and I'm not even going to try that."

"Lace and silk is how it's described, but it all means the same thing," Telm said.

"No, it doesn't," Av said with a shake of his head. "At the palace, we make a cage of silk and lace. We buy them things, jewelry, clothing, give them whatever they could want and things they didn't even know they wanted. We give them fine art and heirlooms. What Raven told me to do was similar, but different. We're going to exert control, not over Aren, but over her environment. Anyone who questions her sanity is to be removed. Which means you all need to be trained and ready. I'm looking at Laeder and Wena in that comment."

"We've been training with the guard," Wena said, looking down her nose at Av. "Does that mean I can smack people?"

"Out of Aren's sight, I'll even let you kill them," Av said quickly. "Out of sight only because witnessing that sort of thing, so suddenly, can cause ranks beside warrior and healer to have instability. We want as much stability as possible."

"You want us to monitor what she eats as well?" Jer asked.

"Not what she eats, but that she eats. I don't care if it's carrots six days in a row, as long as she eats. Not eating needs to be reported because it could be a sign of the stone working its way into her gut. Which I suppose is a reason, Nae, to have a healer on hand who is a part of the family. But any healer would do."

"I see, how will I know it's doing that to her?" Nae asked. "I touched her at your mating feast, and nothing appeared unusual."

"It'll look like a tumour, but feel like nothing," Av said. "Does that make sense to you?"

Nae sighed. "Yes, it does. How do you know it would be like that?"

"Raven described it to me as several healers described it to her ten hundred years ago," Av said.

"A thousand," Laeder said quietly, raising his hand until Av turned to him. "This is fine and dandy. I learn fighting, we keep an eye on all the things, makes sense, she's the one who sits the throne, we should watch that sort of thing. But I think you need to learn the things that are going on behind this all. How can you tell us what we're to do, if you don't understand what our function is in the cage itself? How can you, just for example, go to Wena about one of her girls, uh, I don't know, misappropriating funds when you don't know the reasons why those funds might have gone missing in the first place?"

"Misappropriation sounds like theft," Av said.

"It's not," Wena said. "I'm guessing in this example I'm head of the handmaids. I tell one to go and purchase something for Aren. She purchases the wrong thing, so I have to send her back out to purchase the right thing. Now in the meantime, Aren could use the first item, and let's say it's a cream for her belly. Each lady seems to need a different one, and each healer recommends a different one. The wrong cream could cause an allergic reaction, or make her nauseas. Then I'm upset, and you're upset, and she's really upset, and the poor maid is weeping her eyes out."

"You lost me at purchase," Av said. "Which I'm assuming makes Laeder's point?"

"It does," Laeder said.

"Fine, but you're teaching me," Av said to Laeder.

"What exactly are the rules to this cage?" Danya asked.

"Besides removal of idiots and making certain she eats, I don't know."

"You aren't going to dictate how she dresses?" Danya asked.

"I might insist she wear something I know she'll look good in, but otherwise no. And she still has the right to say no to my insistence."

"And if she wishes to leave palace grounds again?" Danya said quietly.

"If this works properly, she shouldn't want to leave the way she did before, but I have no intentions of stopping her unless there's an army outside the walls," Av said. "This isn't about restricting her, Danya."

"What about the children?" Ervam asked.

"Anue is best as your ward," Av said. "You grew up with queens, you were raised by one. Aren's never raised a child, and I wouldn't feel comfortable raising her sister as my own."

"I meant in this whole thing, where do the children stand in this?"

"They're children," Av said.

"Children are always a distraction," Telm said.

"Well, these ones aren't."

"You didn't think this over, did you?" Nae asked.

"You know what I did think over? I thought of us keeping her sane. I'm sorry if my rules seem simple. We could have problems arise and decide along the way to change the rules, or Mar could arrive and point something out. As time goes on, we might learn things that we shouldn't do and add that to the list. Do not buy her things except special occasions; the moment you do she'll know, and we're all dead then. Or at the very least on the receiving end of her special brand of anger."

"Fair enough," Wena said. "But then why the meeting? You could have just told us not to mention crazy and to make certain no one else did. This 'cage' of yours is exactly what we have been doing."

"I want you to pair with Telm and find Aren several handmaids. Ranked queens. They should be young, capable, intelligent. I don't want anyone to be promiscuous, and if they are they need to be removed unless Aren requests they stay. Make absolutely certain they know that I'm not there for their entertainment and they aren't there for mine."

Ervam chuckled. "Er tell you that tale, did he?"

"The wall is still stained from Aunt Olea's magic," Av said with a growl.

"So not the new queen?" Olea asked.

"If Cara steps foot in Aren's rooms you are to get me and the guard and anyone else you can to separate them immediately," Av said quickly. "And... uh, then possibly you won't hear from half the males for the next day or so."

"What is it about women fighting that does that," Wena muttered.

"I need Jer to behave like a brother would, not like I did when you mated Em. She needs a good role model for good relationships. So don't cry on her for at least the first year."

"Jer cries?" Laeder asked.

"You, Laeder, I need you to find Raven's room."

Laeder shook his head. "Everything on Raven was locked up in the private archives of the highest order. As the baron's son, I had no right to see them, ever. I saw some mentions of the palace and even some as if it were something more than just a building, but nothing like what Aren came to me asking about."

"How long would it take you to find that information if we took the archives?" Av asked.

"The archivists follow their processes to the letter. They will not allow the information to fall into the hands of an invading army just because you fight for the throne," Laeder said.

"Processes?" Av asked. "What are those?"

"It's the way they do things, the process of doing their duties and daily tasks," Laeder said.

"What happens when a process is broken?"

"If a mistake is made or a step missed, it reverberates through the archivists. The scribes need to pick up the slack and put everything back to where it belongs otherwise they start repeating unnecessary processes. These are folk who can't live in the outside world because everything has to be very, very controlled. Turn around three times, absolute perfection every time, sort of thing."

"So they... change mood suddenly and start shouting at people?" Av asked.

"Some of them, yes. Once the processes are placed back, they act as if nothing happened. They recall the incident, but bringing it up can make it happen again, so we're taught not to mention it."

Av sat forward and looked at Laeder. "You know anything about compulsion? Or writing into a person's mind?"

"From what Aren said, only Raven can do that. It's a replication of the way healers teach one another, except to a concentrated degree. Healers show over and over, but none of what they show can ever be seen by another rank."

"I think you know more about Raven than you say, but I also believe that you have no idea that you know."

"What do you mean?" Laeder asked.

"Raven is in twelve anchor stones at Castle Grey, with a majority of her linked back here somewhere. She is the archives, which means our archivist touches Raven with each request. They just can't talk."

"I suppose that might make sense?" Laeder said hesitantly.

"Raven talks a great deal about her processes, how they've been damaged by not enough magic, fractured over time. Olea and her daughters had to put a great deal into her before she could function at a capacity which Raven herself says isn't the full power."

"The archivists may have incorporated her type of magic into their behaviour in case the books were lost," Laeder gasped out. "They taught us things from our earliest lessons which were actual important topics, hidden in stories."

"I need you to pick out whatever you can because it might help us bring Raven back to us."

"Why?" Telm asked. "I mean besides the right thing to do, bring the part of the palace back to us that's been gone for so long."

"One of Raven's base, and most important, processes is to replicate magic. Or stretch it, or whatever. She and Aren believe that the reason for the short-lived queens was the removal of that process. The queens before were no stronger or weaker. They simply didn't have Raven making a drop of their magic reach to the horizon."

Laeder raised his hand again. "What if Aren asks about all this, about anything?"

"Under absolutely no circumstance can Aren know about what we talk about when she's not in the room. It's not her burden to carry. She has the throne, she has the court, she doesn't need to know about the circles we run in behind her back trying to figure out how she did what she did."

Chapter Thirty-Four

Aren pushed the puppy away, only then aware that it had been licking at her face for quite some time. She set it on the floor and stared at it as it stared back up at her.

"Yappy," she said sternly, unfolding from the chair with a groan.

When Jer had retrieved Wena, Aren had known something was going on. She had sat in the chair, meaning to take a quick look but had forgotten that she had to consciously pull away from such a thing. Raven had always pulled her away at Castle Grey, as she practised using that particular magic.

The second puppy trotted up to her with a ripped up slipper in its mouth. Happily, the beastie dropped the slipper at Aren's feet and wagged its tail.

Both puppies looked the same to Aren. It wasn't until she flipped them over that she could tell them apart. One was male, one female. Because she had trouble distinguishing them when they were on their feet, she hadn't been able to get a name to stick to either of them.

She went over to the wardrobe absently and searched about in it until she found two hair ribbons of different colours. Moving back to the puppies, she rolled them and tied the purple one around the female's neck and the blue one around the male's neck.

"I'm going to get you two proper collars," she said sternly to the puppies.

The female barked at her loudly, hopping up and down when Aren moved away to the small table with food on it by the fire. She ate a bit and almost fed the whining puppies but recalled what Er had said to her about them.

Not to feed them at the table least they always beg for scraps.

"No begging," she said to them, then turned her body away from them.

They continued to whine while she ate, even yapped a few times but Aren resolutely ignored them while she finished her meal and set the dishes by the door of her rooms.

It felt wrong.

To continue on with life as if she didn't know.

Raven had told Aren to use the magic whenever she felt something was going on, to settle her mind and see the truth of things. Without seeing the truth of the matter, it would be very easy for her to jump to conclusions and cause problems for herself by confronting the wrong people.

She wasn't certain if she was supposed to tell Av that she knew what was going on.

Then again, they weren't going to be honest with *her* as to what was going on.

Aren looked up as Wena and Av entered the room together. She stared at them as both of them stared back at her, startled. Aren wondered what to say.

"I'm not sleeping with him," Wena said with a grimace.

"If I wanted a threesome I'd ask Url to join us," Aren said, smiling innocently at Av.

The warrior made a high-pitched whining sound. He turned as the puppies responded with yips, and looked down at them when they came running to him.

"They have ribbons around their necks," Av said.

"To tell them apart," Aren said. "What should I name them? What does one name their dogs?"

"Fluffy is popular," Wena grumbled, picking up the empty dishes to take to the kitchen. "Or name them after a marking on their coats like spot or boot. Fleck. Pooper might be a good one."

"They're trained to go outside," Av said. "Er was kind enough to help with that before we left."

Wena made a sound and left the rooms. The sound was pointedly grumpy. Aren looked to Av, who could only shrug in response.

"She seemed fine when we were discussing her finding handmaids for you," Av said.

"She's my handmaid," Aren said.

"Of rank, to help support you should you decide to have children."

"I will, in a few moments…" Aren frowned as the word came out of her mouth. "Years. A few years. Or a mistake happens, that would just be what happens then, wouldn't it?"

Av smiled. "Only way to have an accident is try, try again."

"Not right now. I'm tired because someone got us up well before dawn to get here before the sun went down," Aren grumbled, moving towards the bed.

"Well, we have some time to rest. Wars move slowly, is what I've learned over the past month."

"Once we have an army we should march it south," Aren said. "Which is that way, I believe."

Av took Aren gently and turned her. "It's that way."

Aren shrugged. "I'm not leading the army. You are."

"I am, yes," Av said with a small smile. "Any chance of my winning a war, and then we talk about children?"

"Win the war tomorrow, and I'll jump your bones for breeding within six months," Aren said, pulling away. "How long until Mar comes back to the palace?"

"Who told you she was gone?" Av asked.

"She hasn't come beating down my door to hear all about Castle Grey," Aren said quickly. "Obviously she's not at the palace. She should be here, so naturally, you've already sent a command for her to return, correct?"

"I… have… yes."

Aren watched Av study her and wondered if he would figure it out. He shook his head and kissed her forehead.

"You may want to know that Jer visited the vineyard while we were up north," Av said as he pulled away and headed to the bed. "The boy from the vineyard is here, but they're strongly suggesting we move him to someplace safer. He looks a great deal like you."

"Any other problems?" Aren asked.

"All sorts," Av responded, pulling back the blankets to the bed. "I get the feeling that there will always be problems, however. So could I offer some sleep followed by early morning sex and then training?"

"You want me just to go on as if there isn't a war going on outside the walls of the palace?" Aren asked.

"No, I want you to live your life. After all, you aren't fighting in the war and you not sleeping isn't going to change the fact that people are going to die."

Aren stiffened as Av swore at the bedspread. The warrior took a moment to draw in a long breath before he turned to her.

"I probably should have worded that differently," he said.

"You're right though, my staying up won't change that fact."

Sometimes knowing about a cage means not acknowledging it until you need to use it to help others.

Raven's words. It was in a warrior's nature to contain and control his queen, to what extent depended on both the warrior and the queen. But Raven had also warned Aren that there would be times when those who helped maintain it would need looking after.

The easiest way to look after those around her was to allow them to believe she had no idea what they were doing, to learn the rules to their little arrangement and then turn it against them without being obvious about it.

"Sleeping alone won't change the fact that at this point, people could be dying because the barons or other warriors aren't moving fast enough."

"You mean, you want me to sleep with you?" Av asked, sounding hesitant.

"Yes," Aren said, though she almost asked.

"That was the plan. It's always the plan. Unless you're worn out because some event and I need to go hunting who did it, but then I'll still come join you just as soon as I can."

"Oh..." Aren said. "Should we walk the puppies before bed?"

Av stiffened and looked down at the male, sitting at his feet with both paws in the air. The pup whined and pawed at Av.

"Probably should, and feed them," Av said.

Wena walked back into the rooms with a basket under one arm and a blanket in the other. She dropped them by the fire and scooped up first one, then the other puppy. With two squirming bundles of fur, the handmaid glared at Av, not Aren.

"I am not cleaning up dog shit."

"Fair enough," Av said.

"Or puke."

"I didn't ask you to," Av said quietly. "The puppies are Aren's anyhow."

Wena continued to glare at Av. The warrior shifted uncomfortably.

"If I'm going to have handmaids, they could do it," Aren said to Wena. "If it happens. They are trained to go outside."

Wena struggled with one, then the other pup. "I'm going to take them out to meet the children, and once they are worn out, I will bring them back."

"The children, or the puppies?" Aren called out as Wena left the rooms.

"I don't think she likes dogs," Av said.

"I'm getting that feeling too," Aren muttered. "Other ladies at court do have untrained rats."

"How long do you think it'll take to clear them out?" Av asked.

Aren scrunched up her nose, thinking about what Raven had said to her. "Unfortunately those lords and ladies at court are the ones we need to support us financially over the coming years. Until we've paid back the loans, we're stuck with them."

"Are we still doing the borrow money, pay it back and immediately kill them?" Av asked with a smile.

"If you'd like..." Aren said, watching Av do a little dance on the other side of the bed. "This is years from now, and you have to win a war. And we have to find the coin to pay them back."

"I'll pay them out of pocket," Av said. "Some of them donate a hundred coins and think they deserve a seat at the head table."

"Keep your coin," Aren grumbled. "You never know when we might want to run away and buy an estate somewhere."

"What do we do in the meantime?" Av asked. "While we wait for war to start?"

Aren smiled slowly. "I have an idea."

R.J. Price

RJ Price lives in Canada where she works and writes full time. When not doing either of those things she attempts to navigate social media and resists the urge to return to writing. She has published novels in the fantasy genre and insists she is also a science fiction author, but has been too caught up in her Seat of Magic series to actually complete a science fiction novel for publishing.